PRAISE FOR THE BLACK MIDNIGHT

"A thrilling, beguiling read rich in historical research and featuring many of my favourite ingredients: an atmospheric gas lit Victorian London, an assured voice and intelligent heroine, gripping suspense, and things that go bump in the night. An imaginative plot laced with romance, royalty, and a Ripper-esque twist. Fans of Jaime Jo Wright and Michelle Griep won't be able to keep their hands off it. I certainly couldn't!"

–Rachel McMillan, author of *The London Restoration*

"*The Black Midnight* blends history, romance, and just the right dose of suspense to create the perfect story that will keep readers turning pages long into the night. History buffs will be riveted by this intriguing glimpse into the Midnight Assassin murders, and romance fans will cheer for Ike and Annie as they work to solve the case. . .and lose their hearts along the way."

–Amanda Barratt, author of *My Dearest Dietrich:*
A Novel of Dietrich Bonhoeffer's Lost Love

"*The Black Midnight* is chock-full of historical tidbits that make the account of Jack the Ripper come eerily, vibrantly to life. Another intriguing tale from talented storyteller, Kathleen Y'Barbo."

–Elizabeth Ludwig, *USA Today* bestselling author

"Impeccably researched and thoroughly captivating, Kathleen Y'Barbo's *The Black Midnight* puts a pair of star-crossed Pinkerton detectives on the trail of a Texas killer who may also be the notorious Jack the Ripper. Very highly recommended!"

–Colleen Thompson, RITA-nominated author of *Deadly Texas Summer*

"With a killer plot and an unpredictable romance, unlikely heroes team up for a fast-paced historical suspense. Warning! Don't read this at night!"

–DiAnn Mills, Christy Award–winning author

P9-DXJ-268

"*The Black Midnight* is Y'Barbo at her finest. True crime mixed with romance, and just the perfect blend of modern-day suspense make this book one not to be missed! Highly recommend."

—Robin Caroll, bestselling author of the Darkwater Inn series

"What a clever idea, using two distant and distinct settings and two unsolved, real life murder cases to create a fun possibility. Isn't the challenge of a mystery deciding who did it and why? You'll get your money's worth with *The Black Midnight.*"

—Gayle Roper, author of *Hide and Seek, Lost and Found*

"In *The Black Midnight*, Kathleen Y'Barbo weaves between fact and fiction to make 19th century history come alive on the page. Annie and Ike's story is a page-turning combination of whip-smart dialogue, push-and-pull romance, and intriguing murder mystery. Whether fans of true crime stories enjoy Jack the Ripper's tale, rich historical detail, or stunning storytelling, readers will add Kathleen Y'Barbo to their must-read author list after *The Black Midnight.*"

—Laurie Tomlinson, author of *With No Reservations*

"You're in for a wild ride as Kathleen Y'Barbo takes you on a story through some of America's and Britain's grisliest murders while somehow managing to weave in a delicious romance. From Texas to London, the ties that bind may be more linked than you previously believed. And who better to unravel them than a brash American Pinkerton agent and the granddaughter of a queen? Settle in for a novel of suspense and romance—just be sure to look over your shoulder every now and then!"

—Jaime Jo Wright, 2018 Christy Award–Winning author of *The House on Foster Hill* and 2020 Inspy Award-Nominated *The Curse of Misty Wayfair*

"In *The Black Midnight*, Kathleen Y'Barbo has crafted a page-turning novel. I love that it is based on a historical event. I love even more that it's an event I was unaware of. The characters and setting absolutely sing. This book will delight readers of historical fiction who love romance, mystery, and a touch of suspense."

—Cara Putman, bestselling and award-winning author of *Flight Risk*

the BLACK MIDNIGHT

KATHLEEN Y'BARBO

BARBOUR BOOKS
An Imprint of Barbour Publishing, Inc.

©2020 by Kathleen Y'Barbo

Print ISBN 978-1-64352-595-2

eBook Editions:
Adobe Digital Edition (.epub) 978-1-64352-597-6
Kindle and MobiPocket Edition (.prc) 978-1-64352-596-9

This book is a work of fiction. Names, characters, places, and incidents are either products of the author's imagination or used fictitiously. Any similarity to actual people, organizations, and/or events is purely coincidental.

All scripture quotations are taken from the King James Version of the Bible.

Cover image © Ildiko Neer / Trevillion Images

Published by Barbour Books, an imprint of Barbour Publishing, Inc., 1810 Barbour Drive, Uhrichsville, Ohio 44683, www.barbourbooks.com

Our mission is to inspire the world with the life-changing message of the Bible.

ecpa Member of the
Evangelical Christian
Publishers Association

Printed in the United States of America.

In a moment shall they die, and the people shall be troubled at midnight, and pass away: and the mighty shall be taken away without hand.
JOB 34:20

I have faith that the authors of these crimes will as yet be uncovered. No human heart is strong enough to hold such secrets.
JOHN ROBERTSON, MAYOR OF AUSTIN, TEXAS
STATE OF THE CITY ADDRESS
NOVEMBER 10, 1885

This new most ghastly murder shows the absolute necessity for some very decided action. All these courts must be lit, and our detectives improved.
QUEEN VICTORIA
LETTER TO THE PRIME MINISTER, THE MARQUESS OF SALISBURY, REGARDING THE JACK THE RIPPER KILLINGS
NOVEMBER 1888

London
1889

Chapter 1

The lush carpets kept her footsteps from being heard, but the thudding of Alice Anne von Wettin's heart surely echoed throughout the hallowed halls of Buckingham Palace. Though Queen Victoria was her great-grandmother, she had spent very little time in Her Majesty's presence of late. Somewhere between being the little girl unaware of protocol and the young woman who was keenly aware of the importance of who Granny was, the relationship had suffered.

Their last contact had been some three years ago through palace messengers who delivered the news that Her Majesty was most distressed upon learning of her great-granddaughter's flirtation with the American who had garnered such attention in the newspapers. Distressed? Granny hadn't so much as raised an eyebrow over her mother's death, but a meaningful romance with a fellow who just happened to be from another country distressed her?

With each step, Alice Anne gathered her complaints, watering them with a list of slights and other arguments until they grew into full bloom. Armed with this list and all the responses she would make to her great-grandmother's protests, she paused just long enough for the footmen to open the doors.

Double doors gilded in what was certainly pure gold swung open on perfectly oiled hinges. Twin footmen in regal attire stepped forward to bid her entrance to the innermost sanctum of the most powerful person in all of Europe. Instantly Alice Anne was transported to her childhood and the grand Christmases

7

spent here and at Windsor Castle. Though she could not recall meeting her great-grandfather—she was an infant when he died—his hand had been in every part of the decorations, as it seemed it was here.

Floor-to-ceiling windows on two sides were draped in yards of golden silk woven through with threads of burgundy and puddled atop carpets of a similar hue. Settees that surely belonged to the first owner of the castle huddled around fireplaces set at either end of the room, while a tea set, also made of gold, had been laid out on a table nearest the westernmost set of windows. Overhead three massive chandeliers, wrought from sparkling gold, blazed.

Alice Anne smiled. The effect was very much like standing inside one of the cherished golden orbs that decorated Mama's bedchamber mantelpiece, and it served as a contrast to the dreary afternoon rains pelting the glass.

The doors closed behind her, leaving Alice Anne in a hushed silence that only the crackle of the fire and the pinging of rain against the window dared break. She moved toward the windows and the massive painting that hung between them.

Measuring more than seven feet in width and nearly that in height, the painting of ships in a harbor was Jules Achille Noël's depiction of her great-grandparents meeting with Napoleon III and the Empress Eugénie at Cherbourg some thirty years ago.

"We were all so very young then."

She turned at the sound and found Granny watching her intently, a half dozen minders of all sorts standing behind her. As her great-grandmother moved forward to join her, Alice Anne lowered her eyes from the tiny woman in black to the carpet and executed the curtsy she had learned almost before she could walk.

"Well done, kitten." Granny continued to study her while her courtiers remained gathered near the door. Finally, a smile lifted her mouth at the corners. "Indeed, we do approve of the young woman you have become."

The compliment was both unexpected and very much appreciated.

"Thank you, Your Majesty," she said. "Your praise is gratefully received."

The queen turned her back to move slowly toward the tea table. Though she had few memories of her great-grandmother as an active woman, she did seem to have aged greatly since their last encounter.

Granny looked back over her shoulder. "Alice Anne, do come and sit with us."

"Yes, Gran. . .er, ma'am," she managed as she moved at a dignified but hurried pace to do as she was told.

As soon as her grandmother was seated, Alice Anne took the chair opposite. Instantly, the servants jumped into action. In what seemed only a moment's time, food and drinks had been dispensed, and Granny had dismissed all her minders.

Silence fell between them, but the queen made no move to touch any of the delectable treats stacked before her. Instead, she took a sip of her tea and seemed lost in thought. Since custom dictated that no one could eat before the queen chose to do so, Alice Anne sat very still and waited.

The woman across from her might be Victoria Regina, Queen of all Britain and a good portion of the rest of the world, but at the moment she looked very small and worried. Annie could guess why.

Rumors and headlines involving the royal family had been disseminated practically since the dawn of time. Nothing new, to be sure. But this time the scandal was murder.

Or rather, murders.

Once again, Granny studied her. Finally, she placed the teacup back into the saucer and dropped her hand into her lap. "I have been told you have some talent in solving puzzles."

How could she possibly know? Using techniques Alice Anne had committed to memory over the past few years, she kept her expression neutral and her smile in place while she watched for clues.

"Whatever gives you that idea?" she managed to ask, taking on the persona of her sister, Beatrice—one she used frequently when the situation warranted and who indeed would have responded in exactly that manner.

"Not *what*, kitten. *Who*." The queen shifted positions and gathered her dark shawl closer as she kept her attention focused on her. "Much like your fellow Pinkertons, those in my employ never sleep."

"I see." She schooled her expression to give no indication of her discomfort.

"There is no need for us to make mention of this to your father," Granny said. "We are merely curious as to your willingness to pursue the solution to a conundrum that has recently vexed us."

What else could she say to the reigning Queen of England? "Of course, ma'am. How may I be of service?"

"We have heard of a series of unfortunate occurrences in Whitechapel. Are you aware of them?"

"I am, ma'am," she said. It would be impossible to live in London and not have heard about the man who had been called Jack the Ripper since his letters to the Metropolitan Police using that signature had been made public.

"I have entreated my ministers to do something about finding this man who has committed these atrocities, but they have done nothing but make excuses. It is time for another plan."

Annie sat very still and waited for Granny to say more. "We are also aware that you had a considerable reputation as a detective in America. That ridiculous news story from several years ago notwithstanding, Mr. Pinkerton speaks highly of you."

She tried not to wince at the reminder of the news article written by a disgruntled reporter. At least Granny did not dwell on the embarrassment.

"Thus the responsibility for the new plan to capture him shall be yours."

"Thank you, Granny. I will not disappoint you. Might I ask for clarification? I will need to assemble a few key members of a team. Do I have your permission?"

"You do, but with one caveat."

"Anything," she said.

"Stay out of the newspapers and keep a low profile. When the time comes to unveil the culprit, we shall allow one of our members of the Metropolitan Police to deliver the good news. My great-granddaughter is not to be mentioned."

"Yes, Granny. Absolutely."

"How long do you expect it will take to assemble your team?" she asked.

"A month, I think." At her grandmother's raised eyebrows, she hurried to add, "Less perhaps. Will there be a specific budget?"

"Can we put a price on such an endeavor?" Granny shook her head. "We cannot. You may have whatever you need."

"Thank you, ma'am."

"We do prefer Granny," she said with a smile. "Now tell me the latest news. Has your sister finally determined which of her beaus she wishes to ask permission to wed?"

A half hour later, as Annie left the palace, she couldn't stop smiling. First she would pay a visit to her former mentor, Simon Kent, at the Metropolitan Police Headquarters. He would be the initial member of her team, if he agreed.

The second member of her team would take a little longer to reach. But she would not attempt to do this without him.

Whether Isaiah Joplin would be willing to help was a question that could not be answered with a telegram or letter. For that conversation, Annie would have to speak to him in person.

Not easily done, though she expected the trip to Austin, Texas, would be less taxing than trying to convince the most frustrating man she had ever met to listen to what she had to say.

Austin
1889

Chapter 2

Austin, Texas
One month later

The last person Ike Joplin expected to walk into his law office on the first decently sunny day in almost a month was former Pinkerton detective Alice Anne Walters. Or as he had discovered through his own means, Special Constable Alice Anne von Wettin of the Criminal Investigation Department of the London Metropolitan Police, great-granddaughter of Queen Victoria and a royal of some sort herself.

It was as if the March clouds had parted as she stepped inside. But he'd welcome the rain and all the mud and trouble it brought over this infuriating female any day.

Never a man to miss out on a lesson learned the hard way, he faced her head-on. "I'd ask what you're doing here, Annie, but I figure you're going to tell me anyway. Get on with it."

"It is wonderful to see you again as well, Isaiah."

With her sharp blue eyes and that way she had of inspecting everything around her without allowing anyone to know whether she was paying any attention or not, the Englishwoman had been a formidable opponent and a valuable asset in an investigation that had, unfortunately, not ended well. But that was nearly three years ago.

Time and good sense had intervened since then. Ike had exchanged the man he used to be—a Pinkerton detective with a talent for finding trouble—for a much improved version, or so he hoped. He'd left the Pinkertons to open a law office in Austin, and just recently he'd begun courting a senator's daughter.

The reason he'd left that world behind was standing in front of him. And heaven help him, as he sat behind a desk filled with legal work that needed his attention, Ike was actually curious as to what she might want.

Annie seated her pretty self in the chair across from him and situated her skirts just so. She'd chosen hunter green for her stylish attire today and completed the ensemble with a matching cloak and hat. His guest removed her kid gloves and placed them in her lap, then rested her hands atop them.

There were times when they'd worked together that he'd managed to forget Annie had descended from royalty. Today was not one of those days.

"I see your conversation skills have not improved since the last time I saw you." She paused to fix him with a look. "Granny sent me."

"Granny," he echoed with a chuckle, "being Queen Victoria, sent you to see me?"

He'd known Annie several years and had fallen head over heels for her before she'd admitted her illustrious great-grandmother was the Queen of England. Even then, it had been a grudging admission to facts he'd gleaned himself. She'd made him swear he would never mention it again.

Until today he hadn't.

"Yes." She silenced any potential comment from him with a regal wave of her hand. "Well, actually, no. Not specifically you."

"Especially not me. As I recall, your great-grandmother was not amused when she discovered you had taken up with an American involved in 'the sordid and tawdry trade of information and such.' " He paused. "Did I get any of that wrong?"

"You did not," she said, her expression unchanged and her blue eyes studying him.

Ike leaned back in his chair and steepled his hands. "So why are you here?"

"A simple proposal," she told him.

"Last time there was a proposal between us, you said no."

Was that the slightest reaction he noticed beneath that cool upper-crust British exterior? Ike held his smile at bay by reminding himself of how easily she'd set him aside back then.

"Sticking to the project at hand," she said, ignoring his comment, "there is a situation in London that has not been remedied. Granny believes I might be able to offer some insight. I have, however, promised to remain out of the spotlight."

"Unlike last time."

Annie shrugged. "I've explained that the American press cannot be controlled. Not that the British press is any better, but they do understand the delicate balance of reporting when the monarchy is involved. And I've promised I will do my best to keep my face and name off their pages. But that is neither here nor there. As I said, I have a proposal. I wish to hire you."

The door opened and someone stepped into the outer office. Since he hadn't gotten around to hiring anyone to work for him just yet, Ike was doing double duty as boss and employee.

"Excuse me for a minute," he told Annie before stepping out of his office to find Theodora Rampling waiting for him.

Dora was a Texas beauty with a pedigree that would make any Austin mama of sons want her to marry into their family. The only child of a senator and his upper-crust Boston bride, the woman smiling at him was pampered, adored, and deserving of both.

For some reason, she also happened to be crazy about him. And she wasn't shy about admitting she was the jealous kind. The kind who wouldn't respond well if she discovered the only woman he'd proposed marriage to was on the other side of the wall.

Ike kicked the door behind him shut with his boot and gave her what was certainly a nervous smile. "What a nice surprise."

Dora looked beyond him to the closed door and then back up at Ike. "I've interrupted something."

"Just a meeting," he hurried to say. "Actually, not a meeting I'd planned. I had someone come in unexpectedly, and we were just discussing what I could do for her."

At the word *her*, Dora's dark eyes narrowed. "Anyone I know?"

The question left him looking for a good response. Knew? No. Knew of? Absolutely.

"I see," she said in that tone he'd learned meant trouble.

Before he could get a word out, the pretty brunette pressed past him to open the door and step into his office. To her credit, Dora's expression never changed, even when she spied Annie.

"Miss Walters," she said in a completely neutral tone. "Ike didn't tell me you were back in Austin."

He stepped into the office in time to watch his past and his present shake hands.

Annie was standing now, her posture straight and her expression friendly. "Isaiah could not have known until I showed up without an appointment a few minutes ago." She shook her head. "I'm sorry. Forgive me, but do I know you? I cannot recall that I do."

"Theodora Rampling." She gave him a sideways look. "I don't suppose Ike has mentioned me."

"No, but then, he hasn't had the chance. I only just arrived." Annie's gaze moved from her to him. "I shouldn't have assumed you would be available upon my whim, Isaiah. I will have my secretary set a proper appointment. Now, if you'll excuse me."

"No," Ike and Dora said in unison.

"There's no need," Dora said. "Continue your meeting. I'm only here to deliver an invitation for Ike to join Papa and me for dinner at the governor's mansion tonight." She fixed him with a look. "If you're free, that is."

"Of course I am," Ike told her as he recalled a similar dinner at the mansion some years ago. He'd ended up with Annie in the garden and had been severely chastised by Mrs. Ireland, their hostess.

He'd also missed out on what might have been a memorable kiss under the stars.

Dora placed her hand on Ike's sleeve, redirecting his thoughts. The smile on her face did not match the look in her eyes. "Excellent.

Then why don't you walk me out?" She turned to Annie. "I do hope you'll have a nice stay in Austin. Are you planning a lengthy visit?"

"I'm not certain," Annie told her. "It all depends. I am here on a matter of urgent business, so one never knows how long these things take."

"Yes, one never knows," Dora echoed. After saying her good-byes to Annie, she led Ike to the door. This time it was Dora's foot that slammed the door behind them.

"What is that woman doing here?" she demanded.

"I have no idea other than what she said. She's here on business, and she just walked through the doors a few minutes before you did. That's all I can tell you."

She shook her head. "Get rid of her."

"I was trying to when you walked in," he said, not certain that was the truth. He'd been curious as to why she'd chosen him for whatever project she and Granny had in mind, but he certainly hadn't committed to helping her.

Listening, yes. Helping? Probably not.

"No, you told me you were finding out what you could do for her." She paused, and Ike realized her silence was more powerful than her words. "Have you decided what that is, dear?"

"Probably nothing, but I won't know until the conversation is finished. As I said, I was trying to get to the end of what she was there for when you came in."

"Then go and finish trying," she said sweetly. "Pick me up at seven tonight. Papa will likely be at the capitol until just before dinner, so he plans to walk over. Wear that nice dark suit, please. You look so handsome in it."

Her voice was a purr now. It was also loud enough to be heard on the other side of the door.

Dora Rampling was nothing if not insistent that she be the center of Ike's world. A world made up of no one else but her, Ike, and anyone else who could further the political and social aspirations she held for the two of them.

"Seven it is," he said, offering her a kiss on the cheek. "Do you need me to escort you to your buggy?"

"I need you to conclude your business with that woman and promise me you'll be on time for dinner." She reached up on tiptoe to whisper into his ear. "And I need you to tell her about me."

"I don't see how I can avoid any of these things," he said, meaning it as a joke.

Her expression told him the joke fell flat. "Just do it, all right?" She swept out, leaving the scent of expensive perfume in her wake.

Ike watched the door close behind her and let out a long breath. Then he made his way back to his office and Annie.

"She's lovely," the Englishwoman said after Ike had settled back in his chair. "And territorial."

Ike refused to grin, even though both statements were true. "You said you wanted to hire me. Do you need legal work? Because that's all I do now."

"Impossible," she said with an imperious wave of her hand. "You're too good to settle for this."

"Contrary to what you may recall, I read the law before I turned to detective work, Annie."

"I do recall," she said. "And you admitted you hated every minute of it."

"And that's what makes you think I'm settling?"

Her response was a look that said everything he figured she was thinking. Ike knew those thoughts. He'd had them himself.

Instead of giving him an answer, Annie stood abruptly, her gloves in one hand. She made quick work of donning those gloves. Finally, she met his gaze.

"I will get right to the point. It is possible that the killer we did not catch here in Austin is responsible for the recent killings in London. Though you appear to have retired from that life, I'm sure this news has not escaped your notice."

It still irked him that the Midnight Assassin had never been caught. The husbands of the last two victims were tried, but neither conviction had stuck, leaving Austin with no answer to the murders that tormented the city back in '84 and '85.

"It has not escaped my notice," Ike agreed. "But according to the newspapers, there have been no more verified killings in London since November."

"And no arrest." Annie paused as if considering her words. "I am willing to pay you enough to set you up nicely so you can pursue whatever political career Theodora seeks for you without any concern for your finances."

Leave it to Annie to cut right to the heart of the matter. It only stung a little that she'd decided he had taken up lawyering to please Dora.

The worst of it was that Annie was not completely wrong.

"Why do you think we can catch him this time?"

"Because I have a plan." She grinned. "Unfortunately, it might make you late for dinner."

"How late?"

"A few weeks." Annie shrugged. "No more than a month. I promise."

Ike laughed. "And if I say no, what will you do?"

Annie didn't miss a beat. "Continue investigating without you until this man is caught, whether on this side of the Atlantic or the other."

Exactly what he'd expected she would say.

Ike rested his elbows on his desk. Dora would kill him. She'd get over it, of course, but she would throw a hissy fit to beat all hissy fits when he broke the news to her.

He let out a long breath and regarded her solemnly. "This had better be worth what I may be walking away from here."

"Oh," she said slowly, "it's worth it. And if you were so worried about what you had here, you wouldn't be considering it."

It was Ike's turn to ignore her. "Tell me about this plan." For if there was one thing Ike had learned while working with her four years ago, it was that Annie always had a plan.

Austin
1885

Chapter 3

Four years earlier
Austin, Texas
December 21, 1885

T he worst thing about ending an investigation one week before Christmas was not the paperwork nor the fact that she would never find a way back to Chicago before the holiday. She looked forward to neither of these, to be certain.

No, the worst of it was the incessant invitations by well-meaning folks who assumed that her status as a single woman alone in the city of Austin at the end of December required repairing. Which it most certainly did not.

Through her most recent investigation—in which Annie managed to ferret out the identities of a half dozen men who were providing subpar materials to contractors for use in the construction of state government buildings here in Texas—she'd been introduced to Governor John Ireland and his wife, Anna. Now the lovely couple was insisting she join them at a dinner being held this evening, with promises of other social events to follow.

Annie was far too well bred to show how she felt about such an inundation, though she did stifle a groan once she'd parted from the dear woman. Other invitations waited for her when she returned to her hotel, seven in all, each written out with perfect penmanship on beautifully monogrammed stationery, and every one of them vying for her company. To the stack of invitations, the clerk added a telegram.

"All the way from Chicago," he announced loud enough for anyone in the lobby to hear. "It's cold there this time of year, you know."

"I, yes, well. . ." She nodded, being careful to keep her American accent intact. "I have heard that it is. Now, if you'll excuse me." Annie tucked the envelopes into her satchel and turned her back on the clerk.

"Wait, miss." The clerk hurried to step in front of her and thrust another envelope toward her. "Sorry, I was looking at all these stamps and forgot to put it back in your box. I'm a collector of unique stamps. Never seen any like these."

She had. Frequently. But then, her great-grandmother had posed for the image they bore.

Annie retrieved the letter from his hand. This time she allowed "Thank you" to trail in her wake as she crossed the lobby and climbed the stairs to her second-floor room.

Once in her room, she made sure the door was bolted, then tossed her bag and the letter onto the desk. After a glance around to confirm the room had not been touched since she left it this morning, Annie went to stand at the window.

Across the way, Mr. Driskill's hotel was going up. Down below, Congress Street was bustling with carts, buggies, and pedestrians. If she strained her neck to look beyond the construction, she could see the capitol.

After a moment, Annie turned away from the window to seat herself at the desk. Between the satchel and paperwork she ought to be completing and the stack of letters and invitations, it was all she could do not to toss all of it into the wastebasket in favor of a nap.

She never slept well on assignments, so the first thing Annie did once a job had come to an end was to return home, close the curtains, soak in a hot bath, then hide away beneath the luxurious bedding she'd brought with her from London.

Her bedding was in Chicago, but she'd brought her lavender bath salts and would use them later. Eventually she would be home again in her bed. The paperwork, however, was here to stay until she dispensed with it.

Rather than dwell on what could very quickly become a topic of self-pity, Annie retrieved both her paperwork and the correspondence from the satchel, then placed it on the floor beside her. After sorting through the invitations, she set them all aside and opened the telegram.

NEW ITEM ADDED. MEET TONIGHT
AT PALM TREES. CI

Frowning, Annie dropped the telegram from Captain Hezekiah Ingram, her superior at the agency, onto the desk. A new item was code for a new case that would be handled by an agent already on the scene.

She let out a long breath. So much for that warm soak and her soft bed in Chicago.

A glance at the clock told her she would have neither in Austin—at least not before the driver came to whisk her away to the governor's mansion.

Failing any chance at a rest, she tackled the work at hand. Then she set her attention on preparations for the remainder of the day.

By the time the messenger knocked to alert her to the presence of the driver downstairs, she had answered half of the correspondence, sent a response to the captain, and changed into a gown suitable for an evening with dignitaries.

The ride up Congress Avenue was uneventful, and the weather was mild compared to December in Chicago or London. It was a lovely evening.

In what seemed like only a few minutes, Annie stood in front of the governor's mansion. There were no palm trees in sight for her meeting, so she made her way up onto the wide front porch of Governor Ireland's home.

A glance at the scene behind her revealed a lovely view of the city at sunset and the sweep of green pastureland beyond.

She turned back toward the door just as it opened, revealing a uniformed butler who bid her enter. Offering her greetings to the governor and his wife at the entrance to the massive double parlor, Annie then moved past them to step inside.

The parlor was decorated in the latest style, with gaslights flickering overhead and fires crackling in the fireplaces that bookended the room. Thick carpets muffled footsteps, while curtains reminiscent of Granny's receiving room at Windsor Castle hung from the windows.

The space was at once elegant yet welcoming, formal yet inviting. For a man whose next stop just might be the White House, the governor's mansion was an excellent start.

After making her way through an obstacle course populated by politicians whose faces she recognized from the newspapers and their beautifully dressed and bejeweled wives, she spied the palm trees—a row of them covering what appeared to be a bank of windows or possibly doors—that allowed for close proximity to two exits as well as a full view of the parlor.

Unfortunately, she wasn't the first one there.

She rolled her eyes at Isaiah Joplin, the Pinkerton detective who had positioned himself behind a collection of potted palms that had been arranged in front of a glass door. While Isaiah was an excellent detective with whom she had worked on multiple occasions, he was also a relentless suitor known to surprise her on occasion.

"You're not the captain."

"Hello, Annie."

Any ill humor she felt at being marooned in Texas vanished at the sight of his broad smile. Still, Annie decided to give him a bit of trouble before she admitted she was glad to see him.

"Why are you hiding, Isaiah? Have you been left off the guest list?"

"Of course I was invited. My family and the governor's go way back." He grasped her wrist and pulled her behind the palm trees.

"Let's get out of here."

"This is highly inappropriate," Annie whispered. "Even for you."

"I resent that remark," he said in a teasing tone that told her he felt the exact opposite. "And I am here on Pinkerton business, same as you. What did you think I was about to do?"

Had she still worn that sheen of British propriety, Annie might have blushed at the thought of the kiss she'd hoped would be forthcoming. But she had been in America long enough to shed all of that proper English nonsense, at least where it had to do with Isaiah Joplin.

Annie slid deeper into the darkness behind the hedge of palms, moving into his arms with ease. It had been several months since she'd seen him, and the nearness of him felt like a homecoming of sorts.

A roar of applause, quickly followed by peals of laughter, went up on the other side of the palm trees. Wedged here beside Isaiah, the parlor and guests seemed a thousand miles away.

"I was expecting the captain," she finally said.

Isaiah's arm snaked behind her. "No, Annie. I'm the man you're looking for."

"You are incorrigible," she whispered, turning herself toward him.

Though the light barely filtered through the trees, Annie could still see his grin. "I am just following orders."

"As am I," she told him. "I was told by the captain that I would get instructions on my next assignment."

"You will. Come with me." A moment later, he slipped out the door and pulled her with him into the garden, lit beautifully by the full moon overhead.

Out of habit, she gave the perimeter a cursory glance. The garden was a fenced area with no visible gates that might allow entry. The only access appeared to be from the doors leading to the house.

Satisfied, Annie returned her attention to Isaiah. Had she been free to pursue more than a passing friendship with the handsome Texan, Annie might have considered it. The detective was smart, funny, and an excellent dancer—as she'd learned on their last assignment together—and when he looked at her, it took all she had not to fall in love. But two significant factors contributed to her resistance.

Isaiah had no idea of her family ties to the British monarchy—no one here in America did other than Mr. Pinkerton. Instead, he believed her to be Annie Walters, an Englishwoman unable to gain entry to the all-male ranks of Scotland Yard and thus forced to do her detective work for Mr. Pinkerton instead. For that she owed a fellow Englishman, Simon Kent, a debt of thanks. But Isaiah was only half the problem.

The other factor was that her family knew nothing of her life here. The moment she was exposed as a Pinkerton detective—or presented one as a potential spouse—would be the moment her parents demanded she return home. A demand that Granny would certainly support.

"I just returned from Chicago," Isaiah finally said. "Cap sent me down to monitor a situation here. This comes all the way from the top, and the boss is not happy."

Her heart lurched. "With me?"

"No," he said quickly. "Nothing any of our agents have done."

Annie released the breath she hadn't realized she was holding. "All right. I thought I successfully concluded the investigation, but you had me worried."

"The person who needs to be worried is Matthew Pinkerton."

At the sound of the name, she made a face. "The fellow with the correspondence courses?" Competition between the agencies had been nearly nonexistent, despite Matthew Pinkerton's best efforts to confuse the public into believing his mail-order detectives at the upstart Pinkerton United States Detective Agency were just as good as the best-of-the-best who worked for the original Pinkerton Detective Agency.

"That's the one." He paused. "Apparently the mayor hired

them to come down here and see if they can catch the Midnight Assassin."

Annie frowned. "Instead of us? That seems odd."

He shrugged. "All I know is that the boss man isn't happy, and he doesn't want anyone to believe that his agents are subpar."

"What is it he wants us to do about all that? If we aren't the ones who were hired to do the job, I mean?"

"That is where discretion comes in." Isaiah looked around the garden and turned back to Annie. "The public has been told that Pinkerton detectives are investigating. They don't have any idea that it isn't us."

"The captain wants us to help them?"

Isaiah shrugged. "We're just going to do what we always do and investigate. Quietly. If the public believes we're working together with these other men, then let them. I doubt the mayor will complain that he's getting extra Pinkertons for his cut-rate price."

"He's getting us for free," she quipped. "I fail to see how that is a good use of two detectives."

"Good publicity is priceless. That's how Cap says the boss is seeing it, anyway. We can talk more about this tomorrow. I'll meet you in the lobby of your hotel at ten." Isaiah paused and seemed to be studying her. "Have I ever told you how beautiful you look in the moonlight?"

"Frequently," she responded lightly. "The last time being in August whilst we were on the Fenton stakeout."

"About the Fenton stakeout." Isaiah reached over to entwine his fingers with hers, then lifted her hand to his lips. "I believe we left some unfinished business between us."

The kiss that almost was.

"Yes, we did," she said softly.

Moonlight slanted across his handsome features, highlighting the determined angle of his jaw. He released her hand and gathered Annie to him.

"I've missed you, Annie Walters," he whispered against her ear. The false name grated on her. She should tell him the truth. Tell him who she really was. But first, she should kiss him.

Chapter 4

"There you are!"

Ike looked up in time to see Anna Ireland, the governor's wife, crossing the lawn toward them.

"It's such a nice night," Isaiah called to his hostess, his eyes still on the lady detective. "I had to come and see the stars for myself. Miss Walters was kind enough to accompany me."

If Mrs. Ireland had an opinion on finding the two of them in her garden, her face did not reveal it. Rather, she offered a smile. "Yes, but perhaps you could enjoy the stars later? The governor has some remarks he wishes to make before we go in to dinner. He prefers that all the guests are in attendance."

Annie offered him a regretful look and joined Mrs. Ireland to walk back toward the house. Ike trailed a few steps behind, ignoring the ladies' banter and considering how close he'd come to kissing Annie Walters.

Again.

She'd felt like heaven in his arms, and her eyes when she looked up at him had begged him to kiss her. If only he hadn't savored that moment. If he'd just kissed her first and then talked about business.

Next time that was how it would happen, of that he would be certain.

Tonight he would play the proper party guest and try not to monopolize Annie's attention. Tomorrow, however, it would be back to work for both of them, for the captain was adamant that he and Annie had best not let Matthew Pinkerton's men humiliate the organization.

How they would manage that remained to be seen.

And so did that kiss.

As Ike expected, the governor's speech went on far too long and evoked a hope for the coming year that involved only good things. There was no mention of the monster preying on the citizens of Austin nor any talk of other less pleasant occurrences around the state.

In short, it was a typical politician's get-me-elected speech that ended with a request for all in attendance to return for his annual New Year's Day open house. "Now do not let me delay this wonderful meal any longer. Won't you join me in the dining room?"

As soon as the governor issued his request, Annie was set upon by William Swain, the state comptroller, who had his eye on Governor Ireland's job. A strapping man of middle years, the bureaucrat was a popular man in Austin and throughout the state. In November's election, he had garnered a massive number of votes, practically guaranteeing that the next time he ran for an office—surely that of governor—he would win by a landslide.

"I see you've met my friend Miss Walters," Ike said as he ambled up.

The comptroller slid his gaze toward Ike, then swiftly returned his attention to the lady detective. "Actually, I was just about to introduce myself."

"Let me do the honors," Ike said with a grin. "Annie Walters, meet Comptroller William Swain, the fellow who plans to move into this mansion next. All he has to do is get past Ireland and the Ross fellow from Waco."

"That's simplifying things somewhat," the older man said, "but I would welcome a chance to take the reins of this government. In the meantime, perhaps I could escort you into dinner, Miss Walters?"

Mrs. Ireland stepped into the circle of their conversation and focused on Ike. "Might I trouble you to escort a young lady whose husband was unable to join us?"

Ike schooled his expression to hide his disappointment. "Yes, of course," he said as he allowed his hostess to lead him away from Annie and Swain.

"Mrs. Eula Phillips, may I introduce Detective Isaiah Joplin of the Pinkerton Detective Agency? He will be escorting you in tonight."

The brunette beauty, a slender woman who looked to be no more than eighteen or nineteen, smiled in his direction. "Pleased to meet you, Mr. Joplin," she said. "And thank you for your courtesy. My husband was indisposed this evening, but I did not wish to miss Governor and Mrs. Ireland's hospitality."

"The pleasure is mine, Mrs. Phillips. I am happy to oblige."

A look passed between Mrs. Phillips and her hostess. Then the younger woman nodded.

Ike offered her his arm, and they fell into line with the others making their way toward the dining room. Temple Houston, an old friend who'd recently been elected to the legislature, bid him a hearty welcome accompanied by a slap on the back. Of all the men in the room, only Swain and Houston could stand eye to eye with Ike's height.

"Well met," Temple said with a chuckle. "I see the Pinkertons are on the case. You are here to solve our mystery of the Midnight Assassin, aren't you?"

His wife, Laura, shook her head. "Truly, you do not have to answer him, Ike."

"I do not intend to," he told her. "Mrs. Phillips, do you know my friends Laura and Temple Houston? His father is the beloved general to whom all of Texas owes a debt. He, however, is merely a lawyer."

Temple laughed as he affected a gallant bow. "Ignore most of what my old friend, also merely a lawyer, though a reformed one by virtue of his association with the Pinkertons, says this evening. He and I tend to jest a bit. I will, however, claim my father and agree to his glory, but I warn you it does not extend to me. I have been labeled incorrigible or worse, and I admit to being a bit proud of that."

Mrs. Phillips appeared flabbergasted at Temple's speech. Or perhaps she was merely a shy woman. In either case, her smile barely hid what appeared to be a great measure of discomfort.

"Pleased to make your acquaintance," she said softly, her eyes looking past him.

The general's son appeared nonplussed. But then, he often did. "I am acquainted with your husband, but it is a pleasure to meet you, Mrs. Phillips."

Eula Phillips appeared at a total loss for words. Her expression went blank.

"Forgive my husband his many faults," Laura Houston said with a grin. "And tell me all about that beautiful son of yours. I understand he is nearing a year old, is he not? That would be close in age to my own little one."

Relief crossed her lovely features. It appeared Laura had hit upon a topic in which the young woman had great interest.

"Ten months," Mrs. Phillips said. "And growing like a weed. I can hardly keep up with him now that he's toddling around."

"I know what you mean," Laura told her. "I'm not sure why we encouraged walking, but now that it is happening, I'm exhausted."

The conversation continued as they walked into the dining room. By the time they reached their seats, Mrs. Phillips and Laura Houston had become fast friends and were planning to meet again for tea the next time the Houstons were in Austin.

Ike helped Eula Phillips into her seat and took the place next to her. Twelve were at the table this evening. He'd been placed midway down from their host with Eula to his right and the Houstons across from them. After another brief speech from the governor, the first course was served.

Annie had been seated across from Swain and next to a man Ike did not recognize, and he found himself watching her rather than keeping up with the conversation swirling around him. When he finally removed his attention from her to look across the table, he found Temple grinning.

"Does she know you're over the moon for her?" he asked.

"I might have mentioned it," he said.

Temple studied him a moment. "Has she turned you down yet?"

"Repeatedly," Ike admitted. "My declarations of affection have not yet convinced her I'm a worthy suitor."

"Well, you're not," he joked. "But then, neither was I, and look who I landed. Chin up, my friend. Mark my words. She'll see the wisdom in giving you a chance."

"I hope you're right. Annie is a smart woman. If she looks too closely, she might see that a life with me isn't what she wants."

Temple sobered. "If you want to have something to offer her, you'll need to consider settling down. Maybe returning to your law practice. Or ranching. Something that will keep you at home most nights. What you're doing now isn't going to make for a happy life or a happy wife." He paused. "Trust me, those two cannot exist without the other, for if the wife is unhappy. . ."

"Yes, I see your point, and I'm not sure whether life as a lawyer's wife would make her any happier than being married to a Pinkerton man." Ike considered elaborating but decided to keep his mouth shut. Any concern on his part regarding Annie's employment as a detective had long ago been discarded after working his first assignment with her. She was whip smart, could take on just about any disguise with ease, and generally did the job as a Pinkerton employee as well as or better than he did.

But that was a fellow detective's thinking. In his heart, Ike knew should he ever become Annie Walters's husband, he would have a whole new set of concerns, chief among them her safety.

Another glance at the object of his thoughts—now entertaining her end of the table with a story of some sort—and he knew she was worth all the worry in the world if she would just agree to be his wife.

Annie caught Isaiah watching her and smiled. Soon she would have to decide exactly how she felt about him. The kiss would happen, of this she was certain. But then what? Would they remain fellow Pinkerton detectives who worked together on assignments and then parted ways?

She obviously did not know his thoughts on the matter, or if he even had considered these things. But taking such a bold step as to allow Isaiah Joplin into her world would never be as simple as making a decision based on what she wanted.

Or even what the two of them might want.

No, if she were to consider Isaiah as a husband, she would also have to consider her family's reaction. When put into that perspective, the situation was impossible.

Thus there was no reason to consider it. Even if it meant forgoing that kiss.

"What do you think of that, Miss Walters?"

Annie jerked her attention toward the fair-haired man on her right. Cameron something-or-other. A reporter, that much she recalled. Thus she had said very little to him since their introduction at the beginning of the meal.

"I'm sorry, what?"

The reporter adjusted his spectacles and regarded her for a moment, his piercing blue eyes studying her with what appeared to be great interest. "Miss Walters, you've missed a spirited debate between me and Comptroller Swain as to whether our Midnight Assassin has been caught."

"I see. And what was the consensus?"

"The consensus is this fellow ought to go back to New York City and stop stirring up trouble among the natives," Swain bellowed, capturing the attention of nearby diners, who nodded.

"There was no consensus in that regard," the reporter snapped. "Rather, I got the impression that Mr. Swain would prefer the horrific crimes perpetrated on the citizens of Austin be forgotten."

"That's nonsense," Swain said. "Anyone who has spent five minutes in this town knows we all want that monster caught. What we don't want is strangers like you coming around to tell us how we ought to think, and yes, maybe we do want to forget it all happened. Can you blame us?"

"Well," Annie said slowly, "I am also a stranger to this city, and as such, I do have an interest as well as an opinion in the matter you are debating."

"And that would be owing to your employment as a Pinkerton detective." The reporter gave her a smug look. "In your esteemed opinion, what is the current state of affairs in regard to the Midnight Assassin? Keep in mind that he has not been heard from for nigh on three months."

"We are all very mindful of this, Mr. Blake," the comptroller said. "Thanks to men like you and papers like the *Daily Gazette*, we are unable to forget even for a moment."

Chapter 5

Of course. Cameron Blake of the *New York Daily Gazette.*
Yes, now she remembered him. Blake wrote a law-and-order column in the paper, but his real fame came in the sensational articles he wrote regarding crimes, most of which he claimed might have been solved sooner if only inept law enforcement personnel had done their jobs.

A fellow Pinkerton who had worked one of those cases had called Blake's claims into question—privately, of course—and his methods. And now here he was seated beside her, wanting to debate a case she was unofficially working.

Annie turned to him and offered a practiced smile. Her words must be chosen carefully.

"The current state of affairs," she said as she turned her attention from the reporter to Mr. Swain, "is that no official blame has been admitted by anyone in police custody, and no deathbed confessions have been recorded. Thus the Midnight Assassin is still at large."

Blake regarded her over the rim of his spectacles. "And you're certain of this?"

"There can be no other assumption until that theory is proven false," she said. "But the constant reminder of this in newspapers and in conversations across dinner tables serves no purpose other than to inflame the fear of the locals and highlight what might be a perceived lack among law enforcement. Is that your purpose in coming to Austin, sir?"

Mr. Swain's guffawing laughter echoed across the dining room. "I believe Miss Walters has gone right to the heart of the matter."

Blake shifted his attention to the man across the table. "And that is?"

"Until someone is swinging from a rope for this crime or otherwise similarly dispatched, then it is unsolved. And newspaper articles frightening the general public will not solve this." Swain fixed his eyes on Annie. "Can you assure us the Pinkertons will?"

Out of the corner of her eye, she caught Isaiah watching her again. She had to tread carefully in any response she might give, especially in front of a reporter. "We offer only the assurance that we will do our best."

"Against a killer that a certain segment of the population is convinced practices voodoo in order to make himself invisible?" The reporter seemed poised to reach for his paper and pencil. "What say you about that?"

"Again," she told him as she focused on the soup course now being served, "I cannot comment on an ongoing investigation except to say that we will do our best."

He shook his head. "That's no answer. It's a political statement. What are you really doing to catch this man, because I've seen nothing but incompetence. I am a better detective than these clowns are."

Annie's eyes narrowed. She regulated her response, casting away the words she wanted to say. "At this moment I am listening to a newspaper reporter with absolutely no training in police or detective work call into question an investigation that is still ongoing. You, sir, are part of the problem, not the solution, if you continue to deride the good people of law enforcement in such a way. And if you have a suspect you've determined should be investigated, do enlighten me or one of the hardworking people who are actively doing something about this menace."

She fixed him with a look that dared him to speak further. To Blake's credit, he did not.

"Bravo, Miss Walters," Swain said before dissolving into great guffaws of laughter once again.

Using the diversionary skills she'd learned from her mother at the many social gatherings she hosted at the castle, Annie was able to ignore both the reporter and the politician for the remainder of the meal. Finally, the evening came to an end, and Annie said her goodbyes to her hosts, then gathered her coat and headed for the door. Unfortunately, Cameron Blake trailed her out into the foyer.

He made a great show of looking around before addressing Annie. "Have you come alone, Miss Walters? I would be honored to see you safely back to your lodgings."

"There is no need."

She moved past him to shrug into her cloak, then stepped out into the cool evening air. Stars dusted the sky overhead. It was a lovely night, and he was an awful man.

Unfortunately, the persistent reporter followed her. Annie gave him a look that generally stopped most fools in their tracks.

Apparently Cameron Blake was not most fools.

"The killer could very well be out here watching us," he said. "Though, as neither of us fits the profile of his preferred victims, I suppose there is less danger to us than to others."

Several less than polite responses occurred. "Thank you for that insight. I see you are intent on proving yourself as good a detective as you claimed at dinner. I fail to be impressed, but you have my permission to continue trying. Good night, Mr. Blake," she said instead.

Still he persisted, tagging a step behind as Annie walked down toward the street to arrange transport back to the hotel. Just as she was about to let him know exactly how she felt about his behavior, Isaiah stepped between them.

"Our carriage is over here, Miss Walters." He took her arm and led her away, then leaned in close. "Or would you prefer to give your admirer a little more time?"

She laughed. "That was no admirer. Cameron Blake is a

reporter digging for a story. Can you feature that his flimsy excuse for following me was that he thought I might need escorting back to my hotel? I am a Pinkerton detective, for goodness' sakes."

"And a good one," he said, nodding to the carriage. "After you."

"Thank you." Annie climbed into the carriage and settled her skirts around her. "I hope the conversation at your end of the table was more interesting than mine. Blake and Swain locked horns about whether the Midnight Assassin had been caught, though neither of them offered much in the way of an argument for his side. I might have snapped at the reporter, though I tried to be fair, and I certainly did not say the first thing I was thinking. That would have made headlines for certain."

Isaiah looked back at the house and then frowned. "Excuse me a minute. I see a young lady who might need a ride home. Do you mind?"

"Of course not." Annie followed the direction of his gaze and spied the young woman who had been seated beside Isaiah at dinner. She did indeed appear overwhelmed. "Yes, do go and see if she might wish to allow us to take her home. She looks like a lost puppy."

Isaiah bolted off and returned a moment later with the woman in tow. "Annie Walters, may I introduce Eula Phillips?"

The dark-haired woman was a great beauty with coffee-brown eyes and a flawless complexion. Her gown, a pale confection in the latest style, glimmered in the moonlight.

Though she wore the latest fashion and was likely considered a prize for whomever might call her his bride, Annie detected a hint of sadness in her smile. This woman was not well loved, nor was she content.

"Pleased to meet you, Miss Phillips," Annie said.

"Mrs. Phillips," she gently corrected. "Normally I would not attend an event like this without my husband, but he was unable to attend tonight."

"I stand corrected," Annie said.

Isaiah helped Mrs. Phillips into the carriage. "Thank you for your kind offer," she told him as she took the seat across from Annie and then turned to look down at the detective. "Are you sure I am not imposing?"

"Mrs. Phillips, it would only be an imposition if I had not been the one to invite you." Isaiah climbed in to take the spot beside Annie, and the carriage lurched forward.

They rode in silence for the short distance it took to arrive at the home of the Phillips family on West Hickory Street. A cursory glance as the carriage stopped and Isaiah jumped out told Annie that Mr. and Mrs. Phillips were quite well-to-do.

"The home belongs to my husband's parents," she said as if she'd read Annie's thoughts. "We live in a wing with our son."

"It's lovely," Annie told her. "I'm sure you're quite happy there."

"Quite," Mrs. Phillips said, though her smile did not reach her eyes.

Isaiah helped the young woman down and watched until she slipped inside. Then he climbed back into the carriage, and they were off again.

"She seems like a very sad creature," Annie said as the carriage slowed to make a turn. "There's something almost hopeless about her. And she's so young."

"Do you think so? She didn't seem that way when she and Temple's wife were talking about their babies."

"Perhaps that's it, then. She loves her little one to the exclusion of anyone and anything else," Annie said. "It might also explain why her husband chose not to accompany her."

Her companion chuckled. "Always analyzing, aren't you?"

Annie lifted one shoulder in a shrug. "It's a habit I can't seem to shake. Not sure I ought to though. I think it makes me a better Pinkerton to know who I am up against. If I can decide what propels him or her, then I am at an advantage."

"Such as why a man kills innocent women in the dead of night, and where he might have learned the trick of escaping without being seen?"

"Exactly," she told him. "And for the record, I do not believe that voodoo rumor for a minute. A lot of rubbish, that."

"Which brings us back to our topic from before Mrs. Phillips joined us," he said. "No one at my end of the table wanted to talk about the killings, and it wasn't for my lack of trying. Anytime I broached the topic, someone changed the subject."

"Funny," Annie said. "The comptroller seemed to be of a similar mind. He wasn't thrilled with the reporter's insistence on discussing the murders. In fact, he turned the discussion around to deride the man for asking questions. Though he did answer a few of them."

"Do you think he behaved that way because he didn't want to discuss the crimes, or because he didn't have the answers?"

"I'm not sure," she told him. "But I think maybe he's tired of the topic. That is likely true of most who live here, don't you think? There hasn't been a murder since September. Perhaps the monster has been arrested on some other charge and is in jail."

"Or he's left town," Isaiah offered. "Either is possible, as are a thousand other scenarios. We've got our work cut out for us investigating this. It won't be easy to find answers."

"If it was easy," Annie said, her gaze never wavering, "there would be no need for Pinkerton detectives to investigate, either us or the other group. Since you're a native Texan and the one more familiar with Austin, how do you propose we begin?"

"Tomorrow we pay a visit to the police for a look at their records. I want to know what they've got that they're not telling the press. Then we go see the sites of the murders ourselves."

"At night?" she asked.

"Still deciding," he said. "It's dark as pitch in most of these places."

"Then we go during the day first with a follow-up visit at night." Annie paused. "I would also like to speak with witnesses."

"Agreed, though two are just children. I'm not sure how much help they will be."

The carriage rolled to a stop in front of Annie's hotel. "Sometimes children see things more clearly than the adults do."

She spied a familiar face and groaned. Isaiah looked past her and frowned.

"Is that Blake? The reporter?"

"It is. I cannot believe that man is so brazen as to show himself at my hotel."

"Did you tell him where you were staying?"

"I most certainly did not," she said.

Without a word, her companion headed off toward the New Yorker, leaving Annie to follow a few steps behind. "Isaiah, wait," she called, capturing the reporter's attention but not her fellow detective's.

"Miss Walters," Blake called. "I was merely making sure you arrived safely."

"How did you know where she was going?" Isaiah demanded, closing in on the smaller man.

"Simple investigative techniques," he said. "I asked the driver who dropped her off at the governor's mansion where he'd picked her up." A shrug. "It's amazing what people are willing to tell you if you slip them a little cash."

Isaiah glanced over his shoulder at Annie and then turned to Blake. His face was a mask of rage. Had he stood any closer, Annie feared he might have grasped the smaller man by the throat and shaken him senseless.

Or worse.

"Women are dying in this town from an as-yet unnamed assailant, Blake," he said, his voice tight and barely controlled. "Think carefully about what you've just done here. Miss Walters did not invite you to her hotel, did she?"

The shake of the reporter's head was barely imperceptible.

"I thought not. Keep yourself clear of her, understand?"

While Isaiah's chivalry was a nice gesture, she could no longer remain silent. She was, after all, a well-trained Pinkerton detective and not some woman who might actually need saving. Thus, using her great-grandmother as her example, she stepped forward to address the now cowering reporter.

"Might I amend Detective Joplin's statement?" At the man's shaky nod, she continued. "If you were here to see that I got to my hotel safely, then I applaud your enterprising way of achieving that goal. If you have any other intent in arriving here or anywhere else I might be, unannounced and uninvited, then I assure you that you will be sorry with the results of your choice."

Blake looked past her, presumably to Isaiah. "These English women are something, aren't they?"

"That one is," her fellow detective said. "If I were you, I'd heed her warning—and mine—and make yourself scarce."

"Or at least bring us some concrete facts to work on," she said. "Do you happen to have any?"

"I might," he told her, his chin jutting out just so. "Nothing I care to share with you now, but perhaps once I have more evidence."

"You do that," Isaiah said with unmistakable sarcasm. "In the meantime, let us do our jobs."

"Rest assured," Blake said with venom in his voice, "while you are doing yours, I will be doing mine."

Chapter 6

Though Ike agreed to meet Annie at the Austin Police Department's offices the next morning at half past nine, he set off a full hour before that. As he stepped inside the police station, he saw the Englishwoman hunched over a pile of papers at the desk where the watch sergeant generally sat.

She looked up as he approached. Her dress today was golden yellow sprigged with tiny red flowers and featured a prim neckline that gave the impression of a schoolteacher rather than a Pinkerton detective.

An absolutely breathtaking Pinkerton detective.

Ike shook off the thought. There would be no covert kisses in the police station. No flirting. Not when they were working.

Last night he'd come dangerously close to crossing the line between being professional and acting on his personal feelings, and he'd had most of a sleepless night to consider it. Today he would behave like a professional even if he felt like a lovesick fool on the inside.

Or at least he would try.

"Good morning, Isaiah," Annie said with the slightest hint of a smile. "I didn't expect you just yet."

"Good morning to you." He moved a chair over to take a seat across from her. "Looks like you had the same idea of arriving early that I had."

"I couldn't sleep, and breakfast at the hotel isn't exactly my favorite. So after two cups of coffee and a poor attempt at finishing the report to the captain on the case I just completed, I decided to put my energy to work by coming down here to read through the reports."

He looked down at the papers littering the sergeant's desk. "Have you found anything interesting?"

"It's all interesting." Annie gestured to the page open in front of her. "Though the reports vary on the details, if you look at the big picture, there is no doubt one person is behind these killings."

Ike nodded. He'd heard enough and read enough about the case to come to the same conclusion. But it was good to have that conclusion confirmed by someone whose opinion he valued.

"So we're working off the theory that we have one assassin," he said. "But who is he?"

Her smile rose. "Ah, that is where it gets really interesting. There are so many possibilities. It could be anyone at this point."

"Why are you smiling?"

She closed the file in front of her. "Because I now know where to start."

"At the beginning?" he offered.

"If you mean by visiting the scene of the first crime, then yes," she told him. "I propose that we take a walking tour of the locations of each of these crimes in order of their occurrence. I want to get into this man's mind."

"So you're determined it's a man?" he said.

"Fairly." She paused. "Aren't you?"

"Based on the strength that would be required to wield an ax in the way the killer used it, yes. I think that speaks to a strength that only a male would possess. If this is a woman, she is an exceptionally strong one."

"Agreed." Annie looked down at the desk and then back up at Ike. "That means our first stop is the Hall residence on Pecan Street." She rose and waved to the sergeant who had been watching them from the other side of the room. "If you don't mind, I would like to leave these here to look at later. Perhaps another day."

He nodded. "I'll let the boss know."

"Thank you." Annie rose and gathered up her hat and cloak. "And give him my thanks as well. This information has been most helpful." She returned her attention to Ike, then frowned. "What am I thinking? I haven't given you any time to go over the records yourself."

"I can catch up later. I would rather do the fieldwork first and let you fill in the blanks with what you've learned this morning." He nodded to the door. "After you, Detective."

They walked the short distance to the Hall home on Pecan Street. "All right, Detective," Ike said. "Tell me what you know about the first murder."

"The date was New Year's Eve 1884 in the early morning hours. The victim was Mollie Smith, approximately twenty-three and a cook and maid for the Hall family. She was described as a hard worker and was well liked by the family. Also injured that night but not killed was Mollie's paramour, a laborer at a brick-yard named Walter Spencer. It was Spencer who alerted the guests staying in the Halls' home that a crime had occurred."

Ike took in the size of the home, the double chimneys and wide expanse of porch, with its surrounding picket fence that marked it as one of the nicer dwellings in the city. Then he looked down at Annie.

"That would be Tom Chalmers, brother-in-law to the Halls, who was a guest in the home along with his wife while the owners were away." At Annie's look of surprise, Ike continued. "Tom and my father served in the Rangers together. When all of this happened, I heard about his part in the events of that night from my father. It was a fearsome cold night. The sky was spitting ice and snow after a norther had blown through. Last thing old Tom wanted to do was get out in that mess. He told Walter to solve his problems without asking for intervention—he had no idea Mollie was lying dead in the yard—and let him go back to bed."

"I'm sure he later regretted that," Annie offered.

"He might have, though if he did, he didn't mention it to my father," Ike said.

"He could have saved his own life. If the killer was still out there with Mollie, Tom might have walked into something he wouldn't have survived."

"Or he could have saved Mollie and possibly caught the killer before he struck again."

Annie shook her head. "All of that is conjecture. Tom couldn't have known any of this on that night."

Ike nodded toward the alley. "Let's go have a look at the scene of the crime."

Annie led him down the alley until they stopped at a small shanty situated in the back corner of the Hall property. "According to the police reports, the body wasn't found here."

"If I remember right, she was found by a passerby over at Ravy's Store a few blocks away."

"No, there was a call to the police station from Ravy's," Annie corrected, "but the body was actually found about here." She indicated a spot a few feet away from what was obviously an outhouse. "A witness thought it was a dead animal until he got close enough to see his error. From here, he ran up to the store and requested a call be put in to the police. After an investigation, the murder weapon was determined to be an ax."

They stood in silence for a moment. Ike glanced around to get a feeling for what the killer would have encountered in his surroundings. Not that he could have actually seen anything in the pitch black of this alley. Unless he had a torch.

All around him were the homes of successful Austinites, the backs of their properties littered with outbuildings and servants' quarters. Most of the servants who inhabited these quarters were women, living either alone or with their children.

Only a few had a male companion of some sort under the same roof. Mollie had, and it hadn't saved her.

"Do you see anything of note?" Ike asked her.

"Nothing that wasn't covered in the reports," she said. "What about you?"

He stepped into the center of the alley and looked both directions. "Unless he managed to climb over a whole lot of fences, the killer went one of two directions down this alley. Both empty out onto very public streets, but those streets would have been empty on a night like that."

"So whichever way he went, he likely went undetected."

Ike nodded. "Unless you need to see more of this place, I say we move on."

"No, I've seen enough."

"Tell me what you know about the second murder. There was a gap in time of several months, if I remember correctly."

Annie tucked an errant curl behind her ear and nodded. "The next murder happened on May 7, although there was an attack on two Swedish maids that has been attributed to the same person."

"But they survived," Ike said.

"Yes." Annie turned around to leave the alley with Ike beside her. "The women survived the attack but saw nothing of value to investigators. The one interesting thing about this attack is that a silver watch belonging to one of the women turned up missing."

"From the condition of the deceased to the choice of weapon and time of day, the killing of Eliza Shelly bore a striking similarity to this one."

They walked in silence until they reached Cypress Street and the home of Dr. Lucien Johnson. Similar to the Hall home, the Johnson residence was indicative of the doctor's social status and wealth. Also like the first crime scene, the second murder took place near the servants' quarters in the dead of night. After a thorough examination of the scene, Ike and Annie moved on to East Linden Street, just across from the Scholz Garden.

"Now we're at May 27," Annie told him. "Irene Cross is the victim this time. Same method of dispatching the victim. No viable description of the perpetrator."

They walked on, stopping at the locations of the August assault against Clara Dick and then, the murder of young Mary Ramey. "Mary was eleven when she was killed on the night of August 30," Annie said when they'd surveyed the scene there. "Her mother, Rebecca, was wounded and could provide no help in identifying their attacker."

"He walked right past the servants' quarters and killed that girl in the kitchen of the house where she and her mother were employed." Isaiah let out a long breath. "This one was the most shocking to me."

"They were all shocking," Annie said. "But yes, he did diverge from his usual methods here."

"He put the town on notice that no one was safe."

"Yes, well, isn't that still the case?" She sighed. "Let's move on, shall we?"

They soon reached the next murder site and paused to look around. As with the others, there was nothing particularly remarkable about the well-kept home and gardens or the neighborhood that surrounded the abode. That in itself was one of the more frightening aspects of the crime spree.

She turned her thoughts toward the specifics of the case. "This is the most recent killing, the murder of Gracie Vance."

"The incident where there were four persons in the servants' quarters when the attacks began," Ike offered, recalling the details he'd read about the September 28 murder in several of the Chicago newspapers and the letters his father and their housekeeper had written to him.

"That's right." Annie glanced around the back of the Dunham residence and then returned her attention to him. "Orange Washington, Gracie's beau, was present in the quarters as well as two other women, Lucinda Boddy and Patsy Gibson. All four were asleep when the attacks began. Orange was knocked senseless and eventually died from his injuries. Gracie was dragged a full hundred yards away from where she'd been sleeping."

"Unlike the other killings," Ike said, "where death happened on the property and nearer to the place where the victim was sleeping."

"Correct," Annie said.

Ike thought a moment. "Could be he wanted privacy and he was afraid one of those three he'd just assaulted might gather their wits and come after him to try to save their friend. Whatever the reason, this indicates another departure from his previous crimes."

"That is possible. And yes, it does." She paused. "Also, the police gave chase to a man who ran from the scene, but they lost him. There was no reliable description, only what I would call unreliable guesses, based on what I read."

"This case has been marked by plenty of those," Ike said. "Starting with the voodoo rumor. Then there was the thought that there were packs of murdering men that descended on the city at night. I could go on, but I won't. The politicians have been so desperate to make an arrest that they've pressed the police department into an untenable position. Not a single arrest they've made has stuck, and not one good description of our killer exists."

Annie nodded. "I got a taste of how the politicians feel about catching this man at the dinner last night. But let's return our focus to Gracie Vance. There is one more thing that is remarkable about this particular murder. Remember the silver watch that was missing from the Swedish woman? It turned up on Gracie's wrist."

Ike frowned. "I didn't read that in the newspaper accounts."

"I suppose the police are holding this new information back from the press to discourage anyone who might want to copy the killer's methods."

"It would be easy to dispatch a woman and blame it on the Midnight Assassin," Annie said. "It's possible that has already happened."

"Which may be why the man has added this new signature to his crimes. He doesn't want anyone else getting away with blaming him for something he hasn't done."

Ike lifted his hand to hail a cab. They'd strayed far afield of downtown, and they needed to sit down and compare notes on what to do next. There was only one place he knew of where privacy could be assured and a planning meeting would not be interrupted.

Also, it was lunchtime.

Chapter 7

Isaiah lifted Annie into the cab and climbed in beside her. Her feet hurt and her head spun with all of the information she'd taken on today, so she was grateful for the respite from walking. Between the police reports she'd read and the experience of seeing each of the crime scenes in person, she was exhausted.

"I don't recognize that address," Annie said when she heard Isaiah's instructions to the driver.

"No, I don't suppose you would." He shrugged. "Trust me, okay?"

"All right, but only because I am too tired to argue right now," she said warily. "Should I not?"

He chuckled. "We've worked together enough. What do you think?"

Annie spared him a sideways glance. "I think we need to get something straight, Isaiah."

"That sounds ominous," he said. "But I agree. I've got something I need to say as well."

"You go first, then," Annie told him, grateful for the brief reprieve.

"All right." He looked down at his hands then over at her. "It's no secret that I've got feelings for you. You're quite a woman, Annie Walters. But I can't be letting those feelings get the best of me like I did last night. It was the governor's wife who walked up on us without me knowing, but it could have been anyone. If I allowed something to happen to you because of a lapse in my attention. . ."

Not at all what she expected he would say. But this did work with her plans to keep their relationship on a business-only level while they were working on this case.

"I understand," she said on an exhale of breath. "Business only. Neither of us wants our judgment called into question."

"We do not," he said.

"Then we are agreed." She rested her hands atop one another on her lap and studied her gloves.

"Good," he said in a tone that unmistakably conveyed his relief.

"Good," she responded as she tried not to think about last night's kiss that almost was. The kiss that now was an impossibility.

The cab lurched to a stop in front of a well-kept home that looked very similar to the residences they had just visited. Isaiah helped her down and turned to pay the driver.

"What is this place?" Annie asked when he joined her on the walkway that led to the front door.

"This place is—"

The door opened, and a lovely woman with red hair mixed with silver stepped out. She wore a dress that matched her green eyes, with a pin in the shape of the letter *H* holding a tartan scarf in shades of red and green around her neck. She studied them a moment until her lips turned up in a smile.

"Ike, I expected ya might be here for lunch, but I didn't think there would be a guest. Who've ya brought?" she called in a thick Irish brogue.

"Annie is a friend, Miss Hattie. Can we make room for her at the table? I promise she won't eat much."

"Don't you be smart with me, Ike Joplin," she said with a chuckle before turning to Annie. "Miss, you're more than welcome here at our table. That lot you've arrived with, I'm not so certain about."

"Annie Walters," Isaiah said, "please meet Miss Hattie. She's been running things around here and taking care of my father and me for as long as I can remember. She's also a decent cook."

There was no mistaking the admiration in the older woman's eyes. And the mischief. Annie had been raised by a nanny with much the same qualities.

"Get on with yourself," Miss Hattie told him. "Welcome to the Joplin home," she said to Annie.

Isaiah grinned at the housekeeper and then escorted Annie inside. The home was every bit as lovely on the inside as she expected.

And something smelled delicious.

Annie's stomach groaned. The coffee she had consumed in lieu of breakfast had not been enough, but she had been too busy focusing on the investigation to notice.

Until now.

Miss Hattie bustled past to disappear behind a door on the far side of the room. Annie followed Isaiah into a beautifully decorated dining room that had been set for one.

"She was expecting you?" Annie asked him.

A look Annie couldn't quite decipher crossed Isaiah's face. As quickly as it arrived, the look was gone.

"No," he said gruffly. "I'm not the one she's hoping will show up."

A moment later, Miss Hattie bustled in with a tray containing two place settings of china to match the one already set up on the table, along with a pitcher of water and two glasses. "You two make yourself at home here, and I'll be right back with lunch. It's beef stew and soda bread. Nothing fancy, but it'll fill you up."

After being served, Annie took her first bite of the sumptuously thick soup and suppressed a groan as she slathered butter on a thick slice of bread. "This is delicious."

"So you like it, then," Miss Hattie said as she poured water into their goblets. "I'm pleased, indeed I am. The bread and the stew, they're my mother's recipes, and I'm proud to serve them, though I do not do them justice."

Miss Hattie cast a glance at the empty plate at the end of the table. Then she sighed and disappeared back into the kitchen.

"Why the empty plate, Isaiah?" Annie asked.

"It's for my father," he said. "She cooks him three meals a day and always sets a place for him at the table."

"Where is he?"

Isaiah shrugged. "Hard to say. He's not an easy man to explain. Best way I can describe him is unique. He, along with Miss Hattie, raised me after my mother died when I was a baby. I didn't realize until I was almost grown that he was odd."

"Odd how, if I might ask?"

"He gets preoccupied and loses track of time. Pop is a professor at the college, and he spends a lot of time there and out in the field doing his research."

"I suppose I can understand that. My father was an occasional lecturer on English history. He often got sidetracked, so perhaps it is a hazard of the profession. Why does she worry so? I could see it on her face."

"Because, from what I understand, she promised my mama she would take care of him, and she took that promise seriously. The rumor is he first asked Miss Hattie to marry him sometime around my second birthday, but she turned him down. Last I heard, he keeps asking and she keeps turning him down. Says if he can't remember to sit down at the table and have at least one civilized meal a day, then he isn't the sort of husband she wants."

Annie stifled a smile. "Well, I do see her point, but I'm very glad she cooked today. This stew is indeed delicious. My mother employed a cook who could make a stew that I thought couldn't be beat, but I was wrong."

Isaiah looked up from his bowl of stew. "Tell me about your mother."

Her heart lurched. "Nothing much to tell, really. She's a wife to my father, a mother to me. Just the usual."

"Nothing usual about that for me," he told her.

"I'm sorry."

"No, it's fine." Isaiah paused to study her. "It's just that I feel like you're not comfortable talking about yourself. Or maybe it's just your family that you don't want to speak about."

The truth, but she did not wish to admit it.

"Truly, I had a normal English upbringing in a normal English family. I have a sister, Beatrice, and no brothers. Papa is a history buff who occasionally spoke to classes at the university level, and Mama loves gardening and buying new hats. My parents are still very much alive and arguing daily over which of them will be allowed to complete the daily crossword puzzle in their morning newspaper." She shrugged. "All very boring."

Except for her relation to the queen and the fact that she was brought up as a royal, albeit a minor one many, many steps removed from the throne. Which she would never mention if it could be avoided.

And it would be.

Isaiah lifted one dark brow. "I am always suspicious when someone tells me there's nothing unusual to be found by looking any closer. They generally mean just the opposite."

"Which is what makes you such a good Pinkerton detective," she said, schooling her features into a neutral expression. "Perhaps we should move the topic of discussion along and take up Pinkerton business. It is what we agreed to stick to."

It was her turn to lift a brow in his direction.

"All right," he said, holding up his hands as if in defeat. "Pinkerton business it is. You've seen the locations where the murders occurred and read the police reports. What are your thoughts?"

"My immediate thought is that whoever this monster is, he must be well schooled in making a quiet entrance and exit. No one ever seems to hear him coming, and except for one occasion when men gave chase—an occasion on which no one has proved they were actually chasing the perpetrator—he has never been seen or heard leaving."

"Would you say he's a career criminal or just sneaky?"

"I'd say neither." She gave consideration to whether a theory she had was worth any merit and determined that it might be. "A career criminal would have left a trail before now. There have been plenty of opportunities for law enforcement in other cities to step up and say that they too have had unsolved murders similar to these. None have done that."

"True," Isaiah said.

"As to sneaky?" She shrugged. "That's an obvious yes, if the qualification is that one can go about undetected. But let's consider this a moment. If this man—and as I have said before, I do believe it is a man, based on sheer size and strength required to do the crimes—wanted to merely kill undetected, he could have easily shot these people from a safe distance and disappeared off into the night. He did not do that."

"No, he didn't. In every case, the victims saw their assailant. He just left most of them in a state where they could not describe him."

"And the others," Annie added, "so befuddled over what they'd seen or so frightened that they could give only the most basic description. We've had hundreds of men arrested for this crime. We have living witnesses in the two Swedish maids. Yet the monster remains uncaught. It's baffling."

"You'll get no argument from me." He sat back and dabbed at the corner of his mouth with his napkin. "I think this ability to remain undetected speaks to some level of planning instead of crimes of passion. Do you agree?"

"I think so." She paused. "To me, the big question is not how but why. Why does he do this? What compels an otherwise unremarkable man to commit such heinous crimes?"

Isaiah frowned. "Unremarkable? How do you figure that?"

"If there was something about him that stood out, might he not have been caught already?"

"Possibly," he said. "But not necessarily."

She shrugged. "Then we shall agree to disagree, because I think our assassin is hiding in plain sight and going about his business in a normal and unremarkable way until he decides to kill again. Which could be tonight, next week, or never."

"I'm not sure if I disagree with you," he said in that slow Texas drawl he sometimes used when he was thinking about something. "I'm just not sure I agree with you either."

"That is fair. So tell me your observations, Isaiah. This is your town, and you know the people here, so I am hoping you have some insights I do not."

"Insights." He said the word on an exhale of breath. "Annie, I've been thinking about this case for a long time now. Since the first round of killings last winter. My father tried to move Miss Hattie into the house to keep her safe, but she thought he was just being fresh and nearly quit."

Annie suppressed a smile. "I can see both sides of that argument."

"Well, neither of them could." He shook his head. "After the third attack at the end of May, Miss Hattie struck a deal. She'd move into the attic, but she wanted a door that locked only on the inside and a dog."

"A dog?"

Isaiah nodded. "A big Irish wolfhound. She got it too, along with the lock on the door. She trained that dog to sleep against the door at night, but that's not all. Before Miss Hattie was done, she'd also talked my father into a brand-new bedroom set for her attic room with Irish linen sheets mailed to her from back home in Armagh and lace curtains for the window."

"Lace curtains in an attic? And an Irish wolfhound to guard the door? Oh my. She is persuasive."

"You have no idea," he told her. "Although Alfie hasn't turned out to be much of a watchdog. He loves his master's cooking too much, so he's grown fat and lazy. Miss Hattie puts his bed in front of the door where she figures he will do the most good tripping anyone who might come in."

Annie chuckled. Her father had a pair of wolfhounds that followed him around like lap dogs and were more interested in getting their bellies scratched than actually keeping anyone safe from an intruder.

"Where is Alfie now?" she asked, oddly homesick for her father's pets.

"Likely in the kitchen." He paused to wink at Annie. "If he isn't in front of the fire gnawing on a bone from the stew, then he's probably sitting at his master's heels right by the door where she's listening to our conversation right now."

Miss Hattie stepped into the dining room. "Shame on you, Isaiah Joplin. I was not listening to your conversation. I merely wanted to be prepared in case your guest wanted more bread or stew. After all, it is my job to take care of you."

"But you've left the stew pot and the bread and butter on the table in front of us."

The older woman shook her head as she turned her attention to Annie. "Insufferable, he is."

"I would agree," Annie admitted. "But I've grown used to him."

"As have I." Miss Hattie's eyes narrowed as she studied Annie. "England, yes?" At her nod, the housekeeper continued. "London would be my guess. Am I right?"

"You are," she said.

"My first husband's people were Londoners. Not a bit of good, the whole lot of them. But you look all right." She narrowed her eyes again. "In fact, you look familiar. Should I know you?"

"I don't see how," Annie said, quickly growing uncomfortable under the scrutiny.

She had been told on more than one occasion that she and

Beatrice strongly favored their great-grandmother when she was young. Annie had never given the similarity much thought, even as the portraits of young Victoria she had seen seemed to offer confirmation.

"No," she said. "I never forget a face, and I've seen yours before."

Chapter 8

W hen Miss Hattie set herself onto a problem that needed solving, she hung on like a dog on a bone. Fortunately, Alfie's frenzied barking in the kitchen distracted her long enough for Ike to save poor Annie from any further Irish inquisition.

At least for the moment.

Ike watched the door close behind the housekeeper and then turned his attention to Annie. "Apparently you've got a twin in London."

The look on her face told him the joke fell flat. "What?"

"Nothing," she said. "I believe you were giving me your insights as a local. Can we continue with that?"

It didn't take a Pinkerton detective to realize Annie had something to hide. Something related to London and a familiar face to Miss Hattie. He'd have to tuck that knowledge away and do his own research someday when he had the chance.

Whatever he'd find, Ike was willing to bet it would be interesting.

"Yes, right. I was saying that by the end of May the women who worked as servants or housekeepers and lived on the property were considering this a crime that could happen to them. They were afraid."

"And with good reason. The mother and daughter who were attacked in the August killing were sleeping in the kitchen of their employer because they were afraid to stay in the servants' quarters." She paused to shudder. "Little Mary was only eleven, and her poor mother will never be right again after what the fiend did to her."

"With that attack, the perpetrator showed he was brave enough not only to raid the unguarded servants' quarters for victims but also to go inside a home where he might encounter a much stronger defense. That's the one that really shook the town, I think." Ike paused. "It is the attack that, in my mind, told me this man had an agenda."

Her brows gathered. "Explain, please."

"Until Mary Ramey was killed and Clara Dick injured, it might be argued that the previous incidents were crimes of opportunity. By that, I mean it could be argued that the man was prowling alleys looking for some sighting of a woman who caught his eye or who maybe he'd seen earlier in the day or the week and followed home. The planning was minimal, if at all, and he never chose to harm a child before."

"I can see that."

"But with Mary Ramey's death, that all changed. Now he's standing in a kitchen. He's leaving the mother injured and killing the daughter. What was it about that night or those two women that provoked such a daring move?"

"Anger," Annie said. "Though that is never the primary reason. Anger is always caused by something else, be it disappointment, grief, revenge." She shook her head. "There can be any number of possible triggers."

"But we agree that this is where the crimes escalate?"

"If you mean in the choice of victim and the means of carrying out the crime, then yes, I agree. It was as if he would do anything to get at the victims, and then oddly he chose the child instead of the mother."

"And then we end up with the Vance murder," Ike said. "And the token from a previous crime that he places on her wrist. Could he have left that watch as a goodbye present for the police? It's been three months, and there's no further sign of him."

Annie sat back and seemed to be considering the question. "It's possible. I do hope so, actually. Though I would prefer if we could identify him and send him away so he doesn't harm anyone in another place or at a later time." She paused. "Today has given me plenty to consider. If you'll excuse me, I think I'll walk back to my hotel and put all of this down in my notes so I can give it closer thought."

Ike rose when she did. "I'll walk with you," he said.

"No, truly, I need the time alone. Might we meet again tomorrow once I've had time to clarify my thoughts?"

"We might," he said with a grin. "You do realize tomorrow is the day before Christmas Eve, right?"

"Yes, I suppose it is." Her tone told him that Annie had not realized this until he pointed it out. "Please convey my thanks to your housekeeper for the delicious meal. It's truly the best thing I've eaten in a very long time."

"I will. And I will put my notes together for us to compare later."

Annie did not respond. Ike fell into step beside her as Annie retraced her steps to the front door. Then he reached around to place his hand on the door.

"I plan to visit your hotel later this afternoon to check on your progress. I will bring my notes."

Not a question. A statement.

Annie looked up into his eyes, and Ike knew she was considering her response. Then she nodded. "If I am there, then I will see you and your notes."

With that cryptic statement, the lady Pinkerton ducked under his arm and slipped out. Ike stood in the door and watched her go, trying to decide whether to follow.

"Queen Victoria!"

Ike turned around to see Miss Hattie standing behind him, her hands resting on her hips and Alfie beside her. "Excuse me?"

"Queen Victoria," she repeated, then gave him a look like he ought to understand her meaning. "As petite as she is with her dark hair, your young lady looks like the queen herself, she does."

Ike chuckled. "Miss Hattie, I have seen pictures of the queen, and I assure you she looks nothing like the monarch currently on the throne. Is there another Queen Victoria you were thinking of?"

The housekeeper shook her head. "Don't be daft, Ikey, there's only the one."

"I will try not to be daft if you'll try not to call me Ikey."

Miss Hattie shuffled back to the kitchen, shaking her head, leaving the wolfhound to settle himself where he'd been sitting. "Too far a walk back to the kitchen?" Ike asked him.

In response, Alfie snorted and closed his eyes.

Shaking his head at the lazy pup, Ike turned back to look out the door in the direction Annie had gone. Over the top of the neighbor's tall shrubs, he spied her hat bobbing along on the sidewalk at a brisk pace.

Annie never had been one to take a leisurely pace, but this was quick even for her. Ike took a step out onto the porch where he could see her fully and noticed there was a man in a suit and bowler hat walking at the same speed a few paces behind her.

His first thought was that Cameron Blake had followed them here and was now attempting to squeeze a story out of whatever meager facts he might cajole Annie into sharing. But that wasn't Blake. The man was too tall. Too broad across the shoulders.

Ike was just about to see for himself who the fellow might be and to satisfy his concern that he wasn't following Annie when the lady Pinkerton abruptly crossed the street. The man in the bowler hat continued on without making the trek across the road, alleviating his concern.

Behind him, Alfie whimpered. Ike stepped back inside. "Need to go out, buddy?" he said, wondering not for the first time why he was talking to a dog.

Alfie whimpered again and cut his eyes toward the dining room.

"Oh, I see how it is. You're waiting for stew."

"Don't feed him any," Miss Hattie called from the kitchen. "He's already had two bowls. If he has another, someone will have to carry him up to the attic tonight, and I promise you that someone will not be me."

Ike chuckled at the thought. "Sorry, Alfie. The boss says no."

Once again, the pup snorted and closed his eyes. Ike took another look outside. Annie was now out of sight, so he closed the door.

He glanced over at the table where his empty bowl awaited another filling. Annie was right. There was not much better than a bowl of Miss Hattie's Irish stew.

But Miss Hattie had already removed the pot. Refilling his bowl would require a trip to the kitchen where the housekeeper would likely continue her chatter about Queen Victoria and who knew what else.

Ike frowned. Like Alfie, he'd be waiting until later for his next meal. Unlike Alfie, he had plenty to do in the meantime.

And the first thing he planned to do was check on Annie and make sure that man with the bowler hat wasn't still trailing her.

❦

Annie was far too busy to be interrupted. Yet the persistent man who had followed her—rather expertly—from Isaiah's family home needed to be stopped.

She sighed. He'd managed to make her think for the slightest of moments that they were merely traveling the same path by some accident of time and occasion. When he continued on after she crossed the street, Annie figured she was done with him.

But here he was again, tracking her just enough paces behind to make the untrained person think he was merely out for a walk and going in the same direction as she was. She stopped, counted to three, and then turned abruptly and stalked toward him.

Rather than skitter away as one with criminal intent might, the man stopped short and met her gaze. She studied his features and found them unremarkable.

Unremarkable.

Her breath caught. Surely not.

Straightening her spine, Annie marched toward the man who'd been following her. "You there," she demanded. "Identify yourself."

Blue eyes and a lazy smile were the first two things she noticed about the stranger. A rather prominent nose, a firm jaw, and a breadth of shoulder that might have rendered him a man who made a living with his fists.

The stranger lifted his hat to reveal a thatch of sandy hair. "Good day, ma'am. I bring greetings."

"From whom?" she asked warily, fully cognizant of the fact that he had yet to comply with her request to identify himself.

"A friend, Miss von Wettin."

Annie stifled a cringe at the sound of her actual name being spoken aloud so casually. So publicly.

The man glanced to his right and then to his left before speaking further. "May I have a word? In private?" he quickly amended.

"No, I think not. Whatever you need to say, you may say it here." She paused. "But I will have your name first since you believe you know mine."

Rather than speak, he retrieved a small leather notebook from his pocket. Inside was a folded piece of paper, which he handed to her. "This should suffice as an answer to all of that. You are to read it now."

She glanced down at the document. Then she turned the document over to look at the seal.

Simon Kent. Of course.

Running her finger under the crimson wax stamped with the Kent coat of arms, Annie unfolded the paper to read the message from the grandfatherly man who had single-handedly managed to extricate her from under the tight control of the British royal family and secure her an interview with Mr. Pinkerton in Chicago some three years ago.

The man without whom this life she now led would have been impossible.

Dispensing with any sort of greeting, the practical Kent went right to the message.

Do not blame the messenger for this missive, my friend.
Pause in your reading to send him along his way with a
thank you from me.

Annie looked up at the man. "I am to offer thanks from Mr. Kent and then send you on your way."

The man gave a curt nod and walked away. After a moment, Annie returned to her reading.

I'm sure you have questions, but I shall be brief. I did not
go to great effort to seek you out. My associate was already
planning a sojourn to the colonies and was glad to oblige me
in this. Thus the situation I am writing about is not yet dire.
However, with inaction on your part, it soon shall be. I bring
a warning in regard to your family.

"Annie."

She jerked her attention from the letter to see Isaiah walking toward her. Folding the letter, she tucked it into her pocket.

"Why are you following me?" she snapped and then thought better of her temper. "Sorry. I am just surprised to see you again so soon."

"You were being followed, but not by me," he said, giving her an appraising look. "Bowler hat, dark suit. Did you notice him?"

The most expedient way out of this conversation would have been to feign innocence and say she did not. But she was truthful in all things, even if it meant having to deal with Isaiah Joplin on this matter.

"I did. He was a messenger sent to deliver a letter. . ." She paused then added, "Which he has. Was there anything else you needed, Isaiah?"

"I, well, that is. . ." He shook his head. "No, nothing else. Although I've never seen a messenger who looked like that."

Annie regarded him with what she hoped would be an expression devoid of emotion. "Like what?"

"Bowler hat, nice suit, looked like a fighter." He shook his head. "Never mind. I'll just go on back home and work on my report to the captain."

"All right."

He looked as if he was trying to think of any reason to continue the conversation. Meanwhile, Annie tried to keep her frustration in check.

"You'll be doing that too," he said.

"I will," she responded.

Isaiah opened his mouth as if to say something further, then appeared to reconsider. With a curt nod, he made his exit.

Annie watched him go and felt the slightest twinge of guilt. He'd only sought her to be certain she was safe.

Her response to his protective gesture had been less than enthusiastic. Annie sighed.

"Isaiah," she called.

He turned around and walked back toward her. "Yes?"

"Thank you. Truly. I appreciate that you followed your instincts to be certain I was safe."

"And you are."

Only the slightest pause before she nodded. "I am. The message was personal. Nothing related to this case or any other one."

Again he was studying her. Possibly trying to decide whether to pry. Finally, without comment, he turned and headed back in the direction he'd come from.

Annie waited until the Pinkerton detective was out of sight and then retrieved the letter from her pocket. *I bring a warning in regard to your family,* she read again.

Your father has come to me with concerns regarding your prolonged trip to America and the explanations which he tells me are wearing thin. I have no answers for him beyond that he should continue to write to you. Now, a warning for you: Answer his letters. Write him frequently. Speak of inconsequential things like flora, fauna, and the friends you've made on your sabbatical. Should you not heed my warning, he will come looking for you. Perhaps he already has.

Annie read that last sentence again, and her heart lurched. Surely not.

Chapter 9

With a sigh, Annie tucked the letter into her pocket and returned to her hotel. Bypassing the desk clerk who was busy trying to speak French to a guest who obviously did not speak English, she hurried upstairs and locked the door to her room behind her.

The letter with the stamps that had intrigued the clerk was still where she'd put it. Annie slid the invitations over to reveal the envelope with her father's familiar handwriting emblazoned on it.

> *Alice A. von Witten*
> *12 VanZant Place*
> *Chicago   United States of America*

She sighed. Part of the arrangement Simon had made with the Pinkerton Agency for her employment was that she would be given an address where her family could write while she was "away." The Pinkertons forwarded any letters from her family to whatever location she'd been sent, as long as it did not compromise the mission.

She picked up the letter and moved to the seat beside the window. The afternoon was warm for December, excessively so. Annie lifted the sash. Instantly the sounds of the street below drifted up to her.

Papa was a dear and was rightly protective of her and Beatrice. Though Granny paid Papa a generous allowance, or so she had overheard, Annie and her sister were the assets that would assure solvency would be maintained into future generations. Keeping a manor house and a country home was no inexpensive endeavor even for royalty, her father often complained.

If only Beatrice would decide on which of her many suitors she would bestow her favor. Then perhaps Papa would not be so frantic to keep track of Annie and have her wed.

When his protective nature kept Annie from accepting the hard-won appointment to the Metropolitan Police's Crime Investigation Department as a special constable, she'd been nearly inconsolable. She had been thrilled by the opportunity. Her parents obviously had disapproved.

Then dear Simon, her godfather and a close friend of the family, called her into a meeting. "Though you are named a special constable, your father has made it impossible for us to put you to work here in London. However, I have a friend in Chicago."

I have a friend in Chicago. Six words that had changed her life. And her address.

Though her father never would have allowed her to take a position as a Pinkerton detective, he had no qualms about placing her under the protection of Simon's friends, Mr. and Mrs. Pinkerton, who would be introducing her to Chicago and New York society.

She weighed the letter in her palm. Another sigh and Annie opened the letter, dated the twentieth of October.

Unlike Simon's terse one-page missive, her father had written a chatty multipage account of life in the English countryside these past few months when the family traditionally returned to the family home for the fall. He described village life at length, including weddings, funerals, and a brief list of births. Then he moved on to their plans for Christmas with Granny in London.

> *Your mother and I would like very much for you to be in attendance. Come home, Daughter. It is time.*

Annie let the letter drop into her lap. Simon was right. What would she do?

She rose to return the letter to the top of the stack on the desk and looked over at the window. The afternoon was not half spent.

Tonight she would put together a draft of her thoughts on today's investigation and write Papa. For now, she had more work to do.

Starting by interviewing as many eyewitnesses to the monster's crimes as she could locate. She began by paying a visit once again to the location of the first murder.

"Tom Chalmers is who you want to speak with," the lady of the house told her. "My husband and I were in Galveston when the events occurred. We have nothing to say other than we felt terrible about the whole thing."

Her experience was similar at every other place. Either the homeowner refused to come to the door, knew nothing, or wanted nothing to do with an investigation. She would have preferred to interview the servants, but that was an impossibility if she could not get inside the door or attract anyone's attention from the alley.

Though she hated to admit it, Mr. Blake's allegation that the people of Austin, both the employers and their servants, wished to forget the awful ordeal seemed to be true. Overhead, dark clouds gathered and the wind had picked up. Dejected, Annie hailed a cab with the intention of returning to her hotel.

The cab that stopped, however, already had a passenger. "Good afternoon, Miss Walters," Cameron Blake said with a smile. "I wonder if you might have a minute."

"I don't actually," she told him.

Blake's smile was swift. "Yet you're standing there hoping to catch a cab to keep out of the rain. I have one. Let me deliver you to your next meeting." He paused but only for a second. "Or wherever it is you might be going."

As the first fat drops of rain began to fall, she looked up the road in hopes of seeing another cab. Nothing.

Annie turned back to the reporter. "I will accept your offer. Thank you."

A moment later, they were headed in the direction of her hotel with the rain pouring against the roof of the cab. "Just in time, I'd say," Blake told her.

She offered a weak smile. "It was indeed."

An awkward silence fell between them. Then the reporter spoke up. "Were any of them willing to talk to you?"

Annie looked up sharply. She briefly considered pretending she did not know to whom he was referring, then changed her mind.

"No," she said. "Not one."

"I could have told you that," he said, leaning back and crossing his arms. "They're circling the wagons. No one wants to talk to an outsider." Blake shook his head. "What am I saying? No one wants to talk about the crime spree, period. You heard what Swain said at the governor's dinner. It's just not a topic anyone wants to think about."

"Until it happens again," she said. "If it does."

"It might not," he said, meeting her gaze. "I pray it doesn't."

"How long have you been working on this story?" she asked him.

"Since the beginning," he said. "Though I finally got the paper to see that this was a big enough story to send me down here. Took a while. I arrived just before the September murder. The big one."

"Why do you call it that?"

"Because he killed a man. That hadn't happened before." He shrugged. "Felt to me like he was either escalating or going out with a bang when he attacked Orange Washington and hauled Gracie Vance a good distance from the place where he grabbed her. I'm still not sure which."

"Have you spoken to any of them? The survivors and witnesses, I mean," Annie clarified. "I wonder if there's some piece of evidence they saw or heard that they do not realize is important."

"I tried. When the alarm was raised about Gracie's murder, I ran off to the scene just like half of Austin did."

"So you were a witness yourself, of a sort."

"I was." He paused as if recalling the moment. "It wasn't anything I want to see again, Miss Walters, and I've looked at some pretty grisly crime scenes in my day. And written about them too. I can tell you that Orange Washington is no small man, so whoever bested him cannot be either. There were two other women there who weren't harmed, but they were too terrified to recount what happened. And what he did to Gracie. . ."

Blake looked away and said nothing for a full minute. Annie left him to his silence.

"Trouble is, it took no time for that crime scene to be trampled beyond repair. If there was any evidence that could be identified by a footprint or something of the like, it was gone." He shook his head. "These people are their own worst enemies when it comes to preserving evidence. But this is Austin, not New York. I guess things like that don't happen much around here."

"No," she said. "This is a first for Austin. Who do you think did it?"

Her abrupt change of direction took him off guard, as it was intended to do. "Now that is the question, isn't it? The interesting thing is, I could make a case for a dozen men—and surely it is a man—off the top of my head. Men in power whose hands never get dirty and working men I've seen hauling more bricks on their shoulders than a human ought to be able to. Any man whose anger can spark—or whatever it is that drives him—sufficient to kill. That's your man."

Annie nodded. "Yes, I agree there appears to be nothing to define him as far as race or station in life. He's a killer who is driven by something we cannot yet determine to murder women who are sleeping in their beds."

She let that thought take hold. There was something to that last statement.

"He only kills women who are sleeping and defenseless," she continued. "That speaks to something inside him. A defect. Or a wound. I just can't quite define it yet."

"Here's how I look at it," Blake said. "I don't care why. That's for the article I will write after he's caught. What matters is who."

"Yes," she said. "Rule out anyone who cannot lift a heavy ax over his head more than once. That's all we've got."

Blake shrugged. "Then we pray that is enough."

The cab pulled to a stop in front of her hotel, and Annie moved to exit. Before she stepped out, she looked back at the reporter. "Thank you for allowing me to share your cab. And for the information. You've kept me out of the rain and given me some things to think about."

He shook his head. "I haven't told you anything you didn't already know. The question is, do you have anything you want to tell me?"

Annie frowned. "What do you mean?"

"I know you've seen the police reports. They're off-limits to reporters, so maybe you saw some interesting fact that isn't being circulated to the general population?"

"Mr. Blake," she said in mock astonishment, "are you priming me for information I am not supposed to be giving out?"

He grinned. "Of course I am. Is it working?"

"It is not," she said firmly.

"A pity. I can pay a generous finder's fee for any information that is usable," he told her. "Even a Pinkerton detective must have expenses. It is nearly Christmas. Perhaps there are gifts to be purchased. Baubles and trinkets to be bought. A new frock or a pretty hat, perhaps."

A new frock or a pretty hat? She stifled a groan. Did he honestly think her conscience could be appeased with baubles and trinkets?

"Thank you, Mr. Blake, but your fee is wasted on me," she said evenly. "If you really want to do something good, however, why don't you advertise that finder's fee in your next column and see if you can get any takers. Someone out there may be in possession of valuable information and in need of ready cash."

"A good point indeed," he said. "Perhaps I shall."

"Then I will leave you to it. Good afternoon, Mr. Blake."

"And I will be certain to credit you with any information you provide, if credit is what you wish."

"Please don't mention you've spoken with me," she said hastily. Too hastily. She could see the interest pique on the reporter's face. "I don't want to compromise an investigation by allowing too much information to go out. I'd rather it not be widely known that I am here."

"I understand."

Annie did not miss the fact that while he said he understood, he made no promises that he would comply with her request. She stepped out of the cab and hurried through the rain to duck beneath the shelter of the hotel's broad green awning.

As the cab pulled away, she spied Cameron Blake watching her. In that moment, she was certain of one thing: she should have chosen to walk back in the rain rather than sharing a cab with Cameron Blake.

She said nothing of value to a reporter. Any question he asked, she deflected. Instead, she had been the one to question him.

Annie went over their conversation in her mind as she reached for the door. It was all fine. All above board.

Why then did she have a knot in the pit of her stomach?

She certainly hadn't worried about speaking with the reporter at the governor's dinner. Others had been seated around them, to be sure, and the comptroller had held sway during most of the conversation.

Perhaps it was because now that she had returned here, the task of writing to her father would be the next item on her list of things to get done. And she definitely needed to write to Papa.

She also had no idea what she planned to say. So perhaps that was the problem.

Annie stepped inside the hotel's lobby and froze. Waiting for her with a newspaper in his lap and a scowl on his face was Isaiah Joplin.

∼

"What are you doing here?" Annie demanded.

"Waiting for you." Ike looked past her to be certain the reporter hadn't spied him as the cab drove away and decided to join them. Then he turned to Annie. "You told me you were going back to your hotel. You didn't mention that you and Blake had plans together today."

"Because we didn't."

"I saw you getting out of the cab just now. Blake looked pleased with himself."

"And that's what I'm worried about." She waved away the comment. "Isaiah, I respect you as a fellow Pinkerton detective. I would hope you do the same for me."

"I do."

The lady Pinkerton fixed him with a look. "Then reconsider the direction this conversation is going. I do not have to account to you for my time, just as I would not require you to account for yours."

She had a point. Yet Ike found himself irrationally bothered by the fact he had caught Annie returning to her hotel with Cameron Blake. Even though he knew where she had been.

"Has Blake been with you all afternoon?"

Her eyes narrowed. "Did you not hear what I just said?"

"I did, but my question remains the same. Was the reporter with you all afternoon?"

"I only met up with him on my way back here," she finally said. "It was about to rain, he had a cab, and I did not. Truly, I find the man insufferable. You, however, are edging very close to insufferable as well."

"Past it, I think," Ike said.

Annie stifled a smile. "You'll get no argument from me on that point."

"A doctor friend of mine sent a message that he would like to speak with me." He paused for emphasis. "I'm certain this has to do with our case, so I thought you ought to come along. Since we're a team."

"Enough, Isaiah," she snapped. "I should have asked you to go along with me today. I admit it. So I am telling you now. I went out to speak with witnesses, though not a one of them wished to speak with me."

"I know."

"How?"

He shook his head. "Austin is a big city, but it is still very much a small town. As soon as the front door closed at the Hall home, the news that a Pinkerton detective was asking questions started spreading. After the first time you knocked on a door, were you able to get anyone else to answer?"

"I was not," she admitted.

"Now you know why."

Annie let out a long breath. "This conspiracy of silence is why that monster has not been caught. Could it be he's one of them?"

A theory Ike had tossed around for a while. "I'm not ruling that out, but I don't have any suspects. Do you?"

"No."

He removed his watch from his vest pocket, checked the time, then looked at Annie. The time was never right on the thing, but replacing it would require a shopping trip he did not wish to take. He looked over and noticed she was wearing a watch.

"What time is it, Annie?"

She told him. "Is your watch broken?"

"More like inconsistent," he said.

"You should get it fixed then."

"I don't like it enough to bother. I don't even remember where I got it." He shrugged. "Anyway, I'm hoping Dr. Langston will have something that will change this. Are you coming with me?"

"I am," she said. "And Isaiah?"

"Yes?"

Her face gave away nothing of what she might be about to say. "Never question me like that again, do you understand?" She paused as the beginnings of a smile rose. "Unless I deserve it. I assure you I will hold you to the same standard."

He grinned. "Yes, ma'am."

Chapter 10

Dr. Langston was not, as Annie expected, a medical doctor. Rather, the bespectacled Langston, with his shock of unruly dark hair and pale blue eyes, was a lecturer in the science of astronomy.

The second-floor room where they met on the University of Texas campus was part classroom and part science lab with chairs set up in rows in the back and a dozen tables filled with scientific equipment in front. Incandescent lighting had been strung up down the center of the room, but gaslights still marched at regular intervals down each side of the deep green walls.

Someone had written a string of equations on the blackboard that extended the length of the wall on the lecture end of the room. As the men chatted about old times, Annie looked out the floor-to-ceiling windows situated behind the chairs to watch a campus bustling with students even as a light rain continued to fall.

The room, for all its size, felt claustrophobic and smelled of chalk dust and chemicals. Laughter turned her attention back toward the two men.

Isaiah was smiling. Oh, but he was handsome when he grinned that way.

"I met your father several decades ago when he was just a young pup and I was a newly employed lecturer in the study of rocks that fall from the sky," he said to Isaiah before turning his piercing gaze on Annie. "That would be what we now call astronomy. The elder Joplin needed my help identifying rocks he'd found on a dig, and now it appears that the younger Joplin could also benefit from my assistance."

"If only finding the culprit was as simple as identifying rocks," Annie said.

The professor's pinched expression quickly told her he did not find her statement amusing. "Miss Walters, I assure you that identifying rocks is no simple matter."

"I don't think either of us believes it is," Isaiah said as he braved a sideways look at Annie. "I know I wouldn't know a piece of mica from an obsidian."

"Hush," the professor said as a grin appeared beneath his drooping black mustache. "You would too, but only because your father taught you." He shook his head then turned to Annie. "Forgive me. I fear I lack a sense of humor when it comes to the study of my passion."

"There is nothing to forgive," she told him. "And I am sorry I made a joke at your expense."

"As you said, there is nothing to forgive." He turned his attention back to Isaiah. "Yes, so I did not bring you here to catch up on old times, Detective Joplin. I've spent the morning with your father, Dr. Joplin, and we've done that already."

"You said you've got information for us that might lead to the identity of the man who has killed these women," Isaiah offered.

"I do," he told them. "Though I am reluctant to share what I know. It isn't safe to accuse certain segments of society."

"Which segments might those be?" Isaiah asked.

"Certainly not the ones who are being arrested for these crimes," the professor said with a sweep of his hands. "Not a one of those men did this, and I do not care what the police say. They are not looking for the killer because they already know who it is."

"With all due respect, Dr. Langston, I have read the police records. There is nothing in them that would indicate they are close to naming a suspect. Hundreds of arrests, to be certain, but none upon whom the murder charge could stick."

"Of course not," he said. "They want this to go away. All of Austin wants it to go away." He shook his head. "Perhaps not the families of those who were the victims, but the rest of the city would just as soon the crimes were forgotten."

"I have noticed that," Annie agreed.

"The police continue to pick up possible murderers off the street in the hopes that this time the charges will not be dropped. Eventually, if this works as they hope, the wrong man will be convicted, and citizens can sleep safely in their beds at night."

"Who did it, Dr. Langston?" Isaiah asked.

"Oh, well. . ." The professor let out a long breath. "Joplin men are notoriously straightforward," he told Annie.

"As am I," she responded evenly. "If you have a name for us, it would be most expedient if you would tell us that name. Then we could let you get back to your study of rocks in a timely fashion."

"It is more of a they than a who, actually," he told her. "I have knowledge of them, not of any one specific man. But I do believe that among them is the one who is guilty of these crimes. The others are merely guilty of helping him to evade arrest."

Isaiah's eyes narrowed. "That is quite the allegation, sir."

"I would call it fact, not allegation, but I suppose since there is not yet proof, I won't argue the point." Dr. Langston straightened his shoulders and looked out into the rainy afternoon. "We have an institution of higher learning here. One of the best." His attention jerked toward Isaiah. "I believe this is happening without the knowledge of anyone associated with any department in this illustrious institution other than a small group of men who are spreading lies and, I believe, covering up for a murderer."

He paused and seemed to be collecting himself. Then the professor drew in a deep breath and let it out slowly.

"*Voodoo* is a term that has been bandied about," Dr. Langston said. "Perhaps in your investigation you've run across that allegation. Men who do not want to bring a poor reputation on the city are the source."

Isaiah shook his head. "You're talking in riddles, sir."

"I am aware of that," Dr. Langston said. "Some of it is a riddle. I thought I would solve that riddle before I turned the information over to you, but recently I've changed my mind."

"Are you in danger?"

He chuckled but quickly sobered. "Nothing like that. I have other more pressing projects calling my name, so looking into this curiosity has not been something I've had much time for."

More pressing projects than stopping a murderer? Annie bit back a response.

"Miss Walters and I are happy to take up where you've left off in your investigation," Isaiah said. "Once we've had the facts."

The door opened and a fresh-faced young man stuck his head in. "Oh, sorry, Professor. I'll come back when you're finished with your meeting."

"Yes, please do, Mr. Stevens. And if you're wondering about grades, they're not yet ready." When the door closed again, Dr. Langston shook his head. "That one is a worrier, but worriers make for good students when properly managed. Now where was I? Oh, yes. Shortly after my visiting professorship began, I was trying to find my way around and stumbled into the wrong office. There was a meeting going on. Four men. They were arguing, which is why none of them noticed me. I stepped back out and closed the door as quietly as I could. But I heard them, Isaiah. I heard every word very clearly."

All evidence of any prior joviality was gone. In its place, the professor's face was a mask of fear. Then, just as quickly, it was gone.

"These men are protecting one of their own and this city. I stood outside the door and heard them plot to spread the lie that voodoo was involved and that someone who circulated freely among these serving girls was to blame. It was all to cover up for someone they knew."

"One of the professors?" Annie asked.

He turned a frightened look her way. "Possibly. One of those men or someone the four know well. Either way, I cannot have misunderstood. They called their campaign the Black Midnight, and they spoke at length about it. Or perhaps that was their code name for the killer himself. In the context of the conversation, either could have been the case."

"Who was in the room?" Isaiah snapped, his patience at the professor's meandering way of telling his tale obviously at an end.

"Four men whose names I will give you only if my anonymity is assured." He paused. "All of whom you know."

"I can assure you of that." Isaiah reached into his vest pocket to retrieve a small notebook and pencil. "Write them here." At Dr. Langston's confused expression, the Pinkerton detective continued. "Apparently the doors are thin in this building."

"Yes, of course." The professor accepted the notebook and pencil and moved to a lab table to begin writing.

Annie followed, unwilling to accept only the meager details the older man was offering. "What specifically was said to give you the impression that four men were protecting a murderer?"

Dr. Langston looked up from his writing. "Four men speaking about how to cover up a murder is a conversation that is difficult to misinterpret. As I said, they talked about the misinformation they would offer to police and the newspaper to draw them off the track of the real killer. To handle the Black Midnight. Those words were actually spoken."

"By whom?" Isaiah said.

"All of them in one form or another during the conversation," he exclaimed. "The men agreed that the real perpetrator of these crimes was not to be caught and that the city was better off to believe they were permanently rid of the stain of this crime spree."

"Dr. Langston, is this meeting you've called with Mr. Joplin and me part of that campaign of misinformation?" Annie asked, watching the professor's expression carefully. "Because you've told us nothing concrete and appear to be nervous about what you have told us. Are you part of the Black Midnight?"

"That is ridiculous," he said in a huff. "Of course not."

"And yet you speak in circles and seem reluctant to give us much," Isaiah countered. "Too reluctant for a man who claimed he wants to help us."

The professor snatched up his list and walked past Annie to thrust the paper at Isaiah. "That's because your father is one of them."

❦

Ike looked down at the list and then back up at the professor, keeping his expression neutral. The man was a liar, of this he was almost certain.

But he would have to prove what he already knew: that his father was no killer. They had spoken about the crimes at length, with Pop theorizing on who might be committing the atrocities and speaking at length on his horror that the city had to endure such a madman on the loose.

Rather than say any of these things, Ike kept his silence as he folded the list and tucked it into his pocket. There was a time and place to delve into the proving of this claim.

"You'd better be ready to stake your life on this, Dr. Langston," Ike said evenly.

"It is likely I already have." He paused. "If I turn up dead, know that it was no accident, Ike. I call every man on that list a friend, but I certainly wouldn't put it past them to see that I was silenced on this matter. Not after what I heard."

"From the other side of a closed door?" Annie offered.

Ike walked over to the door, thinking he would check the theory that a conversation could be heard from the hallway. To his surprise, the Stevens fellow reeled backward as Ike swung the door open.

"Hello there," Ike said, grasping the student by the wrist and hauling him inside the classroom. "Stevens, isn't it?"

"Yes, sir," the skinny fellow squeaked as crimson flooded his face.

"How long have you been out there, boy?" Professor Langston demanded.

Ike released Stevens, and he scrambled to his feet. His eyes cut toward Ike then returned to Dr. Langston. "Since you agreed I should wait until you were finished with your meeting, Professor. Should I not have done that?"

"That depends," Ike told him, crowding the young fellow just enough to let him know who was in charge. "What did you hear?"

"Hear?" His brow furrowed. "Where?"

"He is asking if you eavesdropped on our conversation, Mr. Stevens," the professor offered. "If you heard anything of what we were discussing, it would be advisable for you to let these two Pinkerton detectives know."

"Pinkerton detectives?" came out in another squeak. "Gosh, Dr. Langston, are these the Pinkertons I read about in the *Statesman* that the mayor sent for?"

Since Ike couldn't answer that in the affirmative without bending the truth, he said nothing. Annie also remained silent.

"Gosh, I've never met real Pinkerton detectives. I've heard of you, but then, who hasn't?" He stuck out a skinny arm. "I'd like to shake your hand, sir."

Ike complied then took a step back. "Miss Walters and I would like an answer to the question you've been asked. How much did you hear while you were waiting in the hall?"

"I guess I might have heard plenty except that I wasn't exactly telling the truth about waiting out there for your meeting to be done, Dr. Langston. See, I was doing what you told me to do, and then. . . ."The flush on his face deepened. "Well, I was just standing there, and Miss Ellis—she came out of her father's office at the end of the hall."

"Miss Ellis?" Annie asked.

"The dean's daughter," Dr. Langston supplied. "A pretty girl just about Mr. Stevens's age. She often visits her father here." He glanced over at the student. "She's very popular with the young men at the university, though I understand she rarely bestows the gift of conversation upon them. She must like you, Mr. Stevens."

The compliment apparently rendered the poor lad unable to speak. Instead, he managed a nod. Finally, he added, "I reckon so."

"Did you and Miss Ellis hold your conversation outside the door?" Annie asked. "Or did you go somewhere more private?"

Stevens swallowed hard and braved a look at Annie. "There's an out-of-the-way spot at the end of the east hall that allows for"—he paused—"well, for private conversations, I guess you'd say."

Ike tried not to grin as he watched the poor lad squirm under Annie's scrutinizing gaze. If what he said was true, the student had been too busy spending time with a pretty girl over in the east hall to hear anything that had been said in the classroom.

If indeed anything could be heard through the door.

"Dr. Langston," Ike said. "Miss Walters and I will leave you and Mr. Stevens to have your meeting now. If we have any more questions, I hope you will make yourself available to us."

The professor looked him in the eyes, then clasped his hand to shake it. "You have my word."

Ike ushered Annie out of the classroom and closed the door behind them. When he set off down the hall, Annie took a moment to catch up.

"Aren't you going to wait and see if you can hear them?"

"Too easy," he said. "And probably what Dr. Langston expects us to do."

Annie grinned. "So we walk away and then come back in a few minutes."

"Exactly." He matched her grin. "I hear there's a spot we can wait over in the east hall."

"You are incorrigible," she told him.

"I am, but if we weren't working on a case, I bet you'd kiss me anyway."

Her laughter echoed in the hallway. "I refuse to answer that theoretical question, Isaiah. We are working on a case, and we'd both better remember that. And I stand by my claim that you are incorrigible."

He gestured toward the stairwell. "Give him a minute to decide we're gone," he whispered. "Then come back up here very quietly."

At her nod, they set off downstairs and then turned around to retrace their path to the top of the stairs. Once there, Ike made sure the hallway was clear and then inched his way back to the door leading to Dr. Langston's classroom with Annie two steps behind him.

Silence greeted them. Ike frowned.

Annie pressed past him to lean her ear against the door. Then she straightened and shook her head. "I don't hear anything," she whispered.

Ike stood there long enough to convince himself Dr. Langston made up the story he'd told them. Anger mixed with relief.

"Let's go," he said softly on an exhale of breath.

Annie held up her hand to stop him. "Wait. I thought I heard a chair scrape on the floor."

He frowned and joined her in pressing his ear against the door. Sure enough, he could hear something, though the sound was muffled.

"We've proved that the professor lied," he told her as he stepped away. "Let's go."

"All right, thank you for waiting patiently, Mr. Stevens," Dr. Langston said, his voice clear enough to be heard a few steps away from the door. "I stand corrected. I found your paper and am ready to discuss your grade."

"Thank you, Dr. Langston. I just couldn't go home for Christmas until I knew how I did on that paper. I've been worried about it ever since I turned it in."

"Not too worried to chat up Miss Ellis in the east hall," the professor said with a chuckle.

Annie met his gaze. Obviously they hadn't heard anything because no one had been speaking.

Ike stifled a groan. The professor was right, at least in the fact that a conversation could be heard through a door in this building. But he wasn't going to be too quick to let himself believe Dr. Langston on the other allegations.

Not without further investigation.

"Ike?" a familiar voice called from behind him. "What are you doing here?"

Chapter 11

Annie turned to see an older version of Isaiah striding toward them from the end of the hall opposite the stairs. This must be the geology professor.

"Pop," Isaiah said, heading him off to lead him down the opposite hallway. "Annie and I were here on Pinkerton business. I wasn't sure you'd still be here this late in the afternoon."

The elder Joplin gave his son a strange look. "I'm always here this late in the afternoon."

Isaiah nodded for her to follow as the pair disappeared into a room at the end of the corridor. She caught up and paused at the door.

The small office was crammed from floor to ceiling with rocks of every kind. Some were large enough to hold a place on the floor, while others were lined up on shelves and labeled. It reminded her a bit of the London museums she'd spent far too much time in as a child: dusty and overfilled with curiosities.

Annie noticed the silence before she realized both men were watching her intently. "I'm sorry," she said. "Did I miss something?"

The man Isaiah had called Pop smiled in her direction. "Not yet. My son was about to make the introductions, I believe."

"Annie, this is my father, Dr. Seth Joplin. Pop, meet Detective Walters. She and I are working a case here."

"So I heard." He stepped forward to shake her hand. "Charmed, Detective Walters."

"Likewise, Dr. Joplin."

He gave Annie an appraising look. "Ike doesn't bring guests

to my office, especially not guests from outside of Texas. You're British, are you not?"

"I am," she said before he asked further questions about her background. "You have an impressive collection. I don't think I've seen so many outside of a natural history museum."

"Thank you. But he didn't bring you here to see my office or he would have come straight here." Dr. Joplin looked over at Isaiah. "So why are you here? Did Hattie send you here because I missed another lunch?"

"Miss Hattie can deliver her own messages," he said. "I told you we are here on a business matter."

"Pinkerton business," the elder Joplin supplied. "I read that the mayor had sent for the Pinkertons. I didn't realize it would be you until I spoke with Hattie."

"I stayed at the house last night, Pop," he said. "Had two out of three meals there yesterday. And if you're keeping track, I got there the night before that."

"I wasn't."

The bluntness of the man's statement shocked Annie. She schooled her features so as not to reveal her surprise. This was a matter between father and son, and unless she missed her guess, it had more to do with some simmering lifelong disagreement than anything currently happening between them.

Dr. Joplin looked away first, adding a sigh as he settled behind his desk. A moment later, he looked up at Annie and then turned to Isaiah. "Sit down and tell me what you're working on. If you can, that is."

A look passed between them. Isaiah would take the lead here. She gave him an almost imperceptible nod before taking a seat across the desk from the geology professor.

"We're working on the Midnight Assassin case," Isaiah said. "Unofficially, that is. Apparently the mayor sent his payment to the wrong Pinkerton Agency, so the men who showed up worked for a fellow named Matt Pinkerton. It's a relatively shoddy outfit with little to recommend it, but you never know. They may come up with an answer anyway. Sometimes that's how it happens. You just stumble onto a clue that leads you to a solution." He paused. "Other times, it is right there in front of you but takes some investigation for anyone to see it."

"Then there are the times when there's no solution at all," his father offered. "Let's hope this isn't one of them. The specter of that madman is hanging over this city even now. It's been three months since he killed, but people still want to talk about it."

"Do you think they shouldn't?" Annie asked gently, acutely aware that there was already sufficient animosity in the room without her adding to it.

"I think it's time to let it go," he said. "It won't bring any of his victims back to name him. For all we know, he's long gone."

"That may be true. He could be gone." Isaiah picked up a small brown rock from the shelf beside where he stood and tossed it into the air, neatly catching it again. "Or he could still be here. Maybe even in this building right now."

Dr. Joplin chuckled. Then he stopped. "You're serious."

"I am." Isaiah returned the rock to its place on the shelf. "You and I have spoken about this case."

"We have." Dr. Joplin steepled his hands in front of him. "On several occasions. Why? Has something happened?"

Isaiah lifted one shoulder in a quick shrug. "Possibly."

"Oh no. Not another murder." He sat back in his chair and shook his head. "I thought for certain we were done with that."

"Who is it, Pop?"

Dr. Joplin froze. After a moment, he shook his head. "I don't understand. Are you asking me who the killer is?"

Isaiah nodded.

"How should I know?"

From the tone of his words to the expression on his face, the professor looked to Annie like he was telling the truth. But to believe Seth Joplin meant she had to disbelieve Dr. Langston. To her, they both seemed credible.

"According to the evidence I got recently, you should, Pop." Isaiah retrieved the list from his pocket and laid it on the desk in front of his father. "A witness overheard these men plotting to cover up a series of crimes their friend committed. The witness was very clear on what was said."

"I see." Dr. Joplin looked down at the paper and then back up at Isaiah. Then he laughed.

Annie was horrified at the man's response but kept her silence. Isaiah lowered himself into the chair beside Annie and stared at his father as if he'd lost his mind.

Finally, he shook his head. "How about you tell me what's so funny in all of this, Pop? Because I don't see it."

"I don't know who gave you that list, and I don't want to know. I do not deny that a discussion occurred between me and these three men regarding the killer. I believe it was right after the last article that fellow from New York wrote, stirring up trouble."

"So you don't deny that the four of you were talking about how to cover up the crimes a friend committed?"

"Hold on now." The professor waved his hands in front of him. "I never said anything of the sort."

"My witness says otherwise."

"Your witness is wrong."

"My witness said you four were considering a campaign of misinformation to lead anyone away from the person who was committing the crimes. The witness couldn't decide if the killer was one of the men in the room or a friend."

Once again, Dr. Joplin laughed. This time there was no humor in the sound. "Your witness has quite the imagination."

"Does the name Black Midnight mean anything to you, Pop?"

Annie knew at once that it did. The proof was in the older man's expression.

His face went ashen. "Where did you hear that term?" he asked, his voice rough.

"From my witness. Want to reconsider the lies you've just told me?"

"I've told you no lies," he said. "And yes, Black Midnight means something to me." He stood up and walked to the door, looked outside, and then closed it. "But it doesn't mean what you think it does."

"Go on," Ike said. "I'm listening."

Pop returned to his desk and settled there. After a moment, he met Ike's steady gaze. "The police were useless. People were dying. The September killings were the last straw. A few of us—me, those three, and a half dozen others—met to talk about what we could do."

"Just a conversation among friends?" Annie asked.

He swung his attention toward her. "Yes, exactly. We all just wanted to go back to living normal lives in a town that doesn't fear the darkness. To teach students who aren't afraid of the dark and chattering about murders instead of studying for exams. That seemed like an impossibility for much of this year. We were tired of it."

"Yes, I get that," Ike said. "So you called a meeting to tell the killer to stop? Great plan."

"Isaiah, if I knew who the killer was, I'd do a whole lot more than tell him to stop. Orange Washington was a good man." He turned to Annie. "Orange did odd jobs for me before he found regular work, so I knew him well. Those women were hardworking ladies, some of them with children, who didn't ask for such a fate."

"No, of course not," Annie said.

Pop's fist pounded the desk. "I know the Bible says we ought to leave revenge to God, but I sure would ask Him for an exception to that rule if I knew. But I don't."

How like Pop to invoke the Lord's wrath on the death of a stranger but hardly give notice to his own wife's passing or what had gone on under his roof since. It was too much to hear.

Ike snatched up the list and held it where his father could see it. "Why would my witness think you and these men were culpable?"

"I don't have any idea," he said.

"The witness said you called the killer Black Midnight? Why?"

Recognition crossed his face, and Ike knew he had him. The question now was what had Pop really done?

"That's not the killer's name, Son." He paused. "That's what we called our plan. We borrowed the term from a secret society of Englishmen that is whispered about but has never been proven to exist. I first heard about the Black Midnight while teaching at Cambridge. The purpose of its members is to quietly and purposefully aid the police in keeping law and order. The rumor is that all members are sworn to secrecy and to protect one another using any means necessary." He shrugged. "Of course I thought the whole idea of a secret society hogwash, but it did make a good name for us."

Not at all what he'd thought his father would say. Ike turned to Annie. "Have you heard of the Black Midnight?"

Annie shook her head. "I have not."

"Because it's a secret," his father insisted.

"Annie was a police officer in London," Ike countered. "Don't you think she would have heard of a group whose mission it was to protect the officers?"

"Not protect them, Son," Pop said. "Help them. If they're having trouble catching a criminal, the Black Midnight might step in and handle that."

"All right," Ike said. "So your group was formed by the four of you to step in and help. How did you plan to do that?"

"It was simple, really. But first I have a correction. There were just a few of us at first, but we selectively added to our ranks as the weeks went by, so there are more than four."

Ike shook his head. "And what did you do, Pop?"

"We took over where the police left off and did our own

investigating. We spread the word through the community that was most affected by the murders that vengeance was on the way. We hoped it would be. Still do."

Ike folded the paper and tucked it back into his pocket. "So you were a vigilante committee?"

"Of a sort, though we would never take justice into our own hands," he said. "We just used our connections in the community to get the word out that the killer was being searched for by men who were more thorough than the police."

Leave it to his father to believe he could do a better job than a trained police officer. "A bunch of college professors?" Ike shook his head. "Really, Pop?"

His father's eyes narrowed. "Really. Once the word got out that the Black Midnight was after the killer, the killings stopped. Or haven't you noticed?"

The idea that the lull in the murders was attributable to Pop and his band of vigilante professors was questionable. He was about to say so when Annie spoke up.

"So you believe the killer heard about the Black Midnight, some supernatural force for good, and was afraid enough to cease his activities or leave town?" Annie asked. "That's actually brilliant."

"Thank you. We thought so. And for the record, none of us said anything about voodoo or the supernatural. That embellishment happened of its own accord, though none of us wished to correct it. I'm not averse to this monster believing we have some sort of power to find him and stop him. Whatever gets him caught is fine with me."

"Why did my witness insist you were plotting to cover up these crimes?" Ike asked.

Pop let out a long breath. "I have no idea, Son. Truly, I don't. But I assure you the four of us met here in this office to discuss ideas to continue with the work of the Black Midnight." He paused. "Let me see that list again."

Ike complied. A moment later, Pop grinned.

"Well, of course. Dr. Benton was there. He's a psychologist and philosopher who had this theory of trying to understand the mind of the killer in order to come up with ways to deter him."

"Fascinating," Annie said, leaning forward in her chair.

"From the outset he referred to the murderer as 'our friend.' You'd have to ask him why that is."

"Because in theory you know a friend better than an enemy?" Annie offered.

Pop gave her a thoughtful glance. "I suppose so. Did you study psychology or philosophy?"

"I did not," she told him. "But I am greatly interested in the topics and have read up on them frequently."

Pop gave her a look of approval, then handed the list back to Ike. "Are you going to tell me who this witness is?"

"Of course not." Ike tucked the paper back into his pocket. "But I will tell you that he was reluctant to speak with me. He really believed he'd heard something and held on to that information for several days before it weighed too heavily on him and he reported it to me."

"So he knows you and knows you're a detective," his father said. "That means I know him too. And since he heard our conversation through a closed door, I assume he is associated with the university in some way."

"You know I can't answer that, Pop."

He shrugged again. "No matter. I don't care who he is, but I applaud him. What we said was completely misinterpreted, but I appreciate that he felt obligated to report us."

"You do?" Annie asked, surprise coloring her tone.

"Sure," his father said. "If everyone reported what they saw or heard and the police actually acted on the tips, they might have found this man before now."

"Okay, Pop. You and your professor posse want to save the city and all the citizens who live here. You've made your point."

"Isaiah," Annie said sharply. "That isn't necessary. I think it's a brilliant idea."

"Thank you, Detective Walters," Pop said. "It is a harebrained scheme, actually, but it makes us feel like we're doing something worthwhile instead of just complaining about the inept police department. As my son said, we're just a professor posse."

"No," Ike said, regret lacing his words, "Annie is right. My comment wasn't necessary, Pop. I'm sorry."

His father looked as if he had no idea what to say. Then he gave a curt nod and reached for a stack of documents that were resting on the center of his desk, and began to read the first page. "Tell your witness thank you for me. Now, if that's all, I do have some papers to grade."

And just like that they were dismissed. Ike stood and so did Annie.

"It was nice meeting you, Dr. Joplin," she told him.

"And you." He looked up from the papers. "Tomorrow is Christmas Eve. Won't you join us? Might ought to plan on staying over. No one wants to wake up on Christmas morning in a hotel."

Annie cast a quick glance at Ike. "I couldn't possibly intrude on a family celebration."

"Pop is right. You should come. It will be Miss Hattie and me," Ike told her. "I know she would love your help trimming the tree. I'm hopeless at it. She might put you to work threading popcorn. I hate that job. I always end up stabbing my fingers and bleeding on the decorations. Last year Hattie fired me altogether and put me in charge of reaching the top of the tree to put the star on it."

"That does sound safer. What about you, Dr. Joplin?" Annie asked. "What is it Hattie has you do?"

Pop looked up. He was obviously at a loss for words.

"My father doesn't usually show up until after everyone's in bed, so she's given up assigning him anything to do."

"Even on Christmas Eve?" Annie blurted out, then looked sorry she'd said it.

When Pop didn't look up from his work, Ike took it as their cue to leave. "Come on, Annie," he told her. "Time to go."

"It was very nice to meet you, Dr. Joplin," she told him again.

"And you as well," echoed after them once they'd stepped out into the hall.

"Your father is an interesting man, Isaiah," Annie said after they'd made their way out of the building.

"You have no idea," he told her. "Smartest man I know, but sometimes he's the stupidest as well."

Chapter 12

"You're certain I shouldn't have said no?"

"We talked about this yesterday," Ike said as he lifted her bag into the carriage. "You should have said yes, and you did. When I left, Miss Hattie was adding extra quilts to the bed in the guest room just in case you're delicate and get cold easily."

"I'm not, but I appreciate the thought. Miss Hattie is a treasure."

He climbed into the carriage and grasped the reins. "She is, and she likes being reminded of that, so don't forget to tell her at least once."

"Duly noted," Annie said. "But are you sure your father won't mind that I'm staying beyond Christmas Eve?"

"My father won't notice, Annie. But if he did, he would not care. And Hattie was incensed that a lady of your charm and character might possibly have to wake up in a hotel on Christmas Day. Her words, not mine."

Annie's smile would put a bandage on any hurt a man might have. "Then it's settled."

"It is indeed, so hush about it." Her smile turned to laughter as Ike waited for a slow-moving wagon pulled by two sleepy mules to pass. Then he pulled the carriage out onto Pecan Street, where they rode along at a slow pace beneath the festive Christmas garlands that stretched across the road.

Ike looked over at her and noticed she no longer wore her watch. "What happened?"

She looked down at her wrist. "Oh, that. I must have lost it somewhere between the college and the hotel. I noticed it was gone when I sat down to work on my reports. I've asked the hotel clerk to put out the word that it has turned up missing, but he doesn't feel it will be returned."

"I'm sorry," Ike said.

"It's fine. I wasn't particularly attached to it."

Ike shook his head. "No, I'm sorry I won't have you to ask when I need to know what time it is."

Annie laughed and nudged him with her shoulder. "Oh well. I guess we're in the same boat. We'll have to muddle along together."

"I guess we will."

The sky was darkening over the Capitol building up ahead, a portent of the stormy night ahead. Miss Hattie had told him that the cook next door had warned tonight's blue norther would bring sleet and snow. Apparently the next-door neighbor's cook had some sort of special talent at predicting such things.

Because of this, Miss Hattie had him chopping wood until Ezra, the handyman who had replaced Orange, arrived to take over. His arms still ached with the effort.

A companionable silence fell between them. The carriage slowed to a stop to allow a mother carrying a child on one hip and leading another by the hand to cross in front of them.

Annie watched the trio safely arrive on the other side of the street and then spoke up. "What was Christmas Eve like for you as a child, Isaiah?"

He smiled at the thought. Back then the memories were happy. At least until they weren't. "I'll tell you, but first I want to hear yours."

"Mine?"

He nodded. "Yes, tell me about Christmas Eve in England. What was it like?"

"Well, it was. . ." Her eyes went wide. "Wait. Stop!"

He glanced over at her. "What is it?"

"Stop, Isaiah, right now! I need to get out."

"Why?"

"Just do it, please. I cannot be a guest at your home on Christmas Eve without bringing gifts. It's just not done."

He chuckled. "That isn't necessary."

She reached over to grasp his wrist. "Isaiah Joplin, if you do not stop this carriage immediately, I will jump out, I promise you."

One look at her told him she probably would. "All right. I'll stop, but you do not have to bring gifts."

"Thank you," she said. "And we will just have to agree to disagree on this. You'll have to come in with me. I don't have a clue what Miss Hattie and your father would like, so I will need your help."

Once inside Slanton's Department Store, with its Christmas decorations proudly on display, Annie grasped his wrist and hauled him over to the men's department. "What do you think?" she asked. "A tie for your father or cuff links?"

"Cuff links," he said and then watched her choose a pair with the insignia of the university on them. "He will love those," Ike said when she held them up for his inspection.

Annie handed the cuff links to the clerk. "Wrap these, please. I have another gift to buy." Then she was off again with Ike doing his best to keep up. After much debate on Annie's part and a lot of nodding on Ike's, Annie sent a pin in the shape of a shamrock and a matching scarf off to be wrapped for Miss Hattie.

When that was done, Annie turned to face Ike. "Now you have to leave."

"Leave? As in you've changed your mind and aren't coming to Christmas Eve?"

She laughed. "No."

The clerk behind Annie grinned. Then she gestured to the wrapping paper and ribbons in front of her. Ike had no clue what that meant, but apparently the clerk thought it was important.

Ike frowned. The clerk once again gestured toward the gift wrap.

"Isaiah?" Annie said. "Is something wrong?"

"Wrong?" He tore his attention away from the odd motions the clerk was making to focus on Annie. "No, nothing is wrong. Look, I'll just go let the clerk know that she can bring the packages out to the carriage when they're wrapped. You go do whatever it is you need to do."

Annie cast a glance over at the clerk. The moment she did, the woman behind the counter went back to wrapping gifts as if she hadn't just been trying to send some odd signal to Ike.

"All right," she said. "Go straight to the carriage and do not come back in here."

"Why?"

"Christmas surprises, Isaiah. Just do it, please?"

"All right." He watched her hurry off and then quickly made his way over to the counter where the clerk was still staring.

"Good," she told him. "You got my hint. What will you be buying for her?"

"Hint? That's what you were doing?"

She frowned. "I was trying to remind you to buy the lady a gift."

"Oh no, we're not exchanging gifts," he said. "She's just buying my father and the housekeeper something to thank them for inviting her to join us tonight."

The clerk stared. Ike stared.

"I should get her something, shouldn't I?"

She nodded. "Something nice."

His eyes widened. "Like what?"

"What does she like, sir?"

He looked around the ladies' department and then back at the clerk. "I have no idea."

The woman let out a long breath. "I could find out for you. Without her realizing, of course."

"You could do that?" He nodded. "Yes, absolutely. Pick out something nice and put it on my bill. Isaiah Joplin." He told her the address.

"Yes, I recognize you," she said. "You're the Pinkerton detective."

"One of them," he told her. "What's your name?"

"I'm Lucy. I'll see that you get her something nice. Just one question. Is she a wife, girlfriend, or friend?"

"Friend," he reluctantly said. "We work together, else she might fit into one of the other categories."

Lucy grinned. "All right. I'll see what I can find for your friend and have it delivered."

"Thank you," he told her. "And Merry Christmas!" Then he froze. "Oh. I have a housekeeper. I need to get her something."

"What does she like?"

"She likes to smell nice," he said.

"So perfume."

"Yes, good. And my father. I ought to buy for him too. What do you have for a man who does nothing but work?"

"Something for his desk? Maybe a new pen?"

"Yes, pen it is."

The clerk nodded. "I'll have them wrapped and delivered."

"Thank you." He paused to glance around but did not immediately see Annie. Then he turned back to the clerk. "Something nice for her too. And on second thought, let's put her into that middle category, all right? A man can hope."

"Yes, he can," she said. "Do you have a tree? Mr. Slanton still has a few left out back."

"I believe we're all set in that department. Thank you though."

Lucy grinned. "Merry Christmas then, Detective Joplin."

"Merry Christmas, Lucy."

Ike made his way back to the carriage and waited for Annie's return. The wind had picked up, and the air smelled like rain. If the cook from next door was right, they had an hour, maybe two, before the blue norther blew through.

Annie stepped out of the store, her arms empty of any gifts. He jumped down to help her into the carriage. "Did you change your mind?"

She shook her head. "The clerk said she could deliver the packages since they had a delivery going out in the neighborhood soon. I thought that was best."

"Yes, good idea." He picked up the reins and gave her a sideways look. "Hold on tight, Annie, it's getting windy."

Then he chased the weather home, pulling the carriage into the stables just before the air turned frigid. Across the way, the neighbor's cook was wrapped in a quilt and standing outside looking up at the sky. She glanced over at Ike and nodded.

"Gonna be a cold one tonight. Snow too, I believe. Several inches."

He couldn't recall the last time there had been several inches of snow in Austin at Christmastime. Or at any other time, for that matter. Still, he'd been raised to be polite.

"Yes, ma'am," Ike said to her for lack of any better response.

Only the servants came to the back door, his housekeeper insisted, so everyone else who arrived here had to make the trek to the front of the house rather than take the shortened route that led through the kitchen.

It was a silly requirement of Miss Hattie's, but he accommodated her all the same. Again, he had been raised to be polite. And it had been Miss Hattie who had done most of the raising.

The house was aglow with lights, and Ike spied their future Christmas tree waiting in a bucket of water beside the back door.

Annie followed Ike around to the front of the house and then stopped. "It looks so pretty all lit up, Isaiah. Look at it."

He did and saw nothing other than what the home usually looked like at this time of the day. "Miss Hattie likes her lamps," he said. "She claims she needs all the light she can get to finish her work. I just think she likes things bright."

"Well, so do I," Annie exclaimed. "And this is just lovely."

An icy wind tore between them, lifting the ribbons on her cloak. "It's not so lovely out here, Annie. Let's get you inside before the snow starts."

She giggled. "I am sure your neighbor is a very nice lady, but do you think she knows enough about the weather to predict snow? It seems rather unlikely in this part of the country, although it would be wonderful if it did."

"We'll just have to wait and see. Miss Hattie sets great store by the weather predicting that goes on over on the other side of the fence."

"Then I shall as well. I'll be looking forward to the snow."

The front door flew open, and Miss Hattie stood there with a broad grin. "Merry Christmas, you two! Get yourself in the house soon before you catch your death of cold. There's weather coming in, and I do not plan to let it into the house, so let's get that door closed fast."

True to her word, the housekeeper stepped back and closed the door, leaving them standing on the porch.

Ike leaned toward Annie. "Welcome to Miss Hattie's house. The rest of us just live here."

She laughed, and it took everything in him not to kiss her right there. Then he looked up to see that Miss Hattie had hung mistletoe overhead.

❧

Annie had seen the mistletoe before Isaiah did, and she could have avoided standing beneath it. Should have, actually. But it was Christmas Eve. And Isaiah Joplin was the only man she could think of whom she would want to kiss beneath the mistletoe.

Though she absolutely shouldn't. They were fellow Pinkerton detectives working on a matter of the utmost importance. The last thing they needed to do was share a kiss.

Especially with a man her family would heartily disapprove of, not because of his reputation or character—both of which were stellar—but because he was American.

And worse, Texan.

She'd determined she wouldn't kiss him on the first day they were together at the governor's party. Annie was a woman who kept to her decisions once they had been made.

Glancing around, she took note of her surroundings. The rain splattered on the lawn and pinged an uneven cadence on the porch's roof.

Father could be on his way to Austin at this very moment. What would he think to find her like this?

"Annie?"

She looked up into Isaiah's eyes. Took note of his grin. Felt her resolve crumble.

"Merry Christmas," he said as his lips touched hers.

A moment later, though it felt like an eternity, Isaiah was smiling down at her again. She should have had something brilliant to say, something befitting the circumstances.

Instead, all she could manage was a whispered, "Yes, isn't it just?"

"I've waited too long to kiss you, Annie," he said softly.

"We shouldn't, Detective."

"No," he said, his lips so near to her ear that she shivered. "We shouldn't, Detective. Kiss me again anyway."

So she did.

Eventually the door opened again, whether by Isaiah's hand or some other way, and Annie felt herself float inside. It was an odd sensation of coming home mixed with a tinge of dread at where she might be headed.

Chapter 13

Ike wrapped his hand around Annie's and led her toward Miss Hattie's kitchen, following the trail of a delicious mix of scents. The smell of cinnamon and brown sugar floated up from the oven that kept the room at a cozy temperature, while more savory smells emanated from the pots on the stove. A freshly baked loaf of bread sat cooling on the sideboard.

It was what heaven must smell like. Of this, Ike was pretty sure.

"It's about time you two came inside," the queen of this domain said as she gave them both appraising looks. "Miss Walters, I need to show you to your room." She looked around. "Did you bring a bag?"

"I left it on the porch," Ike said with a groan. "I'll go get it."

He loped past Annie to retrace his steps to the front door. Just before he opened it, someone knocked.

Ike recognized the man as the clerk from Annie's hotel. "Telegram came for Miss Walters," he explained. "She left word to forward all correspondence to this address until she returns."

He accepted the telegram and then reached into his pocket and offered a coin to the clerk. The young man tipped his hat and stepped off the porch into the rain. Ike watched him go and retrieved Annie's bag. Before he could return to the warmth of Miss Hattie's kitchen, he spied what appeared to be a messenger coming his way.

"Looking for Miss Walters and Mr. Joplin," the fellow called from beneath the covering of the buggy. "Got packages for them from Slanton's Department Store."

"Yes, just a minute." Ike set down the bag and raced through the rain to retrieve the packages. "Don't get 'em wet," the older gentleman warned. "Else that clerk Lucy will have my hide."

"Yes, all right." He leaned in to accept the packages. "Just give me a second, and I'll put these on the porch and come back with a tip for you."

The fellow grinned. "No need, son. I own the place. Everyone else went home for the day."

"Thank you, Mr. Slanton. I appreciate you delivering these, and while I have you here, I'd like to put in a good word for your clerk Lucy. She was a great help to me today."

"Good to know," he said. "I'll be sure to let her know I appreciate her."

"Yes, thank you. Can I at least offer a hot cup of coffee before you go?"

"My daughter's got that waiting for me at home. And likely a tree to decorate, else I'd take you up on it just to spend time with Hattie. She's something else." He chuckled. "My girl, though, she sweetens the pot with cookies, so I don't mind it so much. You have a merry Christmas, son, and tell Miss Hattie I wish her the same. I slipped a gift to her in with your packages, so if you could make sure it's delivered to her, I'd appreciate it."

"No problem. And merry Christmas to you and your family too," he told Mr. Slanton before hurrying back to the porch.

Slinging the straps of Annie's bag over his shoulder, Ike tucked the smaller packages into his jacket pocket and balanced the rest of them under his left arm. With his right arm, he somehow managed to open the door.

Unfortunately, Alfie had decided to take his nap at the door—his favorite spot—so opening it caused him to yelp and jump up. Ike's legs got tangled up, and he landed in a pile of Christmas presents and giant dog.

Miss Hattie stood over him, a wooden spoon dangling from the hand that was not resting on her hip. "What in the world are you doing, Ikey? I just sent you out to get the bag."

"And I got it. Plus a few other things. Tell me again why you taught that dog to sleep against doors? It is downright annoying."

He heard giggling and looked up to the top of the stairs where Annie was seated. "What's so funny?" he called up to her.

"I remember when my uncle would play Santa for the children on Christmas Eve. The boots that went along with the costume were two sizes too large, but he insisted on wearing them anyway. Always at some point in the evening, he would take a tumble of some sort. You remind me a little of him."

Alfie inched over to lick at Ike's face, likely some sort of apology for causing the whole mess. Then he spied Miss Hattie's spoon and snatched it.

In the ensuing chaos, Ike managed to climb to his feet and gather up the scattered gifts. "I hope nothing was fragile," he said as he stacked them on the nearby table and retrieved Annie's bag.

He climbed the stairs and set the bag on the riser in front of her, then seated himself at her side. As a small child he'd taken cushions off his mother's favorite rosewood parlor set and ridden them down the staircase at full speed. When he was older, he'd often used this vantage point to listen to the goings-on downstairs.

Now it felt absolutely right to be sitting here with Annie. He glanced over and reached for her hand. She smiled, and they settled into a content silence.

Until Alfie appeared at the bottom of the stairs, the wooden spoon firmly between his teeth. "No. Stop," Ike said.

The dog kept coming, though at a relatively slow pace, owing to the animal's overlarge size and love of scraps and second helpings. Annie scrambled out of the way, but Ike refused to move. If the big lug wanted to hide from his owner upstairs, he would have to get past him first.

Alfie, perhaps smarter than he appeared, reached Ike and then lunged over him to race past. "How did he do that?" Ike said as he watched the dog disappear around the corner.

"It was impressive." Annie reached for something on the stairs. "Is this your telegram?"

"No, it's yours. It was delivered by a clerk from your hotel just before the gifts arrived. Sorry about that."

She gave the telegram a curious look and unfolded it. Her eyes scanned the page before she smiled and tucked the paper away in her pocket.

"Good news?"

"Of a sort." Annie met his gaze. "From headquarters," she said. "Good news about a possible issue that might have come up."

"In our case?"

"No," she hurried to say. "Something else. It's all fine though."

Miss Hattie appeared at the bottom of the stairs. "Did that traitorous mutt come up there?"

"He did," Ike told her. "How about we buy you another spoon? He looked awfully happy with that one."

"He ought to look happy. I was stirring my roast gravy before he snatched it from me." She gave them a sideways look. "Why are the two of you sitting up here when we have perfectly good furniture down in the parlor?"

Ike had no time to answer before Alfie plopped himself in between him and Annie, the spoon now notably absent. Annie scratched behind the big dog's ear, causing him to roll over on his back and kick his legs.

"Hey now," he said as he nudged the intruder. "I saw her first. Stop trying to steal my attention."

Annie laughed, but Miss Hattie did not. "Alfie, I'll have that spoon now," she demanded.

At the sound of his master's voice, the pup jumped to attention. His big dark eyes watched the housekeeper closely, but he did not move a muscle.

"Alfie, come."

Nothing.

Finally, the standoff ended when Miss Hattie shook her head.

"Come on down here, ya big lug. I forgive you."

At that, Alfie lumbered down the stairs to nearly knock his owner off her feet. "You better not have hidden that spoon under my pillow again," she muttered as she walked away with the Irish wolfhound close on her heels.

"Welcome to the Joplin house," Ike said. "It is never boring here."

Annie grinned. "It's wonderful. I had no idea you had such an interesting family."

"*Interesting* is certainly a good word for them, although depending on the day, there are others." He paused. "You've never told me about your family, Annie. And if I remember right, we were just about to talk about Christmas at your home when we were sidelined by a shopping trip."

"Speaking of shopping, were the gifts delivered?"

"They were," he said. "I already told you that."

"Oh, yes, of course." She looked away. "The clerk, I believe her name was Lucy. She was very attentive. I must compliment the owner on hiring exemplary staff."

It didn't take a Pinkerton detective to know she was changing the subject.

"I already did," he said. "Mr. Slanton delivered the gifts. Oh, and he had a message for Miss Hattie as well as a gift."

Annie perked up. "Now that is an interesting development. Do you think he's sweet on her?"

"If I had to guess, I would say he might be."

"And she on him?"

"That's harder to determine. I can't see Miss Hattie holding a torch for anyone other than Pop, but now that you've met him, I'm sure you can see how waiting for him to show some affection might get tiresome."

"Isaiah, I have to say I find it odd that your housekeeper is in love with your father and living in the same home with him. Don't the neighbors talk?"

"They all know my pop. Plus I'm certain Miss Hattie hasn't breathed a word of how she feels about him to anyone. Pop may wonder if she's still holding a torch for him, but he's too proud to ask, I'd guess. If he'd just make an effort, he might find out."

Ike shook his head. "Never mind. Forget what I was saying. Miss Hattie's room is at the top of the stairs in the attic with a lock on the inside of the door and a dog that sleeps against doors—as my loud entrance into the house a few minutes ago shows. She moved up there after the murders started last year. Many of the families came up with similar arrangements so that their servants wouldn't be sleeping in their quarters where they were vulnerable to the madman."

"Yes, that does make sense."

"Pop is never here, so it's fine. He sleeps in his office more than he does at home. But enough about us. Tell me about Christmas Eve in England. I'm sure it wasn't anything like this."

"Oh, it was just normal, I suppose. A tree, the trimmings, Christmas pudding, and gifts. My sister and I staying up to peek in on the adults well after we ought to have gone to bed." She shrugged. "Nothing extraordinary."

Ike got the distinct impression Annie Walters did not wish to talk about life back in England. Of course, that made Ike even more determined to get an answer from her.

"I never had a sibling. What was that like?"

"Interesting," she said. "And irritating sometimes. I often wished I were an only child."

"And I wished I had brothers and sisters. When you're the only child at the Christmas Eve celebration, it can get lonely."

"*Lonely* was a word I never used. Between my sister and all the cousins and Granny insisting we gather. . ." Annie shook her head. "Anyway, suffice it to say that chaos was the order of the day."

"Tell me more. I'm interested."

Annie shifted positions to stand and then straightened her

skirts. "Truly, there's nothing to tell. I should go and see if Miss Hattie needs any help in the kitchen."

She wouldn't, but Ike let her go find out for herself. He wouldn't press Annie on the topic of her personal life back home tonight, but considering the kiss they'd shared under the mistletoe, he did plan to find out more about the woman he'd fallen in love with.

Love.

Ike cringed. Yes, there was no denying it. He'd tell her eventually. Not tonight. Maybe tomorrow.

Yes, tomorrow. What better day than Christmas to ask the most beautiful woman in the world if she loved him too?

Annie escaped into Miss Hattie's kitchen with Isaiah's questions chasing her. She'd told him what she could and left out the rest. But with that kiss—oh, that kiss!—she'd opened the door to a need to share her history with the last man who ought to know.

Isaiah Joplin was a dangerous man to be around. She'd known it before, but their moment under the mistletoe removed any doubt she might have had.

What to do about that was a whole other question. Granny would never approve of a romance with him, nor would her parents allow it if they were told. Of course there were many things in her current situation that would meet with their disapproval, chief among them her employment with the Pinkerton Detective Agency.

At least the telegram from Chicago had delivered good news. There was no sign of her father, and it was assumed he had elected not to travel to Illinois to confront her.

Yet, at least.

"Miss Walters?"

The housekeeper's voice cut through her thoughts. "Please," she said to the woman stirring something on the stove with a long metal spoon, "call me Annie."

"Annie it is, child. Now hand me that jar over there, would you, love? Then make yourself at home and take a seat."

She did as the housekeeper requested and stepped back to stay out of the Irishwoman's way. Annie hadn't been granted access to the kitchen at home. That was the domain of the cooks, and no child dare enter.

At least she'd known where it was. Mama was proud of the fact she hadn't a clue where the kitchen was located in the castle where she grew up.

Annie cast a glance around, her gaze landing on the woman at the stove. "It smells delicious in here, Miss Hattie."

"It ought to," she remarked with a grin. "I've made all the menfolk's Christmas favorites and one or two of mine. We'll be eating well now that the weather has hit and we're to be stuck indoors." She leaned over to peer out the window. "Won't be anyone out on an afternoon like this, so don't expect there will be carolers."

"Do you generally have carolers?"

"We do," she said, keeping her attention on her work.

"I read about carolers in books, but the homes were so far apart where I lived, and there was just no. . ." Annie paused. She'd said enough.

"No way to go from house to house on foot?" Miss Hattie offered. "That'd be the problem we children had in Ireland. 'Tis why I do enjoy the singers when they come by."

Annie looked past her to the window where the afternoon was as dark as night. Alfie lay stretched out, already snoring against the door that led to the back of the property. Despite the frantic pace that Miss Hattie kept in moving from pot to pot, the kitchen was the most peaceful place she'd been in a very long time.

"The mistletoe," Miss Hattie said, sliding Annie a sideways glance. "Did it work?"

Instantly, warmth flooded her face.

"Yes, I thought so." Then she went back to stirring.

Isaiah stepped into the kitchen, Alfie's wooden spoon in hand. "Did I miss anything?"

"No, and neither did I," Miss Hattie said, raising the heat in Annie's cheeks.

"All right, well, here's your spoon, Miss Hattie. I found it under my pillow."

At the sound of Isaiah's voice, Alfie lifted tired eyes to give him a brief moment of attention. Then he snorted and rolled back over as if to indicate his opinion of his treasure being unearthed.

"Doesn't look like the one I was using this morning, but then, he's right regular at stealing them. No matter," the housekeeper said. "You'll not be sleeping up there tonight. Not with Annie on the same floor. 'Tisn't proper, and I'll not have it under this roof." She took the spoon from Isaiah and tossed it to Alfie. "You'll bunk in the parlor."

"You'll get no argument from me, Miss Hattie. I've laid down my bedroll in worse places." He walked across the kitchen to look out the window and shake his head. "Besides, I've tried to convince Miss Hattie that I needed to sleep by the fireplace since I was a kid. The better to see if I can catch Santa Claus in the act of coming down the chimney."

He winked at Annie, and she giggled. Miss Hattie merely shook her head. "Why don't you go get the tree off the porch and set it up in the parlor, Ikey? I put it up out of the rain before the downpour started, but it's still going to be a little damp, so shake it off good before you come inside. And watch my floors."

"Yes, ma'am." He nodded to Annie. "Does she have permission to go with me? I might need someone to hold the door."

"You are incorrigible," Miss Hattie said. "Annie can do what she wants in this house." She gave Annie an even look. "Whatever is within the bounds of propriety, that is."

"Oh, Miss Hattie," Isaiah said. "You say that, but which of us hung the mistletoe from the porch roof where she knew we would stand under it? Where was propriety then?"

"Propriety was in the same place then as it was when you and Annie decided to make use of that mistletoe," she said with a mischievous grin. "Not that I am owning up to hanging it there, mind you."

The front door opened, silencing their laughter. Isaiah frowned as Alfie clambered to his feet. "Are you expecting anyone, Miss Hattie?"

Her brows gathered. "I am not."

Before Isaiah could cross the kitchen, the door from the dining room opened. "Merry Christmas," Pop said.

Chapter 14

Not only was Pop home before dinnertime on Christmas Eve, but he'd also brought a wreath for the door and garland made of pine for the mantel. Isaiah tried not to stare.

"What've you got there, Seth?" Miss Hattie called from her place at the stove.

Their housekeeper was doing a much better job of hiding her shock than Ike was. Annie, however, appeared completely unaware of the rarity of seeing Seth Joplin at home at a quarter to four in the afternoon.

"I thought I'd help get things ready for the tree trimming," Pop said. "Hattie, have you popped the popcorn?"

She looked up from her work. "Did that yesterday. There are two buckets filled to the top and ready to be strung and a basket of string and needles. Just don't let Ikey touch a needle. I don't want to have to clean blood out of the carpet again this year."

Ike held his hands out to protest the statement. "Everyone has his talents."

"Yours just doesn't happen to be making the garland for the tree," Miss Hattie interjected.

"I would love to string the popcorn with you, Dr. Joplin," Annie said. "Where are the buckets?"

Miss Hattie directed Annie on where to find them, and once Annie had gone, she turned to Pop. "I don't suppose you know what to do with yourself."

His father's expression turned confused. "I don't know what you mean. I've got a wreath to hang and a pine garland to fix to the mantel. Then I'll go help Miss Walters make the garland for the tree. By then it ought to be time to eat and decorate the tree."

"That isn't what I mean, Seth. You'll kill a few hours' time doing those things, but do you know how to enjoy them?"

"I'm just going to go work on getting the tree inside," Ike said. "I'll leave you to finish this conversation by yourselves. But Pop, I am very glad you're here. If you need any help with the wreath and garland, just let me know."

Ike stepped out into the icy afternoon. True to her promise, Miss Hattie had moved the tree from its spot leaning against the house to a place on the porch where the rain couldn't reach it. Still, the needles were wet, and the water needed to be shaken off.

By the time he had managed his task, his hands were just about frozen and he was wishing for his warm coat rather than the thin jacket he'd worn out onto the porch. This was the kind of cold he would expect in Chicago, not Austin, and it was miserable.

He had just about wrangled the tree into submission when the back door opened and Pop stepped outside. "Need some help?"

Tempted to say no, Ike instead nodded. "Sure. How did you make this look so easy when I was a kid?"

Pop chuckled. "Come on. Together we will manage this."

Ike nodded, and together they urged the tree through the doorway and set it upright. His father took a step backward to survey the scene and then nodded toward the kitchen. "All right. I believe we're ready. Remember, the trick to handling Hattie is not to make eye contact. Just rush the tree through her kitchen and hope for the best."

"Good advice, Pop." Ike paused. "She gave you a hard time in there. I hope you know why she does that."

"I do," he said. "But I cannot change who I am."

Ike looked at him. Really looked at him. Then he shook his head. "Sure you can. You're here, aren't you? That's all we ask." He paused. "That's all she asks. And remember, I am hardly here. My work takes me a lot farther from this place than yours does."

His father seemed to be considering the statement. Then he

nodded. "Let's get this tree set up. I've got a wreath to hang, and I'm sure Miss Hattie will have an opinion on where the pine garland should go too."

"Miss Hattie has an opinion on everything," Ike said. "And sometimes she even keeps them to herself."

They shared a laugh as they hoisted the tree, and Pop took the lead in hauling it through the kitchen. "Nothing to see here, Hattie," Pop told her as he quickly made his way across the room and through the opposite door into the dining room. Finally, they rounded the corner to arrive in the parlor where Annie was busy setting out the supplies for making popcorn garlands.

She looked up from her work and froze, eyes wide. "Oh," she said softly. And then again, "Oh."

"Something wrong?" Ike said as he held the tree until Pop managed to decide how to best place it.

"No." Annie rose and moved toward them. "It's just so pretty."

"Cal Slanton thought so too," Miss Hattie said from the hallway. "He promised to send over the prettiest tree in the bunch he had for sale, and he sure did, didn't he?"

"Slanton picked out this tree? The fellow who owns the department store?" Pop's expression told Ike the name was not only familiar but also not a favorite of his. "Well, I guess he did an acceptable job."

"You know good and well who Cal Slanton is, Seth. And he did just fine." She shook her head. "Now, I want to see that tree standing straight and tall. You've got it leaning to the left."

"I do not," Pop countered. "It looks fine from here."

Ike moved across the parlor to take a seat beside Annie. "Is it like this every year?" she asked softly. At Ike's nod, Annie giggled.

He leaned closer. "Except the part where my father is here before bedtime. It's usually me trying to straighten the tree and Miss Hattie barking instructions," he whispered.

"I heard that," the housekeeper told him.

"Maybe I wanted you to," Ike countered with a grin. "If you

and Pop don't decide how the tree ought to sit in that stand soon, I am going to be forced to take up needle and thread and make popcorn garland in protest."

A few minutes later, the debate was settled and the tree had been set in place. Pop retired to the porch to hang the wreath on the front door, and Miss Hattie returned to the kitchen.

"Are they always like that?" Annie asked.

"No," he said. "Sometimes they argue."

"I'm serious." She glanced at the door where Pop had gone. "They act like an old married couple."

"Because that's what they ought to be," Ike said. "Instead, they're two stubborn people who cannot see what's right under their noses."

"I could say the same for someone else," drifted toward them through the kitchen door.

"Have I mentioned that Miss Hattie has ridiculously good hearing?" Ike said. "It was the bane of my childhood. I couldn't make a single comment under my breath without being caught." He reached into the bucket and drew out a handful of popcorn, then ate a few kernels.

"You're eating the garland," Annie protested when he finished off his first serving and grabbed another. "Leave some for the tree."

He finished that handful and sat back. "Okay, fine. But if I am sitting here, I'll need something to do."

"We could talk about the case," Annie offered. "Neither of us has discussed what happened at the university today."

"Nor should we attempt that now." He gestured in the direction of the kitchen, and Annie nodded.

"All right. You have a point. Then I have questions about local people that you might be able to answer. How about that?"

"Sure," he said. "If I can, I will."

Annie paused to stab a piece of popcorn with her needle and thread it through to the growing garland. She looked up from her work to focus on Ike.

"Yesterday no one wanted to talk to me. Other than a brief 'How do you do?' at the door of the home where the first murder occurred, there was complete silence from every homeowner I could find. And the surviving victims wanted nothing to do with me either. The Brown fellow? He actually saw our killer. Witnessed him with his own eyes. But when I tracked him down and asked if he would allow me to interview him, he claimed I had the wrong man. I didn't, Isaiah. It was him."

"I'm sure it was," he said. "But I think his attitude is the prevailing one. Maybe it's thanks to Pop and his pals and their harebrained schemes, or maybe there's something else that has him scared, but it's not going to change anytime soon. These folks didn't ask for the spotlight and don't like being in it. Remember, a whole lot of other people stood in front of them asking questions before you showed up and tried it."

"I guess so," she said. "It's just so frustrating."

"It is indeed."

The front door opened and Pop stepped inside. "All done," he said. "Now about that garland."

"Let Annie help you two," Miss Hattie called from the kitchen. "And do whatever she says. I know it'll look just fine. She's English, and they have the best of taste."

Annie grinned. "Have I mentioned how much I like Miss Hattie?"

Given the history of unrest between the Irish and the English, Ike could only hope that Miss Hattie meant that as a compliment. He certainly would not disabuse Annie of her belief that it was.

Later, with the tree in place and the pine garland properly situated on the mantel, Pop disappeared into his study, leaving Annie and Ike alone in the parlor. She'd found a book that interested her from the shelf of his mother's favorites and was curled up, reading.

Ike gathered up the latest copy of the *Austin American*

Statesman and joined her. He was halfway through an article on the first page titled "A Romance: The Way a North Texas Youth Got to the Penitentiary" when he heard a pinging sound on the windows.

"It's sleeting out there," he said. "I guess the cook from next door was right."

Annie looked up. "I'm sorry. I just reached my favorite quote and wasn't paying attention. What did you say?"

"Miss Hattie told me the cook next door. . ." He shook his head. "What is your favorite quote?"

"You really want to hear it?" At his nod, she looked down at the book. "All right, then. Here it is: 'If you feel your value lies in being merely decorative, I fear that someday you might find yourself believing that's all that you really are. Time erodes all such beauty, but what it cannot diminish is the wonderful workings of your mind: your humor, your kindness, and your moral courage. These are the things I cherish so in you. I so wish I could give my girls a more just world. But I know you'll make it a better place.'"

She looked up at him. Then she smiled. "That is why I do what I do. I want to make the world a better place, Isaiah. Attending balls and palace tea parties does nothing to right what is wrong in this world. And there is so much wrong." She closed the book but held it in her lap. "We have to catch this killer. He cannot go free after what he's done."

"Agreed." He folded the paper and put it away. "Tell me about these palace tea parties, Annie."

She'd said too much. Annie stood and carefully placed the novel where she'd found it on the shelf, taking her time in doing so in order to avoid turning to face Isaiah.

He saw too much. Knew her too well.

And not merely because he was a Pinkerton detective. She'd allowed too much of herself to show in his presence. Danced far too close to the dangerous line between her well-constructed life as a Pinkerton detective and the life she left behind in England. A life of attending balls and palace tea parties.

Annie let out a long breath. Had she been able to give herself completely to the idea of falling in love with Isaiah Joplin, she might have explained. Might have told him about Mama and Papa, about her grandparents, and most importantly, about Granny.

She turned and braved a look at him. Tall and handsome, brave and kind. All the things she had hoped one day to find in the man she would marry.

And here they were. Here he was. Watching her. Waiting.

Funny how a decision made in a moment could change a lifetime. Annie smiled. Then she shrugged. "It's just a saying, Isaiah."

With those words, she banished the chance to be honest with him. To stand up to a lifetime of learning that she was meant for something that would further the monarchy and nothing else.

That if she found love—or something that passed for it—it would be with "one of us." Or failing that, with a man so wealthy that the influx of cash into the family bank account would wipe out any concerns that the bloodline was being tainted.

"If you don't mind, I think I will go up and rest before dinner. It is at seven, right?"

"Right."

He didn't stand. Didn't move. Just looked up at her, seeing through the words she'd tried to put between them. Seeing Alice Anne von Wettin, great-granddaughter of Queen Victoria, Sovereign of the Realm, instead of Annie Walters, Pinkerton detective.

Something kept her rooted in place. That same something then propelled her past Isaiah to run away.

But he caught her. Slipped his fingers around her wrist and gently hauled her back to him.

"I see you in there," he said, his eyes on hers. "I don't know who you are yet, but I want to. And I am willing to wait."

Words froze in her throat. So did her breath. The *pling-pling-pling* of ice against the windows behind her echoed in the silence.

"I have paperwork that needs to be done. Now seems a good time to tackle that project."

He said nothing. Nor did she add to her pitiful excuse.

Isaiah finally released her with a curt nod. She hurried upstairs, fleeing her chance to be honest with the man she could never admit she might love.

Arriving in the cozy room at the top of the stairs, Annie threw herself on the bed and vowed not to cry. She knew there would be pitfalls to living a life that did not allow for full disclosure to anyone she might wish to befriend.

But she never expected this.

She sighed and grasped her pillow. Then she laughed.

Beneath it was a wooden spoon.

Chapter 15

T rimming the tree was rowdy business, with Ike being called upon to reach the taller part of the tree and Annie doing her part to wrap the garland around the bottom half. Miss Hattie supervised while Pop, his earlier appearance notwithstanding, was nowhere to be found.

Once the garland was in place, Miss Hattie went up to fetch the box of ornaments from the attic. "I can do that, you know," Ike called to her retreating back.

"And let you mess up what I've got organized up there? No, thank you," trailed after her as she disappeared up the stairs.

He turned around to catch Annie tossing a piece of popcorn in her mouth. "Wasn't dinner enough for you, Miss Walters?" he teased as he did the same thing.

"Dinner was wonderful," she said. "But there is something irresistible about popcorn, don't you think?"

Ike leaned closer. "Popcorn and you." Then he gave her a kiss on the cheek.

Before Annie could protest, he nodded toward the stairs. "She's not going to like it, but I'm going to help her with the boxes. Leave me some popcorn."

Annie laughed and waved him away. Ike detoured on his trek to the attic to stop at Pop's office. "We will be putting the decorations on the tree soon. After that comes gifts."

Pop looked up. "Yes, all right."

"You'll be there for that?"

"I will." He returned to his writing, dismissing Ike.

"Hey, Pop."

His father looked up, irritation impossible to miss on his face. "Yes?"

"I don't know if you care, but there's a gift under the tree from Mr. Slanton. He delivered it this afternoon when he brought the things Annie and I purchased." Ike paused to be sure he had his father's attention. "I think he might be sweet on Miss Hattie. She may feel the same. I haven't asked."

Pop's face went blank. A moment later, he offered an almost imperceptible nod and went back to his work.

"Pop?" Ike said. "You heard me, right?"

"I did," he said without looking up.

"All right, then." Ike stepped back into the hall and closed the door behind him. He'd done his good deed. If Pop was too hardheaded to do anything about having a competitor for the affections of Miss Hattie, then that was his own fault.

After wrangling the heavy boxes out of the housekeeper's hands, Ike came down the stairs with her on his heels. They found Annie seated in the place where she'd been this afternoon, the book back in her hands.

"Your father just went out on an errand," she told them. "He said he wouldn't be long and he would prefer we waited to decorate the tree until he returned."

Miss Hattie's brows rose. "Has that man lost his mind? It's sleeting out there and about to turn to snow. He will catch his death of cold, and on Christmas Eve too. Has he any sense?"

"Oh," Ike said slowly, "I think he finally does."

He glanced over at the woodpile and saw it was low. "I'll go get more logs for the fire."

Ike gathered up his gloves and coat and walked through the kitchen to the back door where he spied Alfie happily snoozing against the door of the still-warm room. "You're going to have to give up your spot, mutt."

The dog stared then closed his eyes again. Finally, Ike inched the dog away and stepped out into the cold.

Grumbling against the weather that ought never have come this far south, he traced a path to the woodshed by the light of the lantern. Setting the lantern on an outside table, he gathered up as many logs as he could carry, then placed them out of the weather on the porch. On his next trip, he thought he heard a crunching sound like someone walking in heavy boots on ice in the alley behind the house.

"Someone out there?" he called.

The crunching sound ceased. Then silence.

"Speak up if you're there," Ike said as he gathered up the lantern and moved around the woodshed toward the back fence.

Icy sleet and a few flakes of snow peppered his face. The landscape around him could barely be seen in the yellow circle of light as he navigated his way to the back of the property more from memory than from sight.

Just before the fence line, he spied the tracks of a man's boots and followed them until they ended at the fence. Whoever was there had jumped over into the alley and was likely gone, but he wouldn't take that on assumption.

Hanging the lantern on the fence post, Ike scaled the fence and landed in a puddle of icy slush in the alley. He looked both directions but saw only darkness.

Lifting the lantern, he could just make out the same boot prints he had spied in the yard. Ike followed the prints all the way to the corner where the alley emptied out onto Pecan Street nearly a half mile away.

There the tracks blended in with dozens more until there was no way to know which direction the trespasser had gone. The lights were doused in the shops, and there wasn't a soul on the usually busy street.

The light of the nearly full moon was dimmed by the clouds sweeping past, but he could still make out the Christmas garlands strung across the road and the icy puddles decorating Pecan Street.

Ike turned back toward home. Whatever the man had wanted, he had obviously been interrupted before he found it at the Joplin home. The thought occurred that the intruder may have just been looking for a few pieces of wood to keep a fire going in his home.

When he reached the Joplin property, Ike went over to the woodshed, grabbed three logs, and placed them in the alley where the man's footsteps had led. If the fellow wanted warmth, it was there for the taking. If he wanted something else, he'd have to go through Ike to get it.

After making sure the woodshed and other outbuildings were secured, Ike returned to the porch and stamped off what he could of the ice and mud he'd just slogged through.

His first attempt at opening the back door met with a dull thud. "Alfie," he shouted. "Move your lazy self and let me in."

He tried again with the same result. Then Miss Hattie's face appeared in the window. A moment later, she opened the door.

"Where on earth have you been, Ikey?" she demanded. "Annie and I were wondering if you'd lost your mind too. It's not enough to have your father out wandering around like a fool on Christmas Eve, but now you've got to follow his example? You Joplin men will be the death of me, I do declare it!"

Her complaining, now thick with the Irish brogue that seemed to come and go, quickly ceased when she saw his face. "What is it? You've seen something?"

"Maybe nothing." He looked past her to Annie, who was standing in the kitchen door. "I heard footsteps. Followed the tracks through the yard and over the fence to the alley. I lost them on Pecan."

"Was it a thief or a beggar?" Miss Hattie asked. "The cook next door says she's seen a bit of both lately. Men asking for things for their families, and if the answer is no, then they take. It might be a jar of preserves from the shed or logs for their fire, but it's been something nearly every day. At least that's what she said. I haven't seen it here."

"Maybe they're getting what they want from next door," Ike said. "In any case, I put a few logs out in the alley where the tracks began. If he wants to put up a fire in his home, he can. I didn't think to add preserves, but I am not going back out in that weather to remedy the situation."

"No, of course not." She surveyed him from head to toe and shook her head. "You'll be going upstairs to put on dry clothes, and you'll not grumble about it. I won't have you catching your death of cold because you were out in this awful night and didn't think to get proper warm again."

Annie grinned at him, and he returned the gesture. "Yes, ma'am." He slipped past Miss Hattie before she stopped him.

"Take those boots off, Ikey. I'll not have you tracking mud from all the way to Pecan Street and back all over my clean floors. Not on a regular day, and certainly not on Christmas Eve."

"Yes, ma'am," he said again as he stopped where he was and slipped out of his boots to hold them in his hand. "I'll put them by the stove to dry and clean them up when I can. Does that meet with your approval?"

"It does," she said with a smile. "Now scoot. I'm an old lady. I cannot stay up all night waiting for Seth to come back so we can open gifts. If he's not home soon, I will be taking matters into my own hands. Just watch and see if I don't."

Ike chuckled. "I believe you. I will hurry."

He paused at the door to offer Annie another kiss on the cheek, then hurried off to do as he was told. By the time he'd tossed off his wet clothes and found dry ones, he could hear music wafting up from downstairs.

Padding to the top of the stairs, he paused. Someone was playing the piano, probably Miss Hattie. But who was singing "God Rest Ye Merry, Gentlemen"?

It had to be Annie.

He sat down to put on his clean boots and listened until that song ended and another began. Her tone was clear and bright, a soprano that sounded more like someone with vocal training than a lady Pinkerton detective singing to the accompaniment of an Irish housekeeper.

The front door opened and Pop stepped inside. Immediately he frowned at Ike. "What are you doing?"

"Coming downstairs," Ike said as he climbed to his feet. "I ought to warn you that Miss Hattie is particular about muddy boots, so you might want to. . ." He looked at his father's face and spied what appeared to be the beginnings of a black eye. "Pop? What happened to you?"

"Nothing." He shrugged out of his coat and hung it on the coatrack, then reached into the pocket to retrieve what appeared to be a small wrapped gift.

The music had ceased, but neither Annie nor Miss Hattie spoke. Ike made his way down the stairs in time to see Pop walk over to the piano.

"Seth, what in the world? You've been hurt." She pushed the piano bench back and stood. "I'll just go get something to put on that eye."

"My eye is fine," he said evenly. "Everything is fine. It is Christmas Eve. Let's go finish trimming the tree and then open our gifts."

Miss Hattie looked past Pop to Ike. At his shrug, she nodded. "All right."

"But first I'll leave my muddy boots right here." Pop stepped out of his boots, and before he'd finished, Miss Hattie was back with his slippers. A smile passed between them as she handed them to Pop.

As quickly as the moment happened, it was gone. "All right, the lot of you," Miss Hattie said. "We're wasting Christmas Eve standing here when we could be trimming that tree. Who's going to help me?"

And off she went. Annie followed. Ike remained behind with his father.

"What really happened, Pop?"

He looked toward the tree where the gifts from Slanton's Department Store plus a few others had been laid out. "The gift that was delivered today, which one is it?"

"The one that Mr. Slanton brought?" At Pop's nod, Ike continued. "There with the red stripe and green bow."

Pop nodded again, then marched across the room to retrieve the package. "I spoke to Slanton tonight," he said to Miss Hattie. "He admitted he sent this in error and he'd like to have it back. I told him it would be waiting out front for him."

With that, he marched across the parlor, into the hall, and out onto the front porch where he gave the package a mighty toss. Where it landed was anyone's guess, because Pop closed the door immediately.

He turned around with a smile. "Now, where were we?"

Chapter 16

"We were about to stop waiting for the menfolk to return and take the trimming of the tree into our own hands," Miss Hattie said. "The popcorn garland is a start, but there are two boxes of ornaments to be hung and candles to be placed on the branches."

"Talking about it won't get it done," Pop exclaimed, leading the way. "Come on, let's get busy."

Ike watched the stranger who looked very much like his pop orchestrating the decorating of the Christmas tree with a glee he hadn't seen in a very long time. No, he decided. He'd never seen his father that happy.

Which made the black eye and the tossing of Slanton's Christmas gift to Miss Hattie all the more interesting. And understandable.

After the tree was completely decorated, Pop insisted they move to the piano and sing carols. "I doubt we'll get any carolers tonight, so we'll have to make do," he joked.

Miss Hattie took her place at the piano bench. "What would you like to hear?"

"You know my favorite," Pop said. "Can we start with that one?"

She grinned and plinked out the first bars of "O Little Town of Bethlehem." Annie's beautiful voice was more subdued but still better than any professional he'd heard. "Joy to the World" came next, followed by "Jingle Bells."

Then it was Ike's turn to choose a song. "Annie, would you sing 'O Holy Night'?"

Annie tried to protest, but Pop and Miss Hattie managed to

cajole her into agreeing. As the words rose up in her clear and lovely soprano voice, Annie closed her eyes. Ike did too, allowing the woman he loved to fill the air with his favorite Christmas song.

As soon as she finished, Annie shrugged. "That'll have to do, I suppose."

"You suppose?" Miss Hattie said. "I've never heard such a voice."

"Nor I," Pop agreed. "You've had classical training. I'd stake my rock collection on it."

"Just a teacher who took an interest in some vocal training." She shook her head. "Truly, it's nothing extraordinary. I thank you for saying so though. And thank you for your hospitality. I'm having a wonderful time."

Pop continued to praise her until Ike figured Annie had enough. "Okay, Pop. You're embarrassing her. How about we go open our gifts now?"

"Yes," he said, rubbing his hands together. "That sounds like a great idea. Follow me, family."

Family. Ike looked over at Annie and decided she hadn't caught the reference. Oh, but he had. In that moment, Ike knew he wanted every Christmas to be like this.

He wanted Annie Walters to be his family.

Ike settled next to Annie on the settee, and Miss Hattie took the chair next to the window. That left Pop to pass out the wrapped gifts from beneath the tree.

"Miss Walters, since you're our guest, why don't you go first?"

She still looked embarrassed, but the flush in her cheeks made her even prettier. "I certainly didn't expect anyone to buy me a gift. This is unexpected." Annie looked up at Ike. "Is this from you?"

He smiled. He nodded. Then he panicked when he realized he had no idea what was in the box she so gingerly held in her hands.

Annie lifted the lid, peered into the box, and then looked up at him and smiled. "How did you know it was this one?" came out on a rush of breath.

Ike wisely kept his mouth shut. There was no good and truthful answer he could offer. Nor did he have any idea what she was talking about.

She pulled a silver watch pin from the box, her face now radiant, and quickly attached it to her dress. Then Annie looked over at him. "I was looking at this just this afternoon but couldn't justify such an expensive purchase."

Expensive. Of course. Oh well. It was worth every penny of whatever he'd just spent to make her smile like that.

"Thank you, Isaiah."

He managed a nod, acutely aware he was not worthy of the admiration he saw in her eyes.

"Your turn, Hattie," Pop declared.

"Oh no," she said. "I want to go last so I can see everyone else's first. You go, Ikey."

He opened the first gift, a pen that looked suspiciously like the one he'd purchased for his father. "I thought you might be able to use that in your work," Pop told him. "Hattie picked it out, so it's from both of us."

"I can, yes, thank you both." He reached for the other box and slid Annie a sideways look. "What have you done, Annie Walters?"

"Just looking out for my own interests." She punctuated the statement with a grin as he opened the box.

Inside was a silver pocket watch that almost exactly matched the watch he'd given her. The only exceptions were the size and the silver chain from which it was strung.

"No more having to worry about my partner not knowing the time," she quipped.

Ike held the watch in his palm. The gift was extraordinary. And thoughtful.

Just like her.

He was about to say this when Pop ruined the moment.

"Look what I've got from my son." Pop held up the pen Ike had purchased. "We think alike. That's not surprising."

It also was not completely true since Lucy the clerk had picked out the pen. But Ike went along with the statement and nodded. Pop also exclaimed at length over the cuff links Annie had purchased and the scarf Miss Hattie had knitted for him using her preciously guarded Irish yarn.

Then it was Miss Hattie's turn. "That one first," Pop told her as he delivered the gift from Annie, which was well received. Then Ike's gift, which she exclaimed over.

"Now this one." Pop handed her a small box. "Go on and open it, Hattie."

She lifted the lid on the box and peered inside, then looked back up at Pop. Tears filled her eyes. "Seth, it's beautiful."

"What is it?" Ike asked.

Miss Hattie retrieved something small and shiny from the box, then held it out in her palm. "It's a pin. An emerald pin."

"Emeralds for my Irish lass." Pop stood in front of her and retrieved the pin from her hand. "It'll look lovely on you, Hattie."

"Thank you," she said, dipping her head. "And to think I only knitted a scarf for you."

Pop lifted her chin with his finger and smiled. Then he dropped to one knee in front of her. "And I'm not deserving of that scarf. Or you, Hattie. I've been a blind and crotchety old man since well before I was old. And you've put up with all of it."

She chuckled, tears threatening to spill from her eyes. "When you put it that way, maybe you're right. You don't deserve my Irish yarn. I should have used the stuff I bought at the department store down the road."

They all laughed, but Pop quickly sobered. "Hattie O'Mara. I put a pin in that box that reminded me of you. Emeralds to match your eyes. I would like to have put a ring in there though."

"Why didn't you, Pop?" Ike blurted out before he could stop himself. For a smart man, sometimes his father was stupid.

"Because if she'll have me, she can pick out her own ring. This woman's of the opinionated sort." He paused to smile at her. "And I wouldn't have it any other way. So what's it going to be, Hattie? Dare you take me on and be my wife, knowing what you know about me?"

"Seth, I'll take you on and be your wife in spite of what I know about you. How's that?"

"I'll take that deal," Pop said. "Now to plan a wedding. Nothing outlandish, but we ought to invite the faculty. And the dean too. Oh, and if we're going to do things up right, we will need to settle on a date and a location to celebrate after. What do you say to that, Hattie?"

"I say that sounds dandy," she told him. "But now that we're to be married, I'll be moving out of the attic. Wouldn't be right for me to remain in the house."

Pop looked stricken. "Where will you go? And what will I do without you?"

"I suppose I'll go pay a visit to my sister in Galveston until it is time for the wedding. That'd be the proper way to do it. As to how you'll get along, Seth, that'll be up to you to decide and to remedy. But don't you bring a housemaid into my home. She'd just mess up things, and I won't have it."

Ike laughed, but Pop did not. "All right. That settles it. We'll make a trip to the jeweler's on Monday morning and the courthouse right after to settle up the licenses and such. If I have my way, you'll be Mrs. Joplin by sundown on December 28th. If you still want to see your sister, we can plan a honeymoon in Galveston before the spring semester begins at the university."

"Whatever you think, Seth," Miss Hattie said.

"I think I'd rather go hunt up the judge and have him marry us tonight, but it's Christmas Eve, and I'm afraid I'd end up in jail instead. Now who wants wassail?"

"I would love some," Annie said. "I haven't had any since. . ." Her voice trailed off. "Well, it has been a very long time."

Later that night, Pop insisted on bringing the mistletoe indoors so he could steal a kiss from his future wife. Then the clock struck midnight, and Pop declared it was time to douse the candles on the tree.

"I'll just get those dishes cleaned up," Miss Hattie said.

"Leave them," Pop told her. "They'll wait until tomorrow. You've worked all day. Get some sleep."

"I want to argue, but I won't."

"I don't mind," Annie said. "Ike and I can clean up."

Miss Hattie's expression brightened. "Thank you. Just don't let Ikey break any dishes."

"I haven't broken a dish since I was seven," he protested.

"And you haven't washed dishes since then either," she said with a yawn as she headed for the stairs. "Good night, all, and since we're past midnight and into the next day, Merry Christmas to the lot of you."

Pop bid her good night and disappeared into his office, leaving Annie and Ike to keep their promise to Miss Hattie. "Give me just a minute," he said to Annie. "I need to speak to my father."

Annie frowned. "You're not going to try to talk him out of this, are you? They appear quite happy."

"Not at all," he said. "I'll be right back."

As expected, Pop was at his desk poring over a book on rocks. He looked up at Ike. "I'm not surprised to see you, but are you sure you want to shirk your dishwashing chores? Annie seems awfully nice."

"I'm not shirking, and she is. But I've got to know what changed, Pop."

His brows gathered. "What do you mean?"

"The man I talked to earlier wasn't at all the man I saw tonight.

You proposed marriage to Miss Hattie, for goodness' sakes. Two days ago you couldn't be bothered to come home for a meal or notice the efforts she went to on your behalf."

The wooden desk chair squeaked as he leaned back and grinned. "I cannot disagree with any of that. I guess you could say I had some sense knocked into me tonight."

"By Mr. Slanton?" Ike guessed.

Pop shrugged. "I deserved it. But we're now clear on just which of us will be spending time with Hattie O'Mara. And it won't be Slanton unless Mrs. Joplin decides to do her shopping there. Which I will discourage. Beyond that, I am not prepared to discuss it."

"Okay, so you're not going to give me the details. I understand." Ike chuckled. "I'm just glad it happened. Whatever it was. And congratulations on coming to your senses and marrying Miss Hattie. You two will be happy together."

"We always have been," he said. "Even when we were fussing, we were still happy, if that makes sense. She's a woman of strong opinions, and, well, I'm a man."

"Isaiah," Annie called. "Come quickly, please."

Ike frowned and hurried to find her standing in the front hallway with the door half open and cold air drifting in. "What in the world are you doing?"

"I'm listening to the sound of men shouting. And possibly alarms of some kind?"

He moved to stand beside her, and Pop followed. "What is it?" his father asked.

The sound of men's raised voices echoed toward them from the street. Bells, possibly from the church several blocks away, were ringing.

"Pop, go get the lantern from the porch," Ike said as he reached for his coat. "I'll see what's happening."

Annie snatched up her coat and slipped into it, then pulled her gloves out of the pocket.

Pop returned with the lantern and handed it to Ike. "I'll get my coat and go with you."

"And leave Miss Hattie alone?" he asked. "Do you think that's wise? We don't know what the cause of all the commotion is."

"Last time the alarms sounded like that in the middle of the night, the madman had struck. Surely he hasn't killed again."

"I'm hoping not," Ike told him. "Let's believe that the work of the Black Midnight has chased the murderer off. This may be something as simple as a fire or a brawl that got out of hand."

"On Christmas?" he asked, doubtful.

"A fire? Most likely. A brawl?" Ike shrugged. "It's possible. Annie and I will be back as soon as we've determined what's happening."

Annie stepped out onto the porch, and Ike followed. Pop closed the door behind them, then tapped on the window to wave them on.

The sounds of shouting grew louder, as did the horse hooves of a rider coming down the street. "The Midnight Assassin has killed again," the rider shouted. "He's done killed again."

"Stop! I'm a Pinkerton detective and I need details," Ike demanded. "Where did he strike?"

The rider pulled his mount to a halt and circled back around to meet up with Ike and Annie. He was a young man, likely not out of his teens, and although the clouds had cleared, the bitter cold wind had turned his face a deep crimson.

"Hickory Street," he said. "Mr. Allen, he's the neighbor, told me to fetch the police, but by the time I got there, they'd already heard the commotion and sent someone."

Annie's eyes widened. "Isn't that the street where we delivered the young woman after the governor's dinner a few days ago?"

"Eula Phillips," Ike offered. "And yes."

"Phillips," the rider said. "Yes, that's where the madman struck."

Chapter 17

Annie thought of the quiet girl whom she'd met at the governor's dinner. She'd seemed frail and jumpy, as if a strong wind would blow her away and a loud noise might make her faint.

"Oh, Isaiah, that's horrible. That sweet girl must be terrified. It's not far, as I recall. Should we just walk?"

"It would take too long to hitch a horse to the buggy," he said. "It's this way."

They made their way to Hickory Street on foot, slushing through the ice and mud with a bleak wind blowing out of the north. If Annie didn't know better, she would think she'd stepped into a Chicago winter night, not one in Austin, Texas.

"I thought it was bad out here earlier," Ike said. "But it's even worse now."

A crowd had gathered outside, trampling the wide lawn that had looked pristine and lovely a few days ago. Several members of the police department were doing a poor job of trying to control the crowd while the mayor himself stood on the front porch speaking in angry tones to another man.

The commotion seemed to center on the back of the house, so Annie followed Ike around the side of the structure. Several dozen men stood in the yard, some with lanterns, seeming to be looking for something on the ground. Others stood in groups of two or three.

"Who is in charge here?" Isaiah called, displaying the badge that identified him as a Pinkerton detective. Annie retrieved hers and showed it as well.

"I'm John Abrahamson, sir," a young man said. "The man you're looking for is the city marshal. Likely you'll find him inside."

"What happened here?" Annie asked him. "Has another serving girl been done for?"

"I don't know for sure, ma'am," he told her. "My friends and I were walking down the street, and we heard shouts that someone had been murdered. Two of them went to the police station, and I walked around to the back to see what was going on. It was there I saw the man."

"What man?"

"Jimmy Phillips," he said. "He'd been hurt and was bleeding about the head something awful. I stopped at the door, so that's all I saw. He wasn't dead, but I know the shouts we'd heard earlier were about murder."

"What about his wife and son?" Isaiah said. "Were they victims?"

"I don't know," he said. "I just know I saw Jimmy, and if he's still alive when the sun comes up, it'll be a miracle. I think someone's gone for Dr. Litton, or maybe it was Dr. Cummings, but if either of them can fix this, I'll be surprised."

The young man was babbling, not that Annie blamed him. "We were told the Midnight Assassin had struck again. Why would anyone think that?"

"Might be the ax that was lying on the bed beside Jimmy," he said. "The Assassin killed with an ax, didn't he?"

Annie nodded and stepped away, returning her badge to its place in her pocket. If the Midnight Assassin had indeed struck here, it would fit the pattern to leave a man gravely injured at the hands of an ax. But there would also be a murder victim, whom no one had found yet.

This home, as well as others on the street, had a back lawn that stretched down to a copse of trees at the back of the property beyond the fence line. On the other side of the trees stood another home, as witnessed by the lights she could see when the wind blew.

With the storm over, bright light from the moon made the perimeter easy to see. Several outbuildings were located in different places a distance from the house. All their doors were closed, indicating to Annie that no one had searched inside them yet.

"Look out in the back," she called to the men with the lanterns. "Behind these structures at the fence line and beyond. And check in the smaller structures, but be careful. The killer could be hiding in there."

The men all stopped in their tracks to look at Annie, but none of them moved. "Is there something wrong with your hearing, men?" Isaiah shouted. "You heard the detective. Do it."

"Isaiah, this isn't our crime scene," Annie whispered. "I was just making a suggestion."

"Since I don't see anyone in charge out here, I don't see a problem with suggesting a better alternative to whatever they're doing." He shrugged. "Plus, you're right. If there's a body, it won't be out here in plain sight. The killer has been moving his victims farther from the house with each kill. So it was a good suggestion. Now let's go see what's happening inside and find the city marshal."

Annie nodded in agreement. She got as far as the door, where she spied the victim, Jimmy Phillips, lying in a pool of blood. Next to him was an ax, just as the witness had said.

"There's a trail of blood," someone called. "Get the dogs."

A man with two bloodhounds on leashes came hurrying around the corner. After being shown to the spot in question, he put the animals to their task and released them.

"They'll find something," he shouted as he followed the barking canines. "They always do."

Before she could go inside to investigate further, a shout went up from the back of the property behind what appeared to be an outhouse. "We've got her!"

Annie went running, but Isaiah got there first. The men gathered around something that was draining blood in rivulets in the snow, but she could not see past their tight circle. By the light of the multiple lanterns that were present, she spied a blood spot about an inch long on a plank near the top of the nearby fence. It looked like something left behind by a thumb or finger.

"Let us through," Isaiah demanded. "This is Pinkerton business. Move away unless you're a police officer."

At that, the men stepped back to reveal the victim. Annie's stomach roiled, and she looked away. "Oh Eula," she whispered as she stepped away to find the man with the dogs. "There's a print on that fence board. Set your dogs on a trail on the other side and see if our killer jumped the fence after he. . ." She paused to find the right words. "After Eula was murdered," she finally said.

"Yes, ma'am." The handler lifted his dogs over the fence and into the adjoining yard. Instantly they took off, with the poor man being left behind to try to keep up.

She looked back at the house. The distance was some 140 feet. Not as far as he'd taken his previous victim, but far enough to be out of sight.

Still, Eula Phillips was not a serving girl. Not even close. They might be dealing with the same man, but it was just as possible they were not.

"Are there other victims?" Annie asked the man nearest to her.

"I only knew about Jimmy until they found her," he said, nodding toward the body. "Could be more, but that'd have to be determined."

Annie nodded and moved away from the circle of light. Ike caught her gaze and turned back to the men.

"No one touch her," he shouted. "This is a crime scene, and as such you all are going to have to step back and keep from disturbing anything. A few of you will need to remain with your lanterns." He pointed to an older man with a beard. "You go fetch the lawman in charge inside the house and tell him we've got something he needs to see."

The man hurried away while the others remained. "I told you

to move on," he said to the men. "You in the red shirt and you in the black jacket. You stay here with your lanterns. The rest of you go comb the lawn for clues. There could be a knife or something else hidden in the grass that we need to find."

A few of them murmured until a man shouted from a short distance away. "Do as the Pinkerton detective says, men. We want to find this madman. Standing around talking about it isn't how we do that."

He stuck his hand out to acknowledge Isaiah. "Deputy United States Marshal H. M. White. I believe you're one of the Pinkertons?"

"Isaiah Joplin," he said. "And this is my partner, Annie Walters."

"Please to meet you, Deputy Marshal," Annie said, "though these are tragic circumstances."

"But for poor aim, we might be dealing with two murders," the marshal said. "Or if not poor aim, then something else. I haven't given up on the theory that Jimmy Phillips did that to himself after he killed his wife."

"I haven't examined the crime scene inside," Annie said, "but given the look of Mr. Phillips and the fact there is blood on the fence, isn't it possible that he wasn't the one who did this? Why would there be an indication that an escape was either attempted or made if the perpetrator was so gravely wounded?"

To his credit, the marshal did not seem surprised to hear such a question from a female. "That's what we need to determine, isn't it?"

"There's something you ought to know about your crime scene," Isaiah told him, his expression grave. "The killer left three strategically placed pieces of firewood on the victim."

"He did," Annie agreed. "What do you think the meaning was behind it?"

"I don't know about the meaning," Isaiah continued, "but I believe I know where they came from."

Isaiah told the marshal the story of hearing footsteps and finding tracks in the snow, of the pieces of wood he had left in case the intruder might have needed a source of warmth for a family. Then he let out a long breath. "I think whoever killed Eula Phillips was on my property earlier in the evening."

While the two men discussed the details of Isaiah's possible near-meeting with the killer, Annie became aware of a disturbance in the front of the home. "Excuse me," she told them. "I'm going to go see what's happening."

She walked toward the sound of men shouting until she spied a familiar face: Cameron Blake. "I thought I might find you here, Miss Walters."

"Hello, Mr. Blake. Do you know what's got these men so excited?"

"I do," he said. "We've had a second murder tonight. Susan Hancock over on Water Street. Her girls came home at midnight and found her murdered in her daughter's bed. Her husband, Moses, is a suspect, but my money is on our old friend the Midnight Assassin."

"Why is that? It doesn't sound like Mrs. Hancock was a serving girl. Was she?"

"She was not, but then, neither was Mrs. Phillips." He paused and looked far too pleased with himself. "No, Mrs. Hancock was killed with an ax and her body displayed much like the others. I've heard Eula met a similar fate, except it was Jimmy who was almost killed in the bed, and Eula ended up out in the back of the property like several of our other victims."

"You are a callous man, Mr. Blake. You speak of these people as if they're not human. Have some respect."

He shrugged. "The killer treats them as if they're not human. I'm merely reflecting what he does in an impartial way. My point is, if you remove the fact of who these women are and stick to the details of how they met their demise, you end up with the undeniable fact that our killer has returned."

"How could he kill two women in one night?"

"Given the proximity of the two crime scenes, it isn't impossible to believe. Of course, that all depends on what time the murders happened, I suppose." Blake gave her an even look. "I have a prediction on how this will all end up though."

"What is your prediction?" she asked, only to hear another perspective on the subject.

"No one in this town wants to admit the killer has returned. Not after an absence of murders since the end of September. The powers that be will find a way to charge Jimmy Phillips and Moses Hancock in the deaths of their wives. Case closed. Nothing to see here." He shrugged. "That's my opinion, and I believe it will happen that way."

"Are you planning an article to give your reasons why it shouldn't?" she asked.

Blake grinned. "I haven't decided yet. It might be fun to write, but then, it will also be fun tearing apart whatever theory the police come up with in order to hold these men accountable."

He paused. "What do you think, Detective Walters?"

"I think there's a possibility we are dealing with the return of our madman, but there is also just as strong a possibility that these men took advantage of what they knew about the killer's previous crimes and used that information to their advantage."

"Well said. I suppose we shall see which way it goes. But I have one final prediction."

"What is that?"

"I predict this is the last we see of our killer. He won't be back this time."

"You seem certain of this."

"Do I?" Blake chuckled. "I'm not, truly. But it would make a great ending to my series, wouldn't it? Midnight Assassin's swan song is a double murder. Now he'll never be found. Or something like that."

"I hope he's found," she said. "I want him put away."

A fellow she'd seen holding a lantern at the murder scene loped up. "Miss Walters, you're needed. The marshal would like you to go over your testimony again from the point that you and the other detective arrived on the property."

"Yes, tell him I'll be right there."

Blake chuckled. "They're already looking for holes in the theory that the killer has returned, and they're trying to put Jimmy Phillips away. Mind what you tell them. It will all be twisted."

"Have you always been this cynical, Mr. Blake?"

"Only after I actually figured out what was going on. Until then, I thought justice always prevailed." He paused. "It's never a nice day when you figure out for yourself that it doesn't."

Chapter 18

A few hours later, Ike walked back home with Annie. The two deaths had stirred up the citizens of Austin to the point where they'd taken to the streets. Men and women, and even children, were clustered along Pecan Street talking about the crimes and lamenting the fact they could not be home and safely asleep in their beds.

"I understand," Annie said. "It must be awful to believe the killer has returned."

"He might have," Ike agreed, "but my worry is whether these people would rather prefer believing he hasn't."

As expected, the lights were on, and Pop was likely waiting up for them inside.

Still, Ike slowed as he reached the house.

"I know it's freezing out here," he said, "but I think it's important to discuss what we saw tonight before the details are gone from our minds. As soon as we go inside, we'll have to give an edited version to Pop, and those details may be lost."

"All right, well, my first thought is I am not sure whether Jimmy Phillips injured himself or was a victim as well. I suppose that's for a doctor to determine."

Ike nodded. "It is, but I think Jimmy will be charged with this crime."

"Why?" she asked.

"You know as well as I do that the husband is always the first suspect." He paused. "The problem with that is the issue of the wood. I know what I heard, and I heard someone walking behind our outbuildings."

"I believe you."

"I also found the tracks that had to be made by a man's boot. I hadn't walked out there today once it started snowing, and I know that Pop didn't. If he was headed to Slanton's house when he left here, which he was, then he'd be going the wrong direction if he walked that way. There were no tracks from the house to the outbuildings, only from the fence. So who else was there?"

"If it was the killer, then the wood you put out in the alley will be gone."

"Let's go see." He directed her to the edge of the property so Pop wouldn't see them walking past and join in. The last thing Ike wished to discuss with his father was that something from their home had been used by a killer. Not on a night that should be a happy one.

They traversed the back lawn until Ike stopped at the place where he'd left the wood. The tracks were gone now, erased by the sleet and snow that had fallen in the hours since he'd been there.

As he feared, however, the three pieces of wood he had stacked neatly against the fence in the alley were gone.

"Oh," Annie said. "You were right."

Ike let out a long breath. "I didn't want to be." He looked around on the ground around the missing pile while Annie's eyes scanned the perimeter.

"I don't see anything unusual here," she said. "What about you?"

"Nothing." He frowned. "That's the worst part."

"What do you mean?" Annie asked.

"The hallmark of the Midnight Assassin is that he leaves no trail. No trace of himself other than what he wants to be found." Ike stopped to look around once more. "I'm not ready to say it was him just yet, but I'll admit there are similarities."

"Jimmy being harmed is consistent with previous attacks," Annie said. "We've got witnesses and companions who have been attacked. What we haven't had until tonight is a victim who isn't a servant. And if you believe the reports, two victims in one night. What are your thoughts on the crime scene at the Hancock home?"

"More typical of the previous scenes than the Phillips murder. Same method of killing the victim." He paused. "I'm just not sure. Unlike the Phillips murder, I don't have a reason to disbelieve the allegation that the husband did it."

"I feel the same," she said. "Her husband has no alibi, but he also has no reason."

"That's true, Annie, but we both know sometimes there just is no reason," Ike told her as they retraced their steps to return to the porch.

"I would like to interview him. Maybe I could figure that part out. If there's a cause or not."

"That isn't going to happen anytime soon, Annie," he said. "The police aren't going to let anyone near him. Not when the case is still being built."

"But it all comes back to whether the killer could take down two women and one man on the same night. I just don't know."

"Once the time of death is determined for each of them, that can either be proved or disproved."

The door flew open and Pop stood there with a rifle aimed in their direction.

"Whoa, now, Pop," Ike said. "Put that away. It's just Annie and me."

"Come on in," he groused. "You're letting in the cold air." He put away the rifle then nodded to the parlor. "I want to hear what happened, but keep your voices down. Hattie has slept through everything so far, and I'd rather she not wake up now."

"I'll make some hot coffee," Annie said. "I'm cold, and it won't keep me awake, because there's no way I can sleep anytime soon. Would any of you like some?"

"Not me," Pop said. "But do you need help finding everything?"

"I think I can manage it," she said. "Isaiah? Coffee?"

"Thank you." Once Annie had gone into the kitchen, Ike quietly gave Pop the edited version of the story.

"Jimmy Phillips did it," Pop said. "And I don't know Moses Hancock at all, but I'd wager he is guilty too. It is no secret that Phillips likes to drink, though I'd heard from his mother that he'd given it up."

Ike sat back in the chair and regarded his father incredulously. "Pop, I'll give you your opinion on Phillips, but why say a man is guilty if you don't know him?"

"All right, here's my thought on that. If it comes out that there was any hint of disagreement between Susan Hancock and her husband, he's going to be found guilty. If there's any reason he can be charged, he will be charged. He might not have done it, but he will be guilty. See what I mean?"

Ike let out a long breath. "I do, actually."

"Did you go over to that scene as well as the one at the Phillipses' place?"

"We did," he said. "The deputy marshal took us with him to see what had happened once the news arrived."

"And?"

"And I think it will come down to time of death." He shook his head. "You know, Pop, it's late. Why don't you see if you can get some sleep. Tomorrow is Christmas, and Miss Hattie is going to want us all up for breakfast."

His father yawned. "I suppose I ought to." He rose to walk toward the door and paused to turn. "You know, Son, I had really hoped that our Black Midnight campaign had actually chased off this monster."

Ike regarded him for a moment. "Maybe it has, Pop."

A few minutes later, Annie came out of the kitchen with two mugs of coffee. She handed one to Ike and took the other one over to the chair near the window.

"My mind is going in a thousand directions," Annie said.

"We've got two murders tonight and a possible return of the Midnight Assassin. Or not."

"What did Cameron Blake have to say about it?"

She frowned. "How did you know I spoke with him?"

He shrugged. "I saw him there when we were leaving with the deputy marshal. If he's anywhere near you, he will be talking to you."

"Rubbish," Annie said. "He talks to everyone."

"Not to me."

Annie took a sip of coffee. "That's because you refuse to speak with him."

"You might take a lesson from me," he told her. "The less you say to a reporter, the fewer words of yours he has to twist."

He was right, of course, but Annie wouldn't admit it to him. At least not tonight. She had too many other things on her mind. Too many facts swirling about in her brain that she feared she wouldn't remember.

And one too many images of poor Eula Phillips that she couldn't forget.

"I think we need to write down our notes tonight before we sleep," Annie said. "Same theory as you said outside. Record it while it is fresh."

Ike went to the sideboard and pulled out a pen, ink, and writing paper. "Do you want to write it all down, or should I?"

Annie rose and grabbed her mug, then walked over to the small writing desk in the corner opposite the Christmas tree. "Your writing is unreadable on a good day, Isaiah. Imagine it in the middle of the night."

While he chuckled, she settled behind the desk. "All right, start at the beginning. If you get too far ahead, I'll stop you."

Using that process, Annie was able to record the events of the night in just over an hour's time. She looked at the pages of notes she had written and nodded. "Yes, that's enough for tonight, I think."

When Isaiah didn't answer, she looked up to find him stretched out as much as the settee would accommodate his long frame. Though he wasn't snoring yet, he appeared to be sound asleep.

Annie rose and went over to the chair to retrieve a crocheted afghan from the basket beside it. Covering Isaiah, she turned off the lights and tiptoed out of the room. By the time she reached the second-floor landing, his snoring drifted upward to reach her.

The next morning she rose to the smell of bacon, and her stomach growled. She found Isaiah at the table, his plate empty and his coffee mug full.

"Good morning and merry Christmas," she told him. "I hope you slept well. You snore, by the way."

He shook his head, then winced. "A man of my height should never be made to sleep on anything that small. But it's my own fault, and I'll own up to it. I should have brought my bedroll down."

Miss Hattie came in and replaced Isaiah's empty plate with another one full of eggs, bacon, and biscuits. "Oh, goodness, I didn't hear you in here. Merry Christmas, Annie! Your breakfast is on the way."

"Merry Christmas to you, Miss Hattie. As to breakfast, that's not necessary. I can—" The kitchen door closed on Annie's words. "I guess my breakfast is on the way," she said to Ike. "Does she know what happened last night?"

"Pop told her. She's upset, which is why she's so cheerful. And cooking like crazy. It's what she does."

"I see. Where is your father?"

"Off to an emergency meeting of the Black Midnight." He shook his head. "Not that he phrased it that way, but that was the gist of the explanation he gave to Miss Hattie. I figure they're gathered in an office somewhere on campus, plotting their next move."

"Are you worried about that at all?"

"I should be," he said. "But if it gives him something to do and keeps him out of trouble, I guess there's no harm in it."

Miss Hattie bustled in with a plate overflowing with food and set it in front of Annie. "Enjoy," she said in a singsong voice. "I've got pie in the oven for later, and I'm thinking of making another roast. The last one was delicious."

"Thank you," Annie said.

The future Mrs. Joplin headed back toward the kitchen, then stopped short and turned around to face them. "Annie, I meant to talk to you about something last night, and I completely forgot. The first time I met you, I told Ikey that you reminded me of someone."

Dread rose as Annie tried very hard to keep any sign of it off her face. "Yes, I remember you mentioning it."

"Did he tell you I figured it out?"

"No," she said, cutting a glance in Isaiah's direction. He gave an almost imperceptible shake of his head, and she relaxed slightly. Whatever Miss Hattie had told him, if anything, he had completely discounted it.

"Well, I have. If you're not a copy of Queen Victoria at your age, I'll eat my hat."

"You'd better throw your hat in with the roast so it'll be nice and tasty," Isaiah told her. "Because I guarantee that Annie isn't related to the queen. That's just silly."

Miss Hattie gave her an expectant look. Annie's heart sank.

"Well, as Isaiah said, the idea of that is just silly, isn't it? How would a relative of the queen become a Pinkerton detective? It just isn't done."

The housekeeper gave her another long look, then shrugged. "I suppose it's a silly thought," she said on an exhale of breath. "Well, you two enjoy your breakfast. I need to make sure Alfie doesn't get into the rest of the bacon. I was thinking of adding it to the potatoes I'm making to go with the roast."

Miss Hattie disappeared into the kitchen, and the door closed behind her. Before Annie could speak, she heard Miss Hattie's distinct cry. "Alfie! Bad dog."

"Oh no," Annie said.

"Tell me, Annie," Isaiah said as he peered at her over his coffee cup. "How does a relative of the queen become a Pinkerton detective?"

Her breath froze in her throat. Words failed her.

"Let me guess. First, she has to find someone in the Metropolitan Police to support her in her quest to become a special constable. If I remember right, that's the only way someone who isn't qualified for the police force can serve. From there, all it would take would be a jump across the pond with a letter from your supervising officer, and a Pinkerton detective would be born."

She tried not to gape at how close he had come to the truth. "That's not it at all," she said.

"I don't believe you."

"Fine. Don't believe me."

"Annie." He set down his mug and studied her. "If I have any of this wrong, correct me, please."

She sighed. "I never wanted to leave the Metropolitan Police. I've told you that."

"You have, now that I think of it. Remind me why you had to."

"I never told you that part, but I suppose it doesn't hurt to tell you now." She paused and took a sip of coffee to buy a moment of time and bolster her courage. "My father was appalled when he found out. I hadn't told him or Mama."

"I can understand his reluctance to have a daughter on the police force." He held up a hand to ward off any response from her. "You're more qualified and a better detective than most men I've worked with, but it is a dangerous job. As a father, I would wish to protect my child, not put him or her in danger."

"Yes, well, thank you for the compliment. Papa didn't

care about how well or poorly I performed my duties as special constable. He was more concerned whether I would be discovered."

"By people in his social circle?" Isaiah offered.

"No," she said slowly, "by my great-grandmother the queen."

Chapter 19

I ke could only stare. "Your grandmother is Queen Victoria. *The* Queen Victoria who lives in Buckingham Palace?"

"She is my *great*-grandmother, and easily several hundred people are ahead of me in line for the throne, so if you're interested in me for any potential royal title I might bestow on you, you're out of luck."

"Annie," he said, shaking his head. "I, well. . ." He seemed to be at a loss for words.

"And this is exactly why I never told you." She gave him a look that would have made Granny proud. "I've told you what you wanted to know, and here are the results."

"What do you mean?"

"You're looking at me in a very strange way, Isaiah. Like I'm some sort of species you've never seen but are curious to learn about."

He chuckled. "Well, in a way you are, Annie. I've never met royalty, and I am certainly curious about what it's like."

Annie's temper rose. "You want to know what it's like?" At his nod, she continued. "We are very normal people who live very normal lives."

"Only you live them in castles," he supplied.

"That is enough." Annie stood. "I am the same Annie Walters you have known for more than two years. Nothing about me is different."

"I'm still working on realizing that. I have a question though," he said. "How did you manage the transfer from London to Chicago with your family being who they are, Annie? You couldn't have told them the truth."

"I did not lie," she said, her defenses rising. "I was very unhappy with my parents after my work at the Metropolitan Police was thwarted by them. Thanks to a very kind man who had acted as my mentor when I was going through the process of becoming a special constable, I had an offer to come to Chicago to stay with a family well known to my father. There was some talk of perhaps finding the right man for me to marry, but in general I was allowed to come and experience the social world of the Americas. Simple as that."

"Simple as that," Isaiah echoed, "only your father thought he was sending you here to find a wealthy husband, didn't he? I've read about the American women who go hunting a duke or a viscount in order to bring money into their coffers and a title to the bride. Why wouldn't it go the other way as well?"

"You're ridiculous."

"I am not, and you know it." He paused. "See, Annie, I'm not the only one who can figure out motives by studying someone. The only thing I cannot figure is why your father would believe you would actually go through with that sort of scheme."

"It wasn't a scheme," she told him. "He wanted me happy, but he also wanted me married. Apparently I'd run off every potential bachelor who'd met with the approval of my extended family in England. I had the choice of branching out to settle for lesser European royalty or coming to America and snagging a wealthy industrialist or copper baron." She shook her head. "Or some such nonsense."

"It is nonsense." Isaiah stood. "But it is brilliant. And I'm glad the plan worked. Now do you intend to finish your breakfast, or were you about to give a speech of some sort?"

Annie looked down at her food and back up at Isaiah. She almost managed a smile. "You can never breathe a word of this to anyone, not even your family. No one else knows."

"Mr. Pinkerton knows." A statement, not a question. "He

would have to or he'd never have allowed it."

Annie returned to her seat. "Only he and no one else."

"Fair enough. I agree."

"Good." She reached for the butter on the table in front of her and applied it liberally to her biscuit.

"Just one more thing, Your Grace," he said.

She gave him a cross look. "It's Your Ladyship, but in America I'm just Annie. What?"

"Did you really grow up in a castle?"

"A small one," she admitted.

Isaiah gave her a look. "Is there any such thing as a small castle?"

Annie sighed. "No. Now stop talking about it."

Miss Hattie stepped out of the kitchen with a broad grin on her face and a coffeepot in her hand. "More coffee, Your Ladyship?"

Oh no. She groaned. "Please," she said. "Just Annie."

The housekeeper cackled. "You sure had him going, didn't you, Annie? Ikey bought it all right up to the castle. I know I ought not to be listening, but I know you were pulling his leg." She looked over at Isaiah. "She might not be related, but I still say she looks like her."

When Miss Hattie had returned to the kitchen, Isaiah shook his head. "What just happened? Apparently she missed some of what we were saying."

"I don't care what happened, but I am relieved. Can you imagine if she believed it?" Annie whispered. "Now, if you could just forget, that would be absolutely ideal."

He chuckled. "Not likely, Your Ladyship."

"Isaiah," she snapped. "It isn't funny. Truly, you are insufferable. If you have any care for me at all, I demand you stop."

"Oh." He sat back, obviously surprised. "This really bothers you."

"That is what I have been trying to tell you. Until I came to work for the Pinkertons, no one saw me. They only saw my relation to my family. Here in America, I am judged on what I do, not who I am. Until you've missed that, you have no idea how much it means to have it." She paused. "Please don't take that away from me."

It took a minute, but he finally nodded. "Sure. All right."

She smiled. "Thank you. So should we concentrate on today? Do we tackle the Hancock case or the Phillips case? Or both at once?"

"Actually, I thought we would check and see what the police are saying about the cases. And the deputy marshal, if we can get him to talk. What do you think?"

"Wouldn't it be better to put our own case together?" Annie asked.

"Normally, yes," he said. "But we both agree there's a bias against allowing that the killer has returned. I want to see what they're saying. If there's sufficient case for it, then I am inclined to let this go."

"Let it go?" She paused to take a breath. "I'm sorry. Did you just say you were willing to let two murders go?"

"No," he said patiently, "I am willing to take what the authorities are saying as truth if their arguments are compelling. If there is a solution to the murders, and that solution does not alarm the citizens of Austin, then I am for it."

Annie's eyes narrowed. "You sound exactly like the rest of them. Sweep it under the rug. Look away because there is nothing to see here. Our city is perfectly safe. That is exactly what you're saying. Unlike your father who is trying to do something about it. Even if what he is doing might be quite silly, it is action."

"That is not it at all."

❧

Or was it? The comparison to his father certainly stung. But beyond that, had he become one of the men he had railed against not so long ago?

Ike took another sip of coffee, not because he wanted it but because it gave him something to do while he thought about what she'd said. He did want these cases to be solved, that was true.

And if they were solved in a way that proved Austin's citizens could sleep safely at night, all the better. But did that make him biased as to the possible outcomes?

Ike let out a long breath. He had to admit it did.

"You're right," he told her.

"I'm sorry, what?" She held her biscuit in midair, her gaze locked with his. "Did you just change your mind based on an argument I presented to you? Did that just happen?"

"Don't let it go to your head." He almost added *Your Ladyship* but thought better of it. While she had a point, and he'd certainly keep his agreement not to mention her family connection to anyone else, that didn't mean he wasn't still shocked by it.

Out of all the women he might have been attracted to, he had fallen in love with Queen Victoria's great-granddaughter. Royalty.

And he'd already thought she was the most interesting woman he knew. The most special.

"Isaiah, you're doing it again."

"Doing what?"

"Looking at me strangely."

He shrugged. "I've never seen a woman as tiny as you eat a biscuit that big."

"They're called cathead biscuits," Miss Hattie said as she breezed back in. "I believe it's because they're big as a cat's head. Makes sense that would be it. You two need anything else?"

"Thank you, but no," Annie said. "And the biscuits are delicious."

A short while later, Ike hitched up the buggy and they headed over to the police station. The crowd outside was bigger than any he'd seen, and inside, the small space was crammed with citizens and reporters alongside the meager police force.

"This might not have been the best idea," Annie said. "There are far too many people for us to have any chance of getting information."

"That's the beauty of this." He nodded to the desk where Annie had read the previous police reports a few days ago. "The duty sergeant keeps the records there. I'm sure the others who are working the cases will have their notes, but we can start with him. He likes you. Maybe you could ask."

Annie wove her way through the crowd with Ike a step behind. They found the sergeant deep in conversation with a man who was likely a reporter.

She stepped in between them and smiled. "I'm so sorry. I'm just here for the records."

"Records?" the sergeant said.

"From last night. Both scenes." She turned to the reporter. "Tragic, isn't it?" Then her attention went back to the sergeant. "I just need them for a few minutes. And your desk if you're not terribly busy."

"Well, um. . . ." He scratched his head and seemed to be looking around for someone to confer with.

"They're all busy," she said. "That's why I went directly to you. I don't want to keep you from your interview, so I'll just get to it if you don't mind."

Ike nodded. "We won't be long."

Apparently the ruse worked, for a moment later the sergeant retrieved a thick file from his desk and set it in front of him. Then he rose and stepped aside to continue his conversation with the reporter.

Ike grinned. "And this is why I do not understand the reluctance for anyone to hire a woman. No man could have pulled that off."

She smiled. "I hope you're not saying I played on my feminine wiles."

"Of course not. You read him perfectly and figured out exactly what it would take to get him to hand over the file. That's not wiles, that's brains, Annie. And you've got plenty. Now let's see what's in those files that we might have missed last night."

His companion grinned. Though she was the prettiest woman in the room and could have easily flirted her way to success, Annie was not the kind to do such a thing. He loved that about her.

Annie opened the first file, the case of the death of Susan Hancock, and turned the page so they both could read it. The information was everything the writer of the report had heard or seen at the scene of the crime.

From the information about Mrs. Hancock being found in her daughter's bed to the girls coming home late and finding her there, there was nothing new. Physical evidence was minimal and likely ruined by the mess at the scene, both inside and outside of the home.

"That is disappointing," Annie said.

"It is just the preliminary information. More will come in as the day goes on." He nodded toward the other file. "Let's see what it says about Eula Phillips."

That file too held the facts of the case as she understood them. Jimmy Phillips's words to the first officer on the scene seemed to indicate his guilt, but the doctor who had examined him stated the fellow was not in his right mind and could not be counted on to say anything, either in his defense or to his detriment.

"I wonder what he said." Annie looked over at him. "I don't see a witness name here, so maybe he spoke to the officer in charge?"

Ike looked up to find a man standing before him with pieces of wood. The bloody smudges on the topmost piece in the pile told him this was unmistakably evidence.

"Excuse me, miss, where's the desk sergeant?"

Chapter 20

Ike jumped into action and claimed the wood. "And who are you?" he asked.

"Last night out at the Phillips place, I spoke to some fellow who called himself the deputy marshal. He told me to cut out those floorboards and bring them in. The fence post too. He'll know who I am." Then he disappeared back into the crowd.

Ike looked over at Annie, who moved the police reports out of the way to make room for the evidence. He spread out the pieces of wood—several floorboards and a piece of the back fence—in front of them.

"What do you see?" he asked Annie.

"Fingerprint on the fence board," she said. "I spied that last night. It was found very near the body and looks like a thumbprint." She moved her attention to the floorboards. "That is most definitely a footprint on a section of wood flooring. I wonder what part of the home this was in."

"That would be Jimmy and Eula's bedroom floor," Deputy Marshal White said. "It was found at the end of the bed. Nothing corresponds with it out at the murder site." He shook his head. "Either of you want to tell me why Pinkerton detectives are sitting at a police sergeant's desk holding my evidence?"

"Miss Walters and I were going over reports," Ike told him. "Your informant delivered these just a few minutes ago. You probably passed him as you came in."

The older man gave a harrumph. "I never saw him, but then, there's nothing but chaos in here. Out on the streets too. Not a one of them seems to remember it's Christmas Day. Did you know most of the churches have canceled services? It's madness."

"People are upset," Annie said. "They believe the killer they thought they were safe from has returned."

"Which is why we're determined to catch him," the deputy marshal said. "If you're finished with my evidence, I'll take it now."

Ike took another long look at the pieces of wood and committed the images to memory. Owing to the size, the owner of the footprint was very likely going be a large man. He also had an odd anomaly.

Ike pointed to the oddly shaped portion of the print on the floorboard. "Deputy Marshal," Ike said, "tell me what you see there."

After squinting and leaning forward, the lawman straightened. "Looks to me like the fellow might be missing a toe." He paused. "Or it could be that there wasn't sufficient blood in that one spot to give evidence of the toe that was there. He's a big man though. But that is what the previous witnesses stated."

"How big is Jimmy Phillips?"

The deputy marshal frowned. "I don't know. He was abed all of the time I was there. I guess we need to find that out, don't we?"

"We do," Annie stated.

"You realize, though, that a man carrying something heavy can cause a print to spread," White continued. "So we may have definitive proof of who killed her or we may have a distorted print that will just muddy the waters."

Ike nodded. "But we have something."

"We do." He paused. "I'm going to see that this evidence is preserved. I do hope if either of you Pinkerton detectives were to learn anything important you would have the good sense to tell me about it."

"Of course," Annie said. "Might we expect the same courtesy extended to us?"

He looked down at her, his expression unreadable. "Ma'am, with all due respect, you are a paid employee of the Pinkerton

Detective Agency sent here to try to fix the mess that the lawmen of this city have allowed to go on over the course of a year. You are here because our mayor panicked, and you answer to the man who deposited the money in your boss's bank account. I answer only to the people of Texas. While I am willing to share information, I have no obligation to do so. I hope that you will remember this."

"We are acutely aware of that fact, Deputy Marshal White," Ike said. "But we are all working toward the same goal. We want this killer stopped."

"Yes, well, that is true." He gathered up the evidence, tipped his hat at Annie, then walked away.

"Well," she said, "for the first time in a very long time, I cannot decide what to think about someone. I cannot tell if that man is for us or against us."

"As he said, his obligation is to answer to the people. And the people want to be safe. He's going to make sure they feel that way." Ike shrugged. "Having said all of that, he will do the right thing."

"Which is?" Annie said.

"Tell the truth. Let the evidence speak. And bring in a killer."

"That last part may be a little hopeful," she said. "He has evaded capture for a year and has become brazen enough to venture into the homes of two women who come from a different segment of society than the previous victims. Eula Phillips lived in the best neighborhood in Austin. She was beautiful, loved, and protected. And she ended up dead in the most horrendous way."

"Let's talk about this in the carriage on the way to Hickory Street," he said. "There are too many sets of eyes and ears here." He groaned. "And here comes your friend the reporter."

Annie stood. "See if you can get us through this crowd in the most expedient manner. I will follow behind you."

Ike nodded, then grasped her hand and plowed his way through the throng. Cameron Blake spied them but couldn't get to them owing to the men who milled about.

A moment later, Ike stepped out onto the sidewalk and hurried to the spot where he'd left the carriage. He'd just managed to get Annie situated when Blake caught up to them.

"Running from me? I'm hurt."

He made a gesture like his heart was broken, and it was all Ike could do not to react. Instead, he brushed past the man and climbed into the carriage.

"Miss Walters, you'll be wanting this telegram."

Ike leaned over to snatch the paper Blake was holding. Sure enough, it was a telegram. He handed it to Annie, who looked at it with what appeared to be a mix of curiosity and horror.

"Why would you have this?" she demanded.

Blake shrugged. "I happened to stop in at your hotel to pay a cordial visit and see if we could continue the conversation we were having on the twenty-third. I was told you had checked out. Poor clerk had no idea where you'd gone, and he was in possession of that. So I assured him I would see that you received it." He paused. "And now you have."

"Yes, well. Thank you, I suppose," she managed before looking up from the telegram to focus on the reporter. "However, if you ever are brazen enough to pay for private and personal correspondence of mine to be put into your slimy hands, please know that I will prosecute you to the fullest extent of the law."

"Oh, Miss Walters," he said gently. "Is that any way for a woman of your station to behave?"

❧

A woman of your station.

Annie froze. Surely he couldn't know. Yet she knew he did. It was the only explanation.

"Drive, please," she said to Isaiah, who quickly grasped the reins.

Unfortunately, the throng milling about on the streets prevented the swift exit that Annie desperately desired. Thus

Cameron Blake still stood on the sidewalk smiling at her.

At both of them.

"You're quite the enigma, Miss Walters. A lady Pinkerton detective with a lovely British accent. You do understand I had to investigate. I have been told you're highly thought of at the Chicago office."

She ignored him. Meanwhile, Ike had waved over a young man and was speaking with him about something that appeared to be urgent.

"I am planning a story about last night's murders. Can I get a statement from you or Detective Joplin regarding the allegation that the Midnight Assassin or, as some call him, the Servant Girl Annihilator, has come out of retirement and was well rested enough to take down two Austin wives in their beds?"

Only one was in her bed when she was killed. Annie refused to correct him.

"No, of course you wouldn't comment. It is too early in the investigation. My source says new evidence was brought in today. Any idea what it was?"

Annie sat facing straight ahead.

"Right. Well, okay. If I cannot get enough information on the subject of this investigation and clues that may lead to finding the killer or killers—because we don't know whether there is one or more—then I will have to set my attention elsewhere for my next story."

Ike leaned past Annie to stare down at the reporter. "You obviously have other sources. We are not included in that number, Blake. I have been nice, but that is about to end."

"So you're threatening me?" He grinned. "Please do. I would love to quote you."

A whistle went up on the road, and it was Ike's turn to grin. "Quote away, Blake. Detective Walters might be above prosecuting you for fraud and a list of other things, but I have no such compunctions."

He turned his attention back to the road where a path had been miraculously cleared by the youth and his two friends. Ike tossed the boy three coins, and they were off.

Annie sat very still, clutching the telegram, terrified to open it and see what the reporter had read. Because surely he had read it. What other purpose would he have for assuring a clerk he would make the delivery?

Then she froze as a thought occurred.

"Isaiah, I left a forwarding address with the hotel. They knew where I would be. Remember, I received a telegram yesterday? You accepted it while you were outside retrieving packages."

He frowned. "Yes, I did."

Annie unfolded the telegram and looked down. Due to the rocking of the carriage, the words jumped and swam on the page.

"Would you mind finding a place to stop so I can read this?"

When Isaiah complied a few minutes later, she tried again. This time the words were absolutely clear and readable, though it might have been better if they had not been.

VISIT FROM HRH IMMINENT. HE DEMANDS TO
SEE HIS DAUGHTER. RETURN IMMEDIATELY.

Annie crumpled the telegram and crammed it into her pocket. Though tears threatened, she would not cry. Instead, she straightened her backbone and looked over at Isaiah.

"Has something happened?"

"Not yet," she said. "Would you please stop at the telegraph office before we go any farther?"

Once there, Annie sent a brief response:

CANNOT RETURN. CASE TOO IMPORTANT TO
LEAVE. PLEASE KEEP LOCATION CONFIDENTIAL.

If that did not suffice, she would know very soon. In the

meantime, there was nothing more she could do to stall her father.

Now to handle the other pending issue.

She looked at the telegraph operator and introduced herself, presenting her badge. "I understand I received a telegram this morning from Chicago."

"You did, Miss Walters. I dispatched it to your hotel by messenger."

"And I received it. From a messenger. But not at my hotel. Do you know a reporter named Cameron Blake?"

His guilty expression answered the question for her. Annie offered a stare that riveted him in place.

"Yes, I thought so, although he told me he got it from a clerk at my hotel."

The telegraph operator hung his head. "It was what we arranged."

"I thought so. I will remind you that I am a Pinkerton detective and as such may be receiving confidential information through telegrams. Your release of that information would be considered a serious crime. I have not yet decided if I will prosecute, but be aware that it is a possibility."

"I didn't mean any harm," he protested. "I thought I was helping you get it faster. That's what Mr. Blake said."

"The next time you and Mr. Blake conspire together, I promise you both will be going to jail. And as I said, I haven't decided about this time yet. So from now on you will hand my telegrams, if any should arrive, only to me. Not to a clerk and certainly not to a reporter. If you must send a messenger, it will only be to tell me I have a telegram that must be picked up. Is that clear?"

At his nod, she walked out the door and returned to the carriage where Isaiah gave her a questioning look. She sat very straight, her heart racing.

Finally, she swiveled to look at Isaiah.

"What was in the telegram, Annie?"

"A demand that I return to Chicago because HRH is arriving

and wants to see me."

He let out a long breath. "I see."

"Meanwhile, the telegraph operator has been warned I am prepared to prosecute, and HRH will have to wait. I am working a case."

"Annie," he said, warning in his voice. "Is that wise?"

"I won't even ask which of those things I just told you about you're referring to, and I certainly will not comment further. So if we are going to try to interview Jimmy Phillips, let's get to it." She paused. "I assume that's the reason for returning."

"That and getting a look at the scene during daylight hours. We may see something now that we didn't see earlier."

"Should we intrude on Christmas, Isaiah? It just feels wrong."

"I have a feeling there will be plenty of others there," he said. "The crime scene is fresh. We have to do our jobs."

"Right. Yes."

Annie sat back as Isaiah set the carriage in motion again. Rather than think about the telegrams and the pesky New York reporter, she set her mind on recalling the details of last night's murder. Retracing the steps in her mind, though skipping past the image of Eula, she relived each moment as best she could.

Then her thoughts stuttered to a stop. She hadn't seen the second victim of the crime. Not clearly anyway.

"What was Jimmy Phillips wearing?"

"Wearing?" He shook his head. "I'd have to think about that. All I remember is the blood. His injury was to the head, so that made a mess."

"But he was awake and speaking according to the police reports."

"I suppose, though I did not hear him talking in the brief time I stood in the door." They rode in silence for a few minutes, then Isaiah sat bolt upright. "An overcoat!"

Chapter 21

Annie shook her head. "I don't understand."

"Jimmy Phillips had on trousers, a shirt, red socks—I remember they were red because I thought at first it might be blood—and an overcoat draped over his shoulders."

"Oh," Annie exclaimed. "That is interesting. Why an overcoat and no shoes?"

"Why an overcoat at all?" he mused. "Maybe I'm remembering it wrong."

"Your description fits what I saw too," Isaiah and Annie were told a few minutes later by an Austin police officer who had been on the scene. "Thought it was odd, but then, maybe he got cold sometime before the killer got to him. All I know is that if he survives this, it'll be a miracle."

"We would like to speak with him," Isaiah said.

"Not possible," the officer told them.

"May we just see him, then?"

He thought a minute, then nodded. "The family has moved him out of the room where it happened. Let me check and see what's what." He came back a moment later and said, "Follow me. And make it quick."

They stepped into a darkened room where the bandaged form of a man lay presumably sleeping. Annie held back to survey the room and its contents. She decided that since it was devoid of any personal items or decoration, it must have been used as a guest room.

Isaiah stood over the patient. "Jimmy," he said, "are you awake?"

Nothing. Isaiah said his name again, and this time Jimmy stirred.

"Did you do it, Jimmy?" Isaiah asked.

Jimmy's eyes stared. His mouth moved but no words came out. "What in the world?"

Annie turned around to see an older woman there. The policeman who'd led them to the room scrambled to catch up to her.

"These are the Pinkerton detectives, ma'am. They are here to help."

Annie reached out to touch the woman's sleeve. "Is there anything you can add that would help us find the man who did this to Jimmy and his wife?"

"It all happened so quietly," she said. "For all of this. . ." Tears rose. "Well, for what happened, why didn't I hear anything? I just don't understand."

Mrs. Phillips's tears fell in earnest. The police officer stepped in. "You should go now."

"Just one more question, Mrs. Phillips," Annie said gently. "I wonder if you can recall a detail about your son's clothing last night."

"I will try."

"His socks," she said. "I understand they were red."

"Yes, they were," she replied. "I removed them myself when they finally let me see to him. Oh, my poor boy," she said before the tears fell in earnest.

"About those socks," Annie persisted. "Were they damp or dry? And if they were damp, was it with water or blood?"

"I don't exactly recall." She shook her head. "There was so much blood. So much. I just wasn't thinking clearly. And he was hurting so bad."

"Where are the socks now?"

"I had everything cleaned. I didn't want Jimmy to see the mess when he woke up again."

"Who did that cleaning?" Annie asked.

"Why are there so many questions?" she wailed, and the police officer stepped between them.

"Go now."

Isaiah walked outside with Annie behind him. The room where Jimmy had been injured was locked. "We need to find that maid."

A search turned up a terrified servant girl who confirmed Mrs. Phillips's story. "I did the washing, but it was all put together in a bloody mess. It was the worst thing I've ever seen," she said. "The police took everything."

"So you don't recall if there was blood on the socks or if they were wet?"

"Oh, there was blood," she told them, "but whether that was from the blood that was on everything else or not, I can't say."

"Where are they now?"

"The police collected all the clothing while it was still sopping wet. I'm just waiting for family to come get me," she said. "I can't stay here anymore."

With nothing else to see indoors, Annie led the way to the back of the property where plenty of gawkers were milling about. "This is as bad as the police station," she complained. "There's nothing left of the original crime scene to see."

"You just missed the dogs," one of the men said to Isaiah. "Fellow brought out another set. Says he's going to find the killer. He gave them the scent, and they took off that way." He gestured toward the other side of the fence. "Been gone just a few minutes."

Isaiah leaned toward her. "Let's go see what we can find out at the Hancock home. If the dogs catch someone, we'll hear about it soon enough."

They drove to Water Street where much the same scene of chaos greeted them. "They've had their troubles," one of the men outside said. "But I haven't ever known him to hurt her."

Isaiah quickly took his statement, and they moved inside. There they found the Hancock daughters struggling to keep their composure. Neither could offer any new clues.

"We'd been out at the Presbyterian church Christmas event," the older one said.

"She was like that when we came home," the younger one added before dissolving into tears.

A short while later, they returned to the carriage. "Well?" Annie asked him. "What are your thoughts?"

"My thoughts are that a man cannot cause that much harm to another person and escape undetected." He paused. "But that's what has been said about every other murder the monster is tied to."

"Do you think he did this?"

He paused. "I had hoped we would find something at one of these crime scenes that would sway me one way or another. Unfortunately, my answer is that I don't know. And that means there's room for doubt. What about you?"

"My heart breaks for the Phillips family and for the Hancock girls," she said. "But I'm torn. Why would either of these men want to kill their wives?"

"I didn't know Moses Hancock, but Jimmy had a reputation as a drinker. He and Eula separated a time or two over it. So there's a possible motive. She was planning to leave him again."

"Which we don't know," she reminded him.

"I can only attest to what I saw at the governor's dinner. Eula did not act like a woman who wished her husband was in attendance. At one point, she actually made a joke at his expense. It made a few of us uncomfortable, but she didn't seem to care." He paused. "So if they quarreled, then yes, he could have done this."

"You saw what he looked like. Could he have done that much damage to himself?"

"A drunk man swinging an ax? Yes, he could. If I had to guess how it went down, I would say that they argued, Eula decided to leave him, and he chased her into the yard and did her in."

Annie thought about it. "If that is true, then how do you

account for the footsteps behind your woodshed and the three missing pieces of wood that appeared at the crime scene?"

"Footsteps that could have been made by someone else?" he said. "And wood that was retrieved by whomever I set it out for? The fact there was the same number at the crime scene could be a coincidence. It was freezing out, so I didn't exactly examine the pieces of wood I left in the alley in case I needed to identify them later."

"Isaiah, it is dangerous to form a theory then try to prove it."

"I haven't done that," he snapped.

She stared until he looked away. "I need a new hotel," she told him. "Can you recommend one?"

He whipped his attention toward her. "Why? You are perfectly safe where you are now."

"It is one thing to visit during Christmas and another thing to move into the room at the top of the stairs for the duration of the investigation."

"Why?" He shook his head. "Because you're afraid people will talk? Maybe they will realize I love you?"

Words escaped her. He loved her?

Ike cringed. Had he really just told Annie that he loved her?

What an idiot he was to throw that out in the middle of a conversation like it was nothing. Annie deserved better.

So he pulled the carriage over. Then he inhaled deeply and let it out slowly. After that, he managed to swivel toward her.

Annie was watching closely, likely forming her own opinion of the matter. Studying him in that way she had of making a man feel like he was under a microscope.

"All right," he said. "I have just been very stupid. I shouldn't have blurted out something that important in that way."

"Well," she said after a minute, "I do not disagree."

"And?"

She shook her head. "I am surprised."

"That I love you?" he said.

"No," she said softly, "that you admitted it. I thought we agreed not to get involved as long as we were working together. That was your idea."

"Yes, I did say that," he admitted. "And I meant it. I just can't stick to it, as you might have noticed."

She shrugged. "Of course we kissed under the mistletoe, an action which you might have considered to have voided the agreement. I don't think it did."

"This isn't a business deal, Annie."

"No, it's not. It's much more important than anything like that. We're colleagues, Isaiah. Getting involved would just muddy the waters."

"We're already involved. It wasn't just that kiss. Kisses," he corrected. "There is something between us that is meant to be. And yes, we are colleagues. That's easily remedied though."

Her eyes widened. "How?"

"I'll quit. I can go back to lawyering. Then we're not colleagues." He leaned toward her, but her back remained straight, her posture unbending.

"Don't be absurd. You would hate every minute of that."

"No, I wouldn't," he protested, even as he knew she was right.

"You would, so stop saying that."

"All right, then we can both quit." At this Annie's brows rose, so he kept talking to prevent a response from her. "We're a good team. I'll admit I am fonder of detective work than lawyering, so why not hang out a shingle and open our own agency?"

"Quit the Pinkertons to take on our own cases?"

"I know, it might be slow going at first, but we will be fine. We can call it Joplin & Joplin Detective Agency. What do you think?"

"I think your father will be thrilled that he's being included."

Oh.

"Well, actually. . ."

What? He'd already blurted out that he loved her. He couldn't just admit that the other Joplin would be her. His wife.

"You know what I mean," he managed.

"Do I?" was her swift reply.

"Sure," he said. "I figure if he can come up with that Black Midnight thing, then why not?" Ike set the carriage in motion again, keeping his eyes on the road and away from Annie.

"I would like to find that hotel now, please."

"Annie, don't. I want us to be together. I think that's what you want too, isn't it?"

"Isaiah, I cannot let you turn your life upside down for me."

"Maybe it's the other way around," he said. "You don't want to turn your life upside down for me. I don't fit into that royal life you will go back to someday."

Silence.

"Are you turning me down?"

"You haven't asked," she said.

"If I had?"

"I am."

He slid her a sideways glance and found his fellow Pinkerton detective staring straight ahead. Ike might have argued further, but the likelihood that he would say something else stupid loomed large.

So he did as she asked, depositing her at the best hotel in town with the promise to return with her things. When he arrived home, he ignored Miss Hattie and went straight up to Annie's room. Considering she was neat as a pin, it only took him a second to grab her bag and return to the carriage.

"Where are you going?" Miss Hattie called after him as he stepped out onto the porch.

"Delivering Annie's bag to her hotel," he said.

His future stepmother stood in the doorway, hands on hips,

with that dog of hers a shadow right behind her. "What have you done, Ikey?"

Ignoring the question and its answer, Ike climbed into the carriage and hurried off before the housekeeper had time to ask anything else.

The hotel was dressed in its Christmas finery inside and out, with garlands of red and green draped over the arches and twisted around the ornamental posts on either side of the grand double doors.

A uniformed doorman hurriedly opened one of the doors to let Ike inside. With Annie's bag tucked under his arm, he marched across the thick-carpeted floor and past the ornately framed paintings, hunting for the first clerk he could find.

"Miss Annie Walters is expecting this," Ike told him. "Would you deliver it to her room, please?"

"I'll take that."

Chapter 22

Ike looked over to see a well-dressed Englishman, his dark hair lightly streaked with silver, and recognized him immediately as a relative of Annie's. They shared the same eyes, the same smile, and the same regal bearing.

The gold signet ring on his hand meant something. What that was, Ike did not currently care.

This must be the father who had ended her career as a special constable. Instantly, Ike disliked him.

Depositing the bag on the counter, Ike turned to face him. The man smiled.

"You must be Detective Joplin." He thrust out his hand. "We meet at last."

"You have me at a disadvantage, sir," Ike said. "How is it you know my name?"

"I've hired you for a job," he said. "And I've brought your instructions with me along with a letter from your supervisor."

"The captain?" Ike said.

"No, that would be Mr. William Pinkerton."

"I see," came out on a rush of breath. "And what is it I have been hired to do?"

He waved away the question. "Oh, it's all in the packet. Just mind the time. Your train leaves a few minutes after five this evening."

Ike looked up at the clock above the front desk. "That's in three hours, and it is Christmas Day. When was I going to receive this?"

"I was actually just making the arrangements to have it sent to you." The clerk in front of him nodded. "I suppose the answer is, it would have been shortly."

Ike opened the leather packet, which was emblazoned with his name, and spied one word written across the first page: *Classified*. The second page contained his train tickets.

"Boston?" he said.

"That is your first stop. There are others, but I will let you read all about it in a more secure location." He gave Ike a sweeping glance. "You do understand this is an assignment you cannot turn down."

"That's where you're wrong." He shook his head. "What was your name?"

He chuckled. "I have a number of them. Arthur Henry William George are my given names. But I would rather you know me by my title."

"Your Highness?" he said sarcastically.

"No, Detective Joplin, Alice Anne's father." He nodded to a pair of men in suits standing nearby. "Just so we are clear, they are with me, as are several others I will not point out. And that is just the men who are in the lobby. It would be madness for a man of my stature to travel alone."

"Right." Ike looked over his shoulder at the clerk. "Please go up to Miss Walters's room and have her come down to the lobby. It is urgent."

"I am already here." Ike turned to see Annie standing nearby. "I see you two have met."

"He's a very nice young man," her father said. "But not the fellow for you. I'll give you time to say goodbye, but only just a few minutes. The detective must be on his way. He's been given an assignment."

Annie shook her head. "He already has an assignment, as do I."

"According to William Pinkerton, your presence here is unofficial. There are other Pinkertons being paid to look into the nasty business your local madman is up to, and your jobs were to keep the inept men from looking so inept. Am I wrong?"

"No," Annie said.

"For this reason, there is no official assignment on the books for either of you. Thus Mr. Joplin is being dispatched elsewhere, and so are you."

"Come with me, Annie." Ike told her as he linked arms with her and stepped away. The men in suits made to follow, but Annie's father waved them back.

"I'm being sent to Boston."

"Boston?" She shook her head. "Why?"

"Your father made a deal with William Pinkerton to hire me. The first of many locations," he said. "Unless you want to take me up on that business offer. I haven't told Pop about it yet, so there's still room on the marquee."

The Englishman called to Annie. "I should mention that your assignment is the result of a direct request from Her Majesty to William Pinkerton. There is an agreement upon which your cooperation is required."

"Ignore him," Ike told her. "I love you, and I am pretty sure you love me. If we both quit the Pinkertons, we can continue our investigation here in Austin and maybe help put that monster who is killing women away. Then the Pinkertons and your family will have no say."

Annie looked up at him with tears shimmering in her eyes. "You don't understand, Isaiah. It's just not that simple."

"It is every bit that simple," Ike said. "Just you and me."

"No," she said. "It can never be just you and me. Granny would never allow it."

"I can speak to her. Explain that there is no man on earth who can take better care of her great-granddaughter than me." He held her by the shoulders, desperate. "Annie, I will go to the ends of the earth to make you my wife."

"If my father had anything to do with it, that's where you would be sent." She glanced down at the packet in his hand.

"Read that carefully, because the ends of the earth may be where you are going."

"Let him go now, Daughter," her father said as he moved near to them. "You know you would never get Granny's approval."

Annie turned around to face him. "Give me some privacy, please, Papa. Just another minute."

The Englishman appeared to consider arguing, then thought better of it and nodded. He took several steps back but remained close enough to keep watch.

"Why does her approval mean so much?" he asked, hating the desperation in his voice.

"Honestly, Isaiah, if it was up to me, I wouldn't care. Granny could disapprove and I would be fine. But Papa and Mama and my sister, well. . ." She glanced over at her father and then back at Ike. "She holds the purse strings. If my father allowed me to marry you without her approval, my family would very quickly become destitute."

"You're exaggerating."

She shook her head. "I'm telling the truth. Everything comes from the queen. And with one misstep, that can all go away."

"So that's it then?"

A tear slid down Annie's cheek, and Ike caught it with his thumb. "No one will ever love you like I do," he told her.

"I know," she whispered on an exhale of breath.

Then she kissed him.

New Year's Eve 1885
Chicago

Six days later, Annie walked into the Prairie Avenue home of Marshall Field and his wife, Nannie, to celebrate New Year's Eve at the Mikado Ball. Not that she planned to celebrate. The opposite, in fact.

Annie had barely spoken to her father since she left Austin. It wasn't his fault, and she knew this, but she had been put in an untenable position. She could either walk away from the monarchy and marry the man she loved or put her selfish feelings aside and do what was best for the family.

Having been taught from the cradle that honor and duty were her life's purpose, there had been no question which she would choose. The decision had come at a cost, and Papa knew that when the time was right, she would ask for payment.

Not in money but in permission.

His permission to live her life as she wished as long as Granny did not disapprove.

While her father chatted with the hostess, Annie looked past them to the Japanese-themed room. From the abundant stylized hangings to the bronze stork and miniature pagoda in the center of the room, *Mikado*, a play that had taken the New York theater crowd by storm, heavily influenced the decor.

After making polite conversation, Annie separated from Papa to make her way through to the yellow room where two Japanese flower trees had been placed beneath a giant parasol that hung from the ceiling. She felt ridiculous dressed in full Japanese costume, but that had been the requirement of attending.

And Papa insisted they attend. It was the one thing he requested of her in order to agree to her concessions, the bargain they had struck.

Annie found a table tucked into the corner and settled there in hopes she might be left to her own devices. Reaching into the overlarge pocket that came with the costume, she retrieved the copy of *Little Women* she'd purchased once they arrived in Chicago and disappeared into the world of Jo, Meg, and their sisters.

"Good evening, Annie."

She looked up to see Captain Hezekiah Ingram smiling down at her. "Your father told me you were hiding back here. May I join you?"

"Of course." Annie put away the book. "How are you, Captain?"

"Confused, that's how I am." He shook his head. "Why didn't you heed my warning? Did you want to be pulled out of the Pinkertons and hauled back home to England?"

"Of course not," she said. "Your telegram said 'Visit from HRH imminent. He demands to see his daughter. Return immediately,' " she quoted.

"Exactly. Why didn't you?"

"Captain, now I'm confused. The last thing I wanted to do was return to Chicago because my father demanded to see me." She paused. "I'm sorry I ignored the telegram, but I thought if it was sent in an official capacity, you would have indicated that."

"Oh, Annie, you got it all wrong." He scrubbed his face with his hands. "I did send that exact telegram, but you misunderstood. I meant that you were about to get a visit from your father in Austin and you should return immediately to Chicago to avoid seeing him."

Annie sat back and shook her head. "Captain," she said softly. "No."

"Yes." He paused. "I guess Ike wasn't happy with all this."

"Neither of us were," Annie said. "But it would have happened eventually. Papa would have tracked me down, and it would have all ended badly. At least this way I can go home and Granny won't know what I've been up to."

"About that." He retrieved a folded copy of a newspaper from his jacket and slid it across the table toward her.

Annie looked down at yesterday's copy of the *New York Daily Gazette* where Cameron Blake's column had been given front-page attention. "The Lady and the Pinkerton: An Exposé on the Love Story of Crime-Fighting Pair." She groaned and looked up at the captain. "Has my father seen it?"

"He has, and so has the queen."

"Oh no." Annie sat back and allowed her gaze to rise to the ceiling and the collection of oversized paper parasols hanging there. "Oh no," she repeated.

"Annie," the captain said gently. "It will be fine. Mr. Pinkerton fired off a firm letter to the *Gazette*'s owner and sent Her Majesty his apologies. It has been smoothed over. It will be fine."

"So you said." She folded the paper and left it on the table. "I hope Granny thinks so."

Four Years Later
London
1889

Chapter 23

London
April 1, 1889

It was morning.

Or afternoon.

Or somewhere in between.

Groaning, Ike closed his eyes against the lukewarm rays of sunlight that had sliced through his dreams and jarred him awake. The last thing he remembered was trying to decide whether to find some lunch or give in to the short nap he had been craving ever since the ship docked in London.

Someone knocked. Or so he thought.

Fighting his way out of the tangle of silk to sit up, Ike shook his head to dislodge the sleep from his fogged brain. He looked down and saw that he was fully dressed except for his boots, which were nowhere in sight.

Apparently he'd chosen the nap. Interesting, since he had no recollection of climbing into bed.

He'd managed to fall asleep yesterday at midday only to wake up today with a groggy head and a complete inability to remember how he had come to be sleeping beneath silk sheets with blue sky and wisps of clouds overhead. Upon closer inspection, he determined the clouds had been painted onto a canopy bed situated in the middle of a massive room.

He wrangled the sheet into submission and managed to climb out of bed. Then he found his boots under the bed and stepped into them as the second knock sounded.

"Come in," he called.

A uniformed butler opened the door, followed by another man

in livery who held a silver tray in his gloved hands. He marched to the table beside the window and deposited the tray. With a flourish, he removed the silver dome to reveal breakfast along with a folded note card.

"What time is it?" Ike asked the fellow, realizing his watch was back on the table beside the bed.

"Fifteen minutes past ten, sir."

"Right." He retrieved the note and waited for the hotel employees to leave before he read it.

Meet in the lobby at eleven o'clock. Wear what is in the closet. Please.

Ike opened the gilt-trimmed armoire to locate a dark suit and white shirt hanging there. On the shelf above was a bowler hat and a pair of socks. Below was a pair of leather shoes.

He shook his head but slipped into the suit anyway. Then he donned the socks. He took the hat off the shelf, put it on, and padded to the mirror. "I look like an idiot."

The hat he would wear, Ike decided. The shoes, however, were another matter.

After taking a few bites of breakfast, Ike slipped into his best pair of boots and headed down to the lobby. Annie was waiting.

He spied her before she saw him. Unlike her surprise visit to his office in Austin, he knew she would be here. Still, his heart lurched at the sight of her.

Her hair was tucked up into the latest fashion. She wore white gloves, and her dress was a confection of flowers and bows that seemed unlike her. When she looked his way and smiled, however, Ike knew that she was still his Annie.

That somewhere under the trappings of royalty was the Pinkerton detective he loved. *Had* loved, Ike amended, for he had no business loving her now.

None at all.

"Good morning, Isaiah," she said smoothly. "You're looking well-rested."

"Good morning to you," he said. "Is it Annie, or do I have to call you Alice Anne when I'm on this side of the Atlantic?"

"Annie will do." She offered him a smile. "I'm not that different."

"If you say so," was all he could admit to. Because she was different. She was royal. And she wasn't his.

"If you're ready then."

She led him outside to a fancy carriage with a seal on the side that likely meant something. A coachman opened the door, and Ike climbed inside to settle onto a seat that felt more comfortable than the new settee Hattie had convinced Pop to buy her last year.

"Where are we going?"

"We have a meeting at the palace," she said. "Officially we are meeting with a few of my great-grandmother's advisers to discuss the Whitechapel murders, but knowing Granny, she might be curious enough to pop in. If she does, you'll need to know the protocol."

When she finished going over the rules, she looked down at his feet. "Isaiah, really?"

He shrugged. "I compromised and wore the hat, so something had to give. Let's talk about the Ripper. I've been giving a lot of thought to your theory."

"And?"

"I'm not convinced," he said. "Yet."

"Fine." Annie shrugged. "I welcome your input, but let's save this conversation for later, shall we?"

"Fine." He paused. "Pop and Hattie send their greetings. They were pleased that you paid them a visit while you were in Austin. Hattie was still talking about it when I left. Your gift of a silver tea set and a box of wooden spoons for Alfie from the queen is the talk of the town, at least among Hattie's friends, and I figure any day now I will come home and find that she's framed the congratulatory letter from Her Majesty."

"Her Majesty was very pleased that your parents cared enough to take me in at Christmastime. It was very kind of them. When I told her about Alfie's love of wooden spoons, she had to send them too."

"Where's my gift? I was there too." He punctuated the jest with a grin.

"There was a time when a British monarch had the power to toss a man in jail and throw away the key. Be glad that is not your gift."

They fell into companionable silence. Finally, Annie spoke up. "I am curious. How much trouble are you in with your lady friend over this trip?"

Ike chuckled, even as he recalled Miss Rampling's very vocal response to his announcement that he was temporarily shuttering his office and heading for London. "Let's just say we've gone from her daddy recommending me for political office to neither of them being willing to vote me in as dog catcher."

Annie did a poor job of stifling a smile. "I see. Well, that is unfortunate."

"Probably," Ike said. "But despite my gruff demeanor, I really do like dogs, so I'll be fine."

The carriage turned onto a narrow brick street and slowed to a stop in front of a building marked SCOTLAND YARD. "Simon Kent is joining us. He's the third member of our team. He'll be with us on an as-needed basis."

He knew that name from the research he'd done after Annie left him for England. Simon Kent was a high-level officer of the Metropolitan Police with a great deal of influence in England and abroad. He was also Annie's mentor.

He'd learned from the captain that Kent had been influential in arranging Annie's employment with the Pinkertons. Kent had also been the one who provided information to the captain regarding the movements of Annie's father between the continents. The captain then relayed them to Annie via telegrams.

Cap said he and Kent had tried to save Annie from her family. Ultimately, however, they had failed for lack of communication on his end. He still blamed himself that a poorly worded telegram had ended Annie's Pinkerton career.

Thus Ike had already formed a favorable opinion of Simon Kent before the small bespectacled man slid into the carriage beside Annie. He watched Annie and Kent share a smile before they turned to regard him.

"Isaiah, this is Simon Kent."

"Isaiah Joplin. Well met, sir." Kent reached across the carriage to shake hands. "Well met indeed. Annie speaks highly of you."

"And of you," he said.

"I understand you two met while investigating a series of murders in Texas. I'd be interested in hearing about that case if you don't mind telling me about it."

Annie watched Isaiah closely for any sign of what he might be thinking. From the moment she saw him in the hotel lobby—no, even before, back in Austin—the old feelings had risen. But he and Simon, having become instant friends, were chatting about the Midnight Assassin case and generally ignoring her.

A glimmer of gold at the former detective's pocket and the distinctive chain attached to his vest button told her he still wore the watch she'd given him. What Isaiah couldn't see was that the watch pin he'd gifted her that Christmas was safely tucked out of sight in her bodice.

Once the carriage arrived at the palace, both men fell silent. A footman ushered them up the grand staircase and down the hallowed halls under the painted images of uncountable ancestors of the Crown. Finally, they reached the Yellow Drawing Room on the southeast corner of the palace.

Though relatively small in comparison to most rooms at the

palace, the space could still fit Mama's grand ballroom with plenty of room to spare. With walls covered in golden yellow silk that matched the floor-to-ceiling drapes, the room was bright and cheery against the dreary London weather outside.

A half dozen of Granny's trusted advisers were already assembled, some of whom she recognized and a few others who were unknown to her. She spied Sir Edward Walter Hamilton conferring with a white-haired gentleman whose face was obscured by the man in front of him. When the fellow shifted position, Annie's breath caught at the sight of Lord Salisbury, the prime minister who had turned down Granny's offer of a dukedom a few years ago.

Their eyes met, and the prime minister offered an almost imperceptible nod. Annie responded in kind.

As planned, Simon made the introductions. "Let's get right to it," he said once all names had been announced. "We are here to listen," he said as he glanced first at Isaiah and then at Annie. "So please, do let's continue."

Nigel Kellum, a man with a string of titles she couldn't recall and a long history as an adviser and friend to Granny, stood. "As you can see, we have a varied group here, but we are all united under one cause. The madman plaguing our city must be stopped."

A chorus of ayes mixed with murmurs of agreement. The prime minister sat stone-faced.

"We've been instructed by Her Majesty to abdicate any interest in this investigation to you," the nobleman continued, "so I will speak for all of us, and I will make this brief. There is a particular concern that must be addressed, and it has nothing to do with any worry that our city might be thought unsafe to the rest of the world."

"Is that no longer a concern?" Simon said with more than a touch of surprise in his voice.

"Of course," Kellum exclaimed. Then his gaze fell on Annie. "I must tell you, however, that I wish I did not have to broach this topic, as it might bring some level of distress to you, ma'am."

"You may speak freely here," Annie told him.

"Very well, it concerns your relative, Prince Albert Victor."

Her attention went to the prime minister, who showed no reaction. Then she turned to Kellum.

"I see." Annie folded her hands in front of her. The man she knew as Uncle Eddy, whom the public called Prince Eddy, had a rather interesting reputation, to put it mildly. Still, murder was well beyond anything she would expect of him. "Go on."

"There have been some rumors. . ."

He paused, obviously uncomfortable with the topic. Annie wondered if he'd drawn the short straw in the competition to see which of them would be speaking today.

"That is, it has been whispered. . ."

Annie shook her head. "If you could just say it, that would be most helpful, sir. I assure you I am not the delicate sort, and I prefer a man who speaks his mind plainly and clearly."

Kellum gave Simon a helpless look, prompting the police officer to nod. "What Lord Brixton is saying is that there is a theory that the prince could be the killer we are looking for."

Lord Brixton. Yes, she remembered him now. Papa hadn't particularly cared for him.

"I. . .I. . .I am not advancing that theory," Mr. Kellum stammered. "However sordid or false, which it likely is, it is something that has been spoken about, though not publicly. At least not in the newspapers. I would be remiss if I didn't mention it."

He looked around to the other advisers, and they all nodded. Then he turned to Annie. "That is, if *we* did not mention it," he amended. "Our hope is that this investigation might prove that the prince is innocent of any atrocities. Were it to be found otherwise, I do not know how we would manage to tell Her Majesty."

"So she hasn't heard these rumors?" Annie asked. "Are you certain? I have found that the queen is quite intelligent and generally well informed, even about rumors. Nothing gets past her, so do not underestimate her knowledge on this subject."

"We have heard these rumors." Granny swept into the Yellow Drawing Room with a sea of courtiers following in her wake. "And we are much distressed." She focused on Annie. "Thank you for the compliment, kitten. There must, however, be no preferential treatment for Eddy. I want him properly investigated, and I will not abide any editing of the facts."

"Yes, ma'am," Annie said.

The queen turned to inspect the men in the room. "Prime Minister, we did not expect to see you here."

Lord Salisbury cleared his throat, his hands clasped behind him. "I am here on an unofficial basis, ma'am. What concerns the nation concerns me."

She held his gaze, then nodded. "Yes, of course."

Silence fell. After a moment, her steely gaze landed on Isaiah.

Annie held her breath. The Texan had executed a perfect bow when she entered the room and so far had followed all the rules of protocol he'd learned only a few minutes earlier.

"Detective Joplin of the Pinkerton Agency," the queen said.

"I was, Your Majesty," he told her. "Though I have recently taken up lawyering."

"An unfortunate turn of events," she said. "We'll not need a lawyer here today, thus we hope you have retained some of the knowledge you once possessed when you actually were a detective."

Annie detected the slightest hint of a smile beneath Isaiah's serious expression. "Yes, ma'am. I believe I have."

Granny continued to study him. Unlike the other men in the room, Isaiah did not cower under the queen's icy presence. Rather, he appeared ready to continue their conversation should Her Majesty wish to do so.

"What else have you retained from the time when you were a detective, young man?" Granny glanced down at his footwear and then back up at Isaiah as she waited for his response.

"I have learned that patience is a virtue." He paused. "And

that what is meant to be will be."

One dark brow lifted. "And what cannot be?"

"Takes a little longer, ma'am," he said in his Texas drawl.

Annie wasn't sure whether to gasp or laugh. She decided it best to do neither.

The room fell into silence. Even the courtiers had stopped their whispering. Every eye was on the queen and the Texan who towered over her.

Finally, she spoke. "Have you made the acquaintance of William Cody, Mr. Joplin?"

"Buffalo Bill? Yes, ma'am, I have." He paused. "I understand he performed here for your Jubilee, ma'am."

"We were pleased with that performance." Her gaze slid to the floor and then returned to his eyes. "We were gifted with footwear much like his cowboys wore. Unfortunately, the ornamentation on them has rendered the boots quite decorative and unfit for our stables." She paused. "We would much prefer a pair like yours."

"Ma'am, with your permission, I could see that you have them," he said. "It would be my honor."

The queen never broke her even gaze or showed any indication of her thoughts on the matter. Finally, she offered a very slight dip of her head. "We shall allow it. We must, however, wonder at the advisability of wearing such footwear meant for the stables on our valuable carpets. Do we understand one another?"

Annie held her breath in anticipation of what the detective would say. Knowing Isaiah, it could be anything from a polite response to another of his cheeky comments.

After a moment, he nodded. "Yes, ma'am. We do."

The queen held his gaze a second longer, then turned away to address her advisers. "I will leave you with the admonishment that you will not be a stumbling block to Alice Anne and her team else risk facing our wrath. And to you, kitten, we will require updates of your findings as you have them."

"Yes, ma'am," Annie said.

"Lord Brixton, your presence was appreciated but is no longer required. You all may go. And Prime Minister, I do thank you for your visit."

Lord Salisbury offered a bow before leaving without comment. Lord Brixton and the others filed out behind him, each offering a nod or bow before exiting.

The queen then turned to dismiss her courtiers, leaving just the four of them in the Yellow Drawing Room. Finally, she turned to Annie. "We wish to be kept appraised of your findings, but only us. Thus give us a code name for your team so that we might be the only four persons in this castle who know from whence any information comes."

Without hesitation, Annie said, "The Black Midnight."

If Granny thought the name odd, she did not give any hint. But it was impossible not to note the narrowing of Simon's eyes. Apparently he was not so keen on the name.

"Very well. Just one more thing, kitten. Your safety is the first priority during the entirety of this investigation. We will hold Mr. Kent and Mr. Joplin personally responsible should so much as a hair on your head be harmed. Are we understood, gentlemen?"

"Yes, ma'am," the men said in unison.

Had the speaker been anyone other than the Queen of England, Annie might have spoken up in protest and announced she could take care of herself quite well. But in deference to Granny's position, she kept that tidbit to herself.

"We have arranged for the Black Midnight to have full access to this room at all times for use as a meeting place. As we are sharing Mr. Kent with the Metropolitan Police, he will not be in residence but will be transported as needed."

"Thank you, ma'am," Simon told her.

"Alice Anne and Mr. Joplin, your rooms have been prepared for the length of this matter and are adjacent to this one." She turned to Isaiah. "You will find that everything from your hotel is there, including proper footwear. Anything else that might be needed can be arranged. Do let the staff know."

"Thank you, ma'am," Isaiah said.

"We hope that at the end of this, thanks will have been earned by you and your team, Mr. Joplin. Do keep that in mind."

Without waiting for a response, the queen swept out as regally as she had arrived. The door closed behind her and opened again before anyone could speak.

"Her Majesty has arranged for lunch to be brought in. You will have a carriage at your disposal."

"Please do not send lunch for me," Mr. Kent said. "I must get back to work. Annie, let me know what you need, and I will make the information available."

"Anything you might have on victims, witnesses, and locations of crime scenes that would be outside the normal reports would be helpful," she said. "Especially any leads you think are promising but haven't been chased down yet."

"That is a thick file," Simon told her. "Back in October we had a situation where a fellow claimed he had spoken with a Malay cook named Alaska who was angry at being robbed by one of the local ladies in Whitechapel. He vowed to our witness that until he recovered his property, he would bring harm to every woman he met." His chuckle held no humor. "That is just one of the many witness stories we have not yet been able to follow up on."

"Interesting. I'd like to find this cook." Isaiah shrugged. "Considering I'm not up on the biographies of British royalty, information on Prince Eddy would also be appreciated, now that I think of it."

"I can fill you in on Uncle Eddy," Annie said. "Over lunch."

"And I'll send over what we have," Mr. Kent said. "Though I warn you that file is slim. We aren't encouraged to keep tabs on the future monarch. Now, if you'll both excuse me, I will be off."

"Thank you." Annie paused. "Might I have a word? I'll walk you out." She turned to Isaiah. "I'll just be a minute."

Simon said goodbye to Isaiah. Then he and Annie stepped into the hall where a pair of uniformed footmen waited. One closed the door, and the other led them down the corridor toward the exit.

"You had a reaction to something that surprised me, Simon." They turned the corner to proceed down yet another hallway in the warren of corridors that made up Buckingham Palace. "It appears you were not pleased at my choice of name for our little project. I wish to know why."

Simon chuckled. "Annie, you are very much like your great-grandmother in your directness. I always did appreciate that about you."

She smiled. "Thank you. I will take that as a compliment yet not ask whether you continue to appreciate that quality. Rather, I would ask that you tell me what it is about the Black Midnight that causes you concern."

He continued to stare straight ahead, matching his footsteps to hers. For a moment, Annie wondered if he would respond. Abruptly, he stopped.

"Give us a moment," he called to the footman, who nodded and stepped discreetly away.

After a quick look around, Simon met her gaze. "What causes me concern about the Black Midnight and what bothers me about the name you gave the queen for our investigation are two separate concerns yet the same."

"You're speaking in riddles," Annie protested. "Out with it, please."

Simon looked down at the carpet beneath his feet. He appeared to be considering his words with care.

Finally, he looked up. "This name you've given us, do you realize the meaning of it? There is a segment of our city who would recognize that name, and not in a favorable way."

Annie looked away, sorting out just how much she would tell him. This was a man who had seen something in her before anyone else did. Who had championed her abilities and risked much more than just his friendship with royalty when he'd gone to such great lengths to see that she continued to work as a detective.

Still, she hesitated.

"Tell me the meaning," she finally said. "I prefer facts to rumors."

He muttered something under his breath and sighed. "The less you know, Annie, the better."

"Too late for that—though I had to go to Texas to hear about this rumored secret society, which speaks volumes for the silence of the members here."

Simon's expression offered no indication of his thoughts. "What do you want to know?"

"Who are they, and why are you concerned?" she said.

"Using the name could call out the wrong people," he told her. "Are you ready for that?"

"That's not a full answer, though you've indirectly admitted this group exists. Is their purpose to aid law enforcement, or is something more sinister afoot, Simon?" She paused to give him a direct look. "Because if they were true friends to detectives, mightn't I have heard of them when I was a special constable?"

"Where men are sworn to ignore the law to uphold their own rules, there is always the possibility of something sinister," he told her. "An oath of silence would explain why you hadn't heard of them before."

She glanced around and saw the footman still staring straight ahead and maintaining a discreet distance. Much as she would like to assume they were safe to discuss anything of a secretive nature, Annie knew too well that was unlikely. Still, she pressed on.

"Are you a member, Simon?"

He looked into her eyes. "No."

"If you were, would you be allowed to tell me?"

Without hesitation, he said, "No."

"Will they help us?" she asked.

"I must go now." Simon offered a curt nod and walked away.

"Simon," she called. "A yes or no is all I ask."

He paused, then turned around slowly. "I have neither to give, Annie. I wish I did."

With another nod, Simon set off again. Annie decided to let him go without asking anything else. She hoped he might later relent and provide more information on the Black Midnight.

If not, she would certainly not be shy about asking.

Annie retraced her steps to pause at the door to the Yellow Drawing Room. Isaiah had settled on a yellow chair at a table near the window, his attention focused on what appeared to be some kind of logbook. Several other volumes were stacked beside him.

"When you're tired of standing at the door, you could come on in," he said without lifting his head.

Shaking her head, Annie closed the distance between them to see that he'd already filled a page with notes in his distinctly masculine handwriting. Before she could see what Isaiah had been studying, he closed his notebook and looked up at her. "Let me get this straight. We are investigating the heir to the throne—your uncle—at the request of his grandmother the queen."

Chapter 24

Annie perched on the edge of the fancy yellow velvet sofa like a princess surveying her kingdom. Seeing her so at home in such a grand place confirmed Ike's decision to try to forget how much he loved her. He likely had no potential wife to go home to, though it was possible he would be forgiven.

Not likely, but possible.

Ike forced his attention onto the topic at hand. "We are investigating at the request of his grandmother—your great-grandmother—to decide whether or not your uncle is the man who is killing women in Whitechapel."

"Correct. The good news is that, if my theory is right, our murderer is the same person who attacked those women in Austin. I know my uncle Eddy was not in America during any of those crimes—and yes, I did check his calendar with the palace's social officer—so it would be impossible for him to be a suspect in the Texas murders. Further, he would never be considered large enough in size or strong enough to wield an ax like our Austin killer did."

"That's quite a speech." Ike settled on the sofa across from her, then reached behind him to toss a pillow on the nearest chair.

"My grandmother would not be happy to see you throwing pillows in her drawing room."

"She's already not happy I am walking on her carpets with my boots."

Annie fixed him with a look. "You were given proper footwear along with the suit."

"About this suit. I wore it to humor you, but it's not what I would be conducting an investigation in back home."

Her shrug was barely noticeable. "It's what you'll be wearing here if you don't want to stand out, Isaiah. I'll leave that to you."

The door opened and two footmen arrived with lunch trays, preventing Ike from raising much more of an argument on his change of clothes than he already had. They kept their banter to details of the case and the similarities between the two, which was exactly how Ike wanted it.

The more time he spent with Annie, the less reliable his resolve would be to keep from allowing his feelings for her to return. So when the conversation waned, he started looking for reasons to leave.

"I should go back to the hotel and check out," he said.

"I'm sure Granny had it taken care of," she said.

"How is that possible? I paid for that room with my own money."

"She is the queen, Isaiah." Annie sighed. "She can do whatever she wants. Just be thankful that she does not."

"I suppose."

"No, truly. Be grateful. I'm sure she respects your abilities as a detective or she would not have allowed me to bring you over to assist me with this investigation. But I do not believe she trusts you with me."

"What does she think I will do? Haven't you told her I have a lady friend back home who is sending me strong hints that she wishes to be Mrs. Joplin?"

"Is or was?"

"No comment," he told her.

Annie smiled. "Speaking of Mrs. Joplin, how is Hattie? We didn't talk about her before."

"Hattie is fine. She's fully recovered from the fall she took a few months ago, but I don't think Pop will ever recover from having to be the chef and maid for the two of them."

"Why didn't he hire help?" She held up her hand. "Wait. Let me guess. Miss Hattie wouldn't allow another woman in her kitchen."

"Exactly." Ike rose. "I can't sit around here and talk, Annie. I want to see where these crimes happened. Show me London. Specifically I want to see Whitechapel."

He expected she might be bothered by his dismissal of her conversation about home. Instead, she looked relieved. Maybe Annie wasn't comfortable with him either.

Annie rang for the butler and arranged for a carriage. "We'll be fine during the day, but nighttime is not when you want to make your first visit to Whitechapel."

Their first stop was Buck's Row, where Mary Ann Nichols was found on the last day of August 1888. "Over there," Annie said as she pointed out a wretched gateway. "He started with her."

He looked around. "He didn't bother to hide, did he?"

"No," she said. "Yet he was able to. Right here in plain sight."

Ike had seen the slums of New York and the worst side of Chicago, but he was not prepared for the poverty and desperation he found in the London borough of Whitechapel. When Annie explained the concept of the workhouses, how children lived— and usually worked—alongside their parents for a meager day's food and a dirty cot, he was dumbfounded.

And angry.

"I know," Annie said. "It is impossible to reconcile. Which is why removing the menace who treats women like prey is imperative."

Ike gathered Annie close as they walked the narrow streets. Each of the five murders had taken place within a small distance from the others, leaving Ike to believe that the killer either resided nearby or had a specific tie to the area.

Next they made their way to 29 Hanbury Street. "Mary

Chapman was found back there," Annie said, pointing to the rear yard of the building. "This was eight days after the first murder."

A woman stepped into their path, causing Ike to stop short to keep from avoiding her. The whites of her eyes were as sallow as her skin, and the few teeth she had were brown.

"Hello there, pretty lady," she said to Annie. "Might you have money for food? My children are hungry."

Before Annie could respond, Ike slipped her a coin and she disappeared into the crowd. "Be careful about that," she told him. "There are many more beggars here than any of us has coin, and they will only increase as the sun goes down. Which it will do soon. We should go, Isaiah. We'll be losing daylight soon, so we'll need to take the carriage to Berner Street. That's where our killer ended the life of Elizabeth Stride. From there I'll show you Mitre Square and the location of Catherine Eddowes's murder. Then if the light holds, we'll visit Miller's Court on Dorset Street where he ended Mary Jane Kelley's life."

"Yes, fine. But as to the beggar, if I can help one. . ." He paused as he spied a familiar face. "Hold on. I know that man."

He guided Annie across the crowded thoroughfare to step in front of his father's old friend, Dr. Langston. "Good afternoon, sir," he said. "You're a long way from Austin."

"As are you." He glanced around as if checking to see whether anyone was watching, then looked back at Ike. "What are you and your fellow Pinkerton detective doing in England? Miss Walters, right?"

"Yes. We're working on a case," Ike said for expediency. There was no need to dive into a tale of false names and royal connections at this point. "What brings you to London? The last I heard you were teaching in Connecticut."

"Research," he said. "I have thoroughly enjoyed my time at Greenwich. I've been especially fascinated with the advances made there in the study of astronomy. Have you heard there's a telescope being built that will rival any in the world?"

"I have not," Ike said. "Professor, if you're doing research in Greenwich, why are you in Whitechapel?"

"Well, it's the funniest thing. I was out seeing the sights and wandering about, and the next thing you know, I was here. I'm not sure how to get back to where I was, but I know I'm having no luck on my own."

"We have a carriage waiting," Annie said. "If you'd like, we can take you back to your hotel. Where are you staying?"

Dr. Langston paused only a second, but Ike took note of it. "Thank you for your kind offer, but I'll be fine."

"It isn't safe here after dark, sir," Annie offered. "I'm not sure you're aware of that, and I would feel terrible if something were to happen to you."

"I'm going to insist we deliver you somewhere safe," Ike said. "My father would have my hide if I didn't take care of a friend of his."

Reluctance etched his features. Then he nodded. "I don't suppose I can turn down your offer."

"Come this way, Dr. Langston."

They retraced their steps to where the carriage was waiting, with Dr. Langston chatting away about the details of his research. But when he realized he would be traveling to his accommodations in a royal conveyance, he fell silent.

"I don't understand," he said. "This belongs to the queen."

"It's a long story." Ike relayed the address the professor had given him to the driver and then opened the door for Annie and helped her inside. "After you," he told the professor.

The older man's expression went serious. "Might I have a moment, Isaiah?"

Ike exchanged a look with Annie, who nodded. He led the professor a few steps away. "Is something wrong?"

"It might be." He cast a furtive glance at the carriage and then turned back to Ike. "When you two spied me, I was following someone I recognized from my time in Austin. A fellow named Maurice who cooked at the Pearl House, where I was lodging during my time at the university. He had a talent for searing a steak exactly to my preference, so of course I told him. We struck up a friendship. The last time I saw him was New Year's Eve. I went to the Pearl House for dinner and Maurice came out of the kitchen to say goodbye. He was leaving Austin for good, he said."

A cook named Maurice. Ike tensed as he felt Annie's eyes on his. The claim that a cook had moved from Austin to London to continue the killing he'd begun in Texas was a familiar one. He hadn't reacted when Simon mentioned the tip, but only because he figured there would be time to discuss it later.

"Interesting coincidence that you found him here," he said when he realized the professor was expecting him to say something.

"It was, and I told him so." Dr. Langston paused. "When I last saw him, he said he was leaving to cook on the ships, as he put it. He was from Malaysia and hoped to someday end up back there. After he saw the world."

"Dr. Langston, did you actually speak with Maurice?"

"I did," he said. "I was thrilled to see him and hoped I might have another of his well-cooked steaks. I told him that. He seemed happy to find a familiar face here, and he told me he hadn't yet decided to go back to cooking as he had made enough money to take care of his needs for a while."

"From cooking on ships, I suppose?"

"Yes, I guess so." The professor looked down at the ground and shook his head. "I was curious where he lived, so I followed him."

"Why?" Ike asked.

"I don't know," he said as he shook his head slowly. "I think because I was hoping I could find him again and perhaps learn if he returned to cooking here. His talent with a steak is amazing. He even carves it before he serves it, and his knife skills are stellar."

"Knife skills?"

"Yes," Professor Langston said. "He had a collection of knives, and each one had a purpose. He was very proud of them."

"Did you find out where he lived?" Ike asked him.

"Of a sort," he said. "I followed him until he stepped into the door of one of those awful homes near the workhouse in Whitechapel. It did not look like a place where a man of his quality would live."

"He's a cook. Why wouldn't it be feasible for him to live like that?"

The professor shrugged. "Because he once told me that before he was a cook, he had been a doctor. Not a professor like me, but a medical doctor. There was some mystery as to why he was no longer in that profession, but he hinted it had to do with a woman. I digress. For a man who cooked for a living, he had very refined tastes. We discussed art, music, all the things you would speak about with a gentleman."

"Do you remember the address of this home?"

Dr. Langston recited it back to him. Ike retrieved his pencil and notepad and wrote it down, then returned the items to his pocket. He checked his watch. Half past four. The shadows were lengthening despite the earliness of the hour. He would have to find this location tomorrow.

"Is there anything else, Professor?" Ike asked him.

"Just one thing," he said. "I always wondered about his temper. He had a violent streak. I once saw him throw an ax at the serving girl when he worked at the Pearl."

"Doctor, why are you telling me this?"

He shrugged. "You haven't mentioned what case you're working on, Isaiah, and I haven't asked. But I do know the last time I saw the two of you, you were trying to catch the Midnight Assassin. If that's why you're here in London, I think my cook may be your murderer."

"I think we are safe to discuss this with Annie."

Ike escorted the professor back to the carriage and waited until he was inside to follow suit. After the carriage started rolling, Ike had the professor tell Annie what he had told him.

"So you believe your cook is the link between the two killing sprees," she said. "There is precedent for this theory. Not so long ago the *New York Times* and the *New York Gazette* both put forth the same suggestion."

"Does your friend Blake still work at the *Gazette*?" Ike asked.

"I wouldn't know." Annie frowned. "He is not my friend, and if there is any justice in the world, he is in jail. I should have had him arrested when he stole my telegram and committed fraud."

"Hey now," Dr. Langston said. "Are you talking about the reporter who was nosing around Austin for months at a time?"

"There were a lot of those, sir," Ike said. "But yes, he was there for an extended period of time. He sent in regular dispatches to his newspaper about the killings. From what I read, about half of it was true and the rest was speculation."

The professor grinned. "What about that one he called "The Lady and the Lawman"? How much of that was true?"

"None," Annie snapped at the same time Ike said, "About half."

"Which half?" Annie demanded. "The entire piece was ridiculous. It was a farce. He made us sound like characters in a dime novel. Seriously."

"I stand by my statement," Ike said as the carriage slowed to a halt.

"We've arrived at your guest's address," the driver said. "Will you be getting out here?"

"No, just Dr. Langston. But would you send one of the footmen to escort him to his door?"

"That isn't necessary," he said. "I can find it just fine."

The professor jumped up and hurried out of the carriage so

fast, Ike had to move quickly to catch up to him. "Annie and I are working on the investigation at our London office. If you think of anything that might be of help in determining who the Whitechapel Murderer is, please contact us. And as you guessed, it never set well with me that the monster who killed in Austin was never caught."

"It was a travesty," Dr. Langston agreed. "Those husbands were arrested far too quickly, and Jimmy Phillips even got a guilty verdict, though it was overturned on appeal. Moses Hancock went free. Nobody thought about the others who didn't have justice either." He paused to shake his head. "If I find out anything, I will send word. Where is your office?"

Ike grinned. "Buckingham Palace."

The professor let out a low whistle. "My office is much less grand. I'll be conducting research at the Greenwich Observatory most days. You can find me there."

They exchanged goodbyes, and Ike returned to the carriage. "What do you think of his theory about the cook?" he asked Annie.

"It does fit with what others have theorized, and he seemed adamant about the facts. If Dr. Langston has seen the cook here in Whitechapel, then he has proximity to both sets of murder scenes."

"And motive, if his temper and grudge are to be believed."

"That remains to be seen."

Ike sat back against the seat and closed his eyes. Exhaustion was tugging at him again. He retrieved his watch and realized it was still set to the time in Texas.

"You kept it." Annie smiled. "I'm glad."

"Of course I did," he said. "It reminds me of the half of that ridiculous story that was true."

"What half is that?"

"The half where Blake wrote about you and me. How it was obvious to anyone who cared to notice that I was over the moon in love with you." Ike paused, knowing he was straying into dangerous territory but too tired to care. "Because I was. I probably still am. But you probably know all that."

Chapter 25

Annie sat very still and watched Isaiah's eyes drift shut. His words still hung between them in the silence of the carriage. *I probably still am.*

She hadn't expected that. For all his joking to the contrary, she knew Isaiah had a woman back in Austin waiting for him. A woman who was determined to show Annie just how far he had come since those days when Isaiah was professing his love for her.

A woman who had, on Isaiah's own admission, planned a career for him in politics and convinced her father to finance it. Or something of that sort.

That was not the life of a man who was in love with another woman.

Or was it?

If that other woman spurned his affections and left without ever admitting that she loved him too, then would it be so far out of the realm of possibility that the man would dry his tears on another woman's shoulder?

She knew the answer. It would not.

His breath slowed as he fell deeper into sleep. Thick lashes dusted high cheekbones, and a lock of hair fell onto his forehead. Isaiah looked much younger like this.

Annie thought of that Christmas Eve when she covered him in a blanket and kissed him softly. He hadn't recalled that, most likely, but she hoped he remembered their kisses under the mistletoe.

She would never forget them.

The carriage hit a bump in the road and lurched to one side

as they turned into the grand gates of Buckingham Palace. In an instant, Isaiah was awake.

"Did I miss anything?"

Annie almost said *me*. "No," she said instead, "but we've arrived at the palace, and I think we ought to call it a night. You're exhausted."

"Nonsense," Isaiah said. "I'm fine now. I just needed a little nap."

"Tomorrow," Annie said firmly. "We've got plenty of work to do, and you'll need to have all your wits about you."

He chuckled. "Around you, that is impossible."

The carriage stopped, but the well-trained driver did not make a move to open the door.

"Stop teasing me," she said, "or I'm going to start thinking your Theodora isn't going to keep her man after all."

He froze and turned around. "How would you feel about that?"

"Truly?" she asked.

"Truly," he responded.

"Relieved. She's not the right woman for you, and you know it. You need a woman who will appreciate you for who you are and not what she can turn you into. What in the world were you thinking?"

He leaned closer. "I was thinking that I could never have the woman I loved, so settling for someone else was the next best thing."

"Settling?" Annie looked into his eyes. "How sad."

"I'm a good man, Annie, and I would have treated her well. She never would have known." He paused. "But I'm pretty sure she has figured it out now."

"I would say so," Annie said.

"Why didn't you just say yes?"

She shook her head. "Yes to what?"

"Yes to me," he whispered. "When I asked you to marry me. It would have been a simple thing to just say yes."

Oh, but he was close. Those eyes watching her, not missing a thing.

It would be so easy to fall back in love with him. To inch forward just enough to allow him to kiss her.

And what would one kiss hurt, really?

Isaiah seemed to understand her question even though she hadn't asked it. His hand reached for hers.

"Annie, I still—"

The carriage door opened, and the Buckingham Palace footman appeared in the doorway. "Welcome home, ma'am, sir."

Annie jumped back, her heart thumping. Isaiah gave her a lazy grin and climbed out of the carriage, then reached to help her.

"I can do that, sir," the footman said.

"I would rather you did not." Isaiah's hands spanned her waist as he lifted her down. Had she not been completely certain that Granny or one of her courtiers was watching, she might have continued the journey toward another kiss right there.

But she knew better. And she knew she'd just been saved from something she ought not to have considered.

So she said good night at the door and hurried up the staircase to the room assigned to her. The room she'd always been assigned since she was a little girl.

Dropping her gloves on the table next to the door, Annie wandered toward the window that faced the river. She'd loved the vantage point up here, a lovely view that allowed her to count the boats as they floated past in the distance and to pretend she was in a grand house in the clouds.

Tonight, however, she merely looked out into the darkness and wondered how she would manage to keep herself out of love with Isaiah. Perhaps it was true that they were meant to be. Granny certainly had not been dismissive of her request to hire him as an associate on this investigation.

If she was still adamant that he stay away, why would she allow him here?

Annie went right to work on her notes, allowing her mind to move from the questions she had about Isaiah to the questions she had about her current investigation. The similarities between the two killers filled two pages in her notebook, and then came the details about the Malay cook and the college professor who was his friend.

That's where Annie stopped. Back in Austin, the college professor who was his friend gave them information that turned out to be completely false. He had made an accusation and had come to a conclusion about the killer that turned out to be untrue.

Was he now a reliable witness in this case? Annie wasn't so sure.

The facts were the facts, but something in Dr. Langston's story was not quite right. She just wasn't sure yet what that was.

Annie sighed and rang for the maid. A warm soak in a lavender scented tub would cure what plagued her. Or at least it would pass as a suitable substitute.

After her bath, she returned to her bedchamber to find a silver tray piled high with envelopes. Sorting them while the maid dressed her hair for bed, Annie paused when she found a letter written in her sister's handwriting:

Annie, I've found the most unsuitable man. Papa hates him and Mama swears if I marry him Granny will never give us another shilling. You faced this choice and made your decision. Do you regret the path you took? I don't care about the money, and yes, I know I should. But I do not, nor should Mama and Papa. What should I do? I am in love. Is that wrong?

Bea

"Oh Bea," Annie said on an exhale of breath as she reached for writing paper. "What should I tell you? The truth? Or the story that will keep you from hardship?"

She dipped the pen in ink and wrote two words: *Marry him.*

The she signed the letter. Emboldened, she retrieved another sheet of writing paper and wrote a single sentence: *I should have said yes.*

When the maid finished, Annie turned around and handed her the two letters. "Please have this one delivered to my sister, Beatrice, and the other to Mr. Joplin who is staying here at the castle. Both are urgent."

That done, she climbed into bed and doused the light. Tomorrow was another day, a day when Isaiah would awaken knowing she loved him.

Not that she had actually said this, of course. That might come soon. Or not.

But probably.

She awakened to a maid opening her curtains to allow sunlight to stream in. On the table beside her was a breakfast tray. Beside the tray were two letters.

Annie scrambled into a seated position and reached for both of them, opening the one on top. It was from Beatrice.

Thank you for your honesty. You've helped me decide. Will you do what you can to sway Granny to our side? Perhaps you could mention that he trains horses and loves dogs, two of her favorite things. Or you could remind her how very much we love her, and how we look like her at her age, or something that will make her remember that she was once young and in love and got to marry the man she wanted to marry. Whatever you say will be much appreciated.

She tossed that letter aside and opened the second one. The handwriting was Isaiah's, but the one-sentence response was odd: *Marry who?*

Annie groaned. The maid had mixed up the letters. That worked out fine for Beatrice, who'd been encouraged by her sister's admission that she should have said yes to Isaiah. But that meant that the former Pinkerton had received a note from her telling him to marry someone.

A man.

No wonder he was confused. She sighed again.

Was this a sign that she should forget this line of thought? Perhaps. The best way to handle it, she decided after a few more minutes of debate, would be to laugh off the mistake and go on about their day. He need not know that there was a letter to him that her sister received.

That was information for another time. Or never.

A short while later, Annie made her way down to their temporary office where she found Isaiah and Simon with their heads together and a drawing on the table in front of them. Neither looked up when she came in.

"What have you got there?" she asked cheerily.

"Maps," Isaiah said. "Two of them. Come and look." When Annie drew near enough to see the two maps, one of Austin and one of London, he continued. "See here how the Austin murders are clustered together within a mile of the Pearl House. Three of them are much closer than that."

"I do," she said. "That's interesting."

"Now look at the map of Whitechapel," Simon said. "We agree that while there are a number of killings that are attributed to the madman, there are only the five that are proven to have been him. These are Mary Ann Nichols, Mary Chapman, Elizabeth Stride, Catherine Eddowes, and Mary Jane Kelley. Do you agree, Annie?"

"I do," she said. "There have been others, to be sure, but at this point they seem slightly disconnected in some way. Just not a close match to the manner of death of the others."

"Agreed," Isaiah said. "So with that information, and the

address of the cook given to us by the professor, we put him in the center of the five murder scenes."

"Oh," Annie said, "that is interesting, isn't it?"

"I've sent a detective to bring him in," Simon told her. "We may have our man. Now let's talk about Prince Eddy."

"If we must," Annie said. "What is his alibi, or doesn't he have one?"

"He has an impeccable alibi per his private secretary," Simon said. "The fellow showed me his datebook. Eddy was away from London all five days when women were killed."

"So he has an alibi for all of them," Annie said. "That's good news."

"It is except that I am having trouble verifying these dates. One of them was with the queen at Sandringham, but the queen's private secretary will not confirm Eddy was there. He can only say the queen was there. Others are easier to find a witness for, yet those witnesses are less reliable." He paused. "Shooting party in Norfolk. That sort of thing."

"Places that were private enough to allow only those who were invited to know who was there," Isaiah said. "That's convenient."

"And his friends are not going to say he wasn't there if Eddy says he was."

"Truly, Simon," Annie said. "Do you think my uncle did this? He does not even cut his own meat at dinner. I've seen it myself. And Granny will confirm or deny any dates you present to her."

"I don't think he did," he said. "Your theory that there is a link between Austin and Whitechapel intrigues me. The prince could not have been our killer in Austin. That isn't possible for a number of reasons." He paused. "I've found another person with ties to both places that we haven't spoken with yet."

"Oh?" Isaiah said. "Who is that?"

"Charlie Einhorn."

"The knife thrower in Buffalo Bill's show?" Isaiah shook

his head. "Why him?"

"Because when Bill Cody and his cast and crew left London, not all of them went with him. A few unfortunates got stuck here under circumstances that were not of their making, but they eventually got home a few months later. Charlie Einhorn stayed here."

"Any idea why?" Isaiah asked.

"Something about a woman, is what the newspapers reported." He reached to retrieve a file from the corner of the table and pulled out a clipping. "Here's the article that appeared in the local papers. It was a romantic story that went wrong quickly."

"How so?" Annie asked.

"She died." Isaiah looked up from the clipping. "Under mysterious circumstances. They found her in the river. There were, as the paper said, alterations to her form that might have been made by a knife." He paused. "There's more."

"What's that?"

"Charlie Einhorn was born and raised in Austin. Bill Cody discovered him while Charlie was on a trail drive. He basically took him right out of the stockyards in Fort Worth, and Charlie never went back home to Austin."

"When was that?" Annie asked.

"The spring of 1886."

Annie shook her head. "So within months of the last killings?"

"Exactly." Isaiah shrugged. "What do you think?"

Annie looked over at Simon. "Can you bring him in too?"

"Why don't we pay Einhorn a visit instead, Annie?" Isaiah said. "One Texan to another?"

❧

A short while later, they were knocking on the door of a small but tidy home on a street just barely removed from Whitechapel. When no one answered the door, Ike took several steps back to decide what to do next.

"Who are you?" came from behind him, and he turned around to see a man in boots and buckskins coming toward him. "What do you want?"

The Texan was of average height and build, his face pock-marked, and his dark hair cut short. His angry expression told Ike exactly how glad he was to see strangers on his doorstep.

"Are you Charlie Einhorn?" Ike asked, exaggerating his Texas drawl.

"I might be. Who're you?"

Ike stuck out his hand. "Isaiah Joplin from Austin, Texas. I understand you worked for Bill Cody."

"I might have," he said, his scowl lessening. "You a reporter?"

"Hardly," Ike said. "Annie and I were Pinkerton detectives. Now we do our own investigation. I'm not here on business though. I have a question about boots."

"Boots?" He shook his head. "That's a new one. People usually ask me about the Wild West Show or my wife."

Ike shrugged. "I owe someone a pair of boots. Is there any-place I can get some in London?"

"Not like we can get back home." He glanced down at his footwear then back up at Ike. "I get mine resoled at a shop over on Hanbury Street. Had them done a few months ago, and they've lasted. If you need boots for your friend, you're going to have to go back to Texas to get them."

Hanbury Street was where Mary Chapman had been found in September of last year. Ike studied Charlie. "Thank you. I'm curious, Charlie. Why didn't you go back with the rest of the show?"

"Don't believe what you read in the newspapers," he said. "It wasn't a woman. If it had been, I'd own up to it. And that woman who was supposed to be my wife? That was all for the papers too."

"What do you mean?"

"That woman wasn't my wife. I'd never seen her before, but I was scared to tell anyone. He's why I didn't go back. He told me to take care of her and I didn't. Well, I tried, but I couldn't."

"What are we talking about now, Charlie?"

"I didn't go back because I had a better offer. Red Finney told me he would pay me to stick around here and watch out for his girl until he could return. He offered me a lot of money, and I took it."

Charlie paused as if remembering. "He told me if something happened to his girl, he would ruin me. Well, he did all right. He knew she wasn't one to stay home, but when she went out, it was my fault in his eyes. When she didn't come home, that was my fault too. Red told 'em at the inquest that I'd married his girl and then got jealous. I didn't hang for it because Bill Cody wrote a letter standing up for my character. After all that, knowing Red was back in Texas soured me on going home. So I stayed."

Ike looked over at Annie. She shook her head.

"I'm going to ask you this, Charlie, only because I value your opinion. Do you know who's been killing women in Whitechapel?"

Charlie's eyes widened. "Well, it ain't me. I wouldn't." He shook his head. "And I couldn't." He lifted his arm a few inches and then let it drop again. "I might've been an expert knifesman back then, but last winter I fell off a horse. Landed wrong and broke my arm. Couldn't afford to set it, and it healed like this. So if I'm being honest, that's the other reason I can't go home. I don't have a spot in the show anymore, and I'd just be a burden to my family."

"I'm sorry," Annie said. "That must be difficult."

"Not so much as you would think," he said. "I've made peace with it."

"We won't bother you further," Ike told him. "I'll take your advice on those boots and send them here from Texas."

"It can't be him," Annie said when they'd left Charlie's house. "He's physically unable to make the motions that the killer would have to have made."

"I agree. Right now we've got one suspect, and that's the cook."

"No," Annie said firmly. "Granny wants Uncle Eddy thoroughly investigated. We should pay him a visit."

Chapter 26

I t didn't take long for the detectives to locate Prince Eddy. They found him in the middle of a tennis game, which he immediately stopped when he saw Annie.

"Alice Anne," he called. "Wonderful to see you. To what do I owe the honor?" He paused. "And who have you brought with you?"

Annie made the introductions and smiled. "There are discrepancies in your datebook. I came to find out why."

"Discrepancies?" He shook his head. "Of what sort?"

"Of the sort that would give you an alibi for possible things you would not want to be associated with," Annie said.

"There are several responses I could give you. I will say, however, that whatever you think I did, I assure you I did nothing of the sort."

Annie shook her head. "That isn't an answer, Uncle Eddy."

"It is, dear," he said. "You have come to find out if I spent time in Whitechapel doing things I ought not have done. And the answer is yes, I did. But I am not the man you're looking for."

"You know about that?"

He shrugged. "I find things out. Look, investigate. I will provide people to back up my statements. Truly, whatever is in my datebook is very likely where I was, because I am bound to keep my appointments or Granny will cut off my funding. And I cannot have that. So any mischief I get into is done outside of the days I have committed to represent the Crown."

Annie nodded. "All right, Uncle Eddy. I believe you."

Ike could tell she did. "You said that you find things out, sir. I wonder if you know about the Black Midnight."

The prince's eyes narrowed. Then he looked down at Annie. "You're vouching for this man?"

"I am, Uncle Eddy."

"Yes, I know about them," he said. "And it is only because I don't care one fig for their silliness that I am willing to admit it."

"What silliness?" Annie asked him.

He glanced around and then looked over at Ike. "Oaths and rituals and such nonsense. I understand the purpose is to see justice done, but when the one who should be caught is kept safe because others have taken an oath of silence?" He shrugged. "Nonsense."

"So the Black Midnight is protecting the killer?" Annie asked. "Why?"

"The oath," he said as if she were a child. "They're sworn to protect their brothers to the point of lying, Annie. I suppose you heard about the kerfuffle about the clue that was erased?"

"I read about it," Annie said. "I believe that decision was made by the chief of police."

"That's what they told the papers," he said. "But how often do these reporters get anything right anyway?"

"You have a point, but I must ask, Uncle Eddy. Do you know the name of the man who is killing these women? Is it a cook, perhaps?"

"No idea," he told them. "But if you look at the members, you'll find the man."

"How do we do that, sir?" Ike asked. "We don't know who they are."

"That's the question, now isn't it? They're an exclusive group," he said as he reached over to embrace Annie. "Do take care of yourself and tell your father I am still waiting for his visit. The last time I was in Brighton, he missed me by a day."

"I will," she said.

Without another word, Prince Eddy turned and walked away.

And as he watched the prince go back to his tennis game, Ike had to agree he didn't believe him capable of it either. The man could barely swing a tennis racket with any effectiveness.

Annie climbed into the carriage and Ike followed. As soon as the door closed, he shook his head. "What do you make of all that, Annie?"

"Uncle Eddy is not our killer," she said firmly. "As to the Black Midnight, I believe he's a member."

"Why?"

"A society that exclusive wouldn't exist in that social circle if it excluded Prince Eddy. I also believe he doesn't give a fig about it and has no qualms about telling us the secrets he's bothered to remember."

"Except the identity of the members," Ike said. "He certainly didn't give that information up."

"No, he did not, whether out of loyalty or ignorance." She let out a long breath. "What about the Malaysian cook? Until I spoke with Uncle Eddy, I thought we were on to something. Now I have to wonder."

"It's a convenient theory if you want to believe the killer in Austin is also our killer here." Ike paused to give the idea more thought. "But is he? Your uncle thinks someone in the Black Midnight is covering for a killer in their midst. Would that killer also have struck in Austin?"

"The only way to know that is to compare the membership list to the possible suspects in Austin." Annie shook her head. "Of course that's impossible."

The carriage delivered them to the offices of the Metropolitan Police a short while later. Simon met them in the hallway with a worried look on his face.

"Remember that cook you asked me to check into? I sent a man out to speak with him, but he was gone. Left this morning is what the landlady said. She let us in. He left some things in the room." Simon paused. "Including a set of knives."

Ike let out a long breath. "Any matches to our victims?"

"We're checking on that, but that could take some time." He paused. "What brings you here?"

"We've just come from visiting Uncle Eddy," Annie told him. "It was an interesting conversation."

Simon looked at her for a moment and then nodded. "Come with me."

He led them down a corridor and up a flight of stairs to an office that was too small and devoid of personal items to be his. Indicating they should sit, the police officer closed the door.

"All right," he said as he settled behind the desk and retrieved pencil and paper from the drawer, "what have you learned?"

"He's not our man," Ike offered. "But he may know who is."

Annie shook her head. "Or he may not. Given what I know about my uncle, I think he'd say so if he did."

Simon remained silent for a moment, steepling his hands as if in thought. Then he nodded. "Truly, I've never thought him a viable candidate, especially given your theory, Annie, that our killer and the Austin murderer are one and the same."

She sighed. "It's a good theory, but I'm less certain now than I have been. Though I stand by my assertion regarding the prince."

"I think it safe to remove him from the list," Simon told her. "The queen will wish to know we've cleared him."

"I can tell her that." Annie paused. "There is one more order of business, Simon, and it is a delicate matter."

"Go on," he said, exchanging glances with Ike.

"We need a membership list of the Black Midnight."

Simon laughed. Then he sobered. "You're serious."

"Deadly serious," Annie told him.

The policeman sat back, obviously flabbergasted. "How do you propose I get that?"

"However you can manage it," she said. "Please let me know when you have it." Then she rose with a smile. "We will see ourselves out."

Ike withheld conversation until they'd returned to the carriage and were on their way back to the palace. "Annie, I am impressed," he finally told her. "You made that request without cracking a smile. It was like you were serious."

She looked over at him, her expression somber. "That is because I was."

⤜

The next morning, Annie left a message with Granny's private secretary and then rejoined Isaiah in the Yellow Drawing Room, where she resumed her study of copies of the police reports he had somehow managed to bring from Austin. When a footman appeared, she expected him to be delivering a word from the queen as to when they might speak.

Instead, there was a message that she had a visitor. "The American is waiting in the Green Drawing Room," the footman said.

Isaiah looked up from his work. "An American visitor? Is his name Langston?" he asked the footman.

"No, sir," he said. "He said he is a friend from New York."

Annie took the man's card from the footman and read it. Cameron Blake. Though her first instinct was to tear the card in half and banish the reporter from the castle, she let out a long breath and said instead, "Tell him I'll speak with him."

"Do you need me to come with you?" Isaiah asked.

"Of course not, but you're busy and this is likely a social call that can be quickly ended. I'll have the footman stay close." She nodded toward the door. "Shall we?"

He led her to a smaller reception room where Cameron Blake was inspecting a Gainsborough painting hanging over the fireplace. He jolted and turned toward her when she said his name, acting as if he'd been caught with his finger in the jam jar.

"Thank you for seeing me," he said as his confidence and composure swiftly returned.

"Good sense told me not to."

"I'm glad that you didn't listen to him." The reporter smiled.

"Good sense, that is. I assume his name is Isaiah Joplin, this good sense of yours."

Annie stood her ground, the door still open and the footman easily seen just outside in the corridor. "What do you want, Mr. Blake?"

He affected a pout. "Is this how you treat an old friend come to call? And to think I bring news that may help you with a case I hear you're working on."

"I have no idea what you're talking about."

"Right." He nodded. "Moving on then. What do you know about an organization called Black Midnight?"

She schooled her features. "I understand a group of citizens in Austin dredged up an old myth in trying to flush out the name of the killer who stalked the city several years ago. Their efforts amounted to spreading some misinformation and hoping for the best. Ultimately they were not successful in finding the killer. Beyond that, I know nothing."

"An old myth?" He shook his head. "You're certain?"

"I am certain of very little anymore, Mr. Blake. Please get to the point."

"I was sent over here to find out why Jack the Ripper hasn't been caught. Rumor was that the palace was protecting the killer for reasons that you probably already know. I don't believe that for a minute."

He paused, obviously thinking Annie would respond. She did not.

"Right. Well, anyway, I believe the killer remains at large because there are men who are protecting him. Powerful men." He paused. "And if I knew who those men were, I would also know whether our murderer spent time in Austin practicing his skills before he returned home to continue his craft here."

So he'd come to the same conclusion as she had. Annie refused to let on that she agreed with him. Instead, she shrugged.

"Again, I fail to see what all of this has to do with me. So if you'll excuse me, I'll be getting back to what I interrupted in order to meet with you." Annie turned to go.

"The Black Midnight is no myth," he said just loud enough for her to hear it. "Just ask your father."

She whirled around to face him. "Get out."

"Oh," he said sweetly, "now I have touched on a sore subject. You haven't talked to your father about this. You should. It's why he wanted you home. You weren't safe in Austin. The man who was killing women had become emboldened enough to move from servant girls to ladies of a different class. You might have been next, and he knew it."

Annie summoned the footman. "Please escort Mr. Blake out, and do not allow him to return."

She swept out of the room with her head held high and her fingers tucked into her pockets so the odious reporter would not see her hands shaking. Though she started toward the Yellow Drawing Room, she stopped short and summoned another footman.

"I will need a carriage, please," she told him. "And let Mr. Joplin know I'm paying a visit to my father and will return shortly."

By the time the carriage stopped in front of the family's London townhouse, Annie's courage had begun to wane. What if Cameron Blake was merely goading her? Surely Papa had nothing to do with such an organization.

He wasn't involved in anything remotely related to law enforcement or detective work. Papa was an occasional lecturer in the subject of English history, for goodness' sakes. And a retired one at that.

She found her father in his favorite chair in the library, an unlit pipe next to him and the scent of vanilla and leather in the air. Settling on the cowhide settee across from his chair, she waited for him to speak.

"I rather expected you," he said. "What with that reporter friend of yours being turned away from my house a few hours ago. Did he complain to you that your father refused to speak with him?" He shook his head. "I am still upset that he saw fit to publish that piece of fiction about you and that Texan. I tried to pay him not to, you know."

"I did not know," she managed, immediately wondering why Papa's offer of a payment wasn't included in the story as well. "But that isn't why I am here." Annie paused a moment. "What do you know about the Black Midnight?"

He stared but did not speak at first. "Swirled in rumors that go back as far as time and keepers of an oath to see to the country's safety however they see fit," he finally said in that professorial way of his. "Why?"

"There has been an accusation that you are a member."

His face gave away nothing. Then he laughed. "And that is why you are here? To find out if your father has joined such a group?" He shrugged. "Any answer I give will be suspect. You've already made up your mind. What do you think?"

"I think you know who is killing those women in London, or you know people who know. And you were aware that that same person was in Austin. When you discovered I was there too, you panicked and sent for me. When I did not immediately respond, you came for me yourself. Am I wrong?"

The fire crackled in the fireplace. Papa reached for his pipe. Still he did not speak.

In that moment, she knew she was right. Yet none of it made sense.

"Tell me about it," she said, pleading. "About them. And about him."

He met her gaze. "I cannot."

"You cannot or you will not? There is a difference."

"Not in the results," he told her. "Let it go, Annie. And if the queen is behind this, tell her I said the same. There's no good to be found at the end of this trail."

Annie rose, fumbling with her thoughts until she managed

one last question. "Who is he?"

But Papa only shook his head.

A door opened and closed downstairs. "Papa," a familiar voice called. "Papa, are you here?"

Annie stepped out into the open corridor to look down at the foyer where her sister Bea was handing off her hat and cloak to the maid.

"Annie," she said, looking up. "You're here. Good. You can help me talk sense into Papa."

"I'm afraid I'm the last person for that job," she said, glancing over her shoulder at her father, who was studiously ignoring her. She descended the stairs to envelop her sister in an embrace.

"We've done it," Bea said. "We're to be wed, and I don't care what he says about it. If we have to live in a hovel, we'll do that."

Annie squared her shoulders and shook her head. "Come with me. I don't think living in a hovel will be necessary."

Annie marched back up the stairs to stand in the door of Papa's library. He made a great show of ignoring her until Bea pressed past them.

"Papa, I've come to talk to you, and this time it's just me. You won't be telling me I cannot wed, because that'll just make me hide it from you. I want you and Mama to be there, but I will do what I have to. And I'll live in a hovel if that's where we have to live."

His weary gaze shifted to Bea and then returned to Annie. "I suppose you've got something to say about this."

"Let Bea marry the man she loves and give them a good start to their lives together by deeding over Blinn Cottage to them as a wedding gift." She looked over at Bea. "You always liked Blinn Cottage, yes?" At her sister's nod, Annie spoke to her father. "Do this and I won't press my case to Granny regarding what we've spoken about. My guess is she's got no idea about it."

Annie winked at her sister, then turned and walked away. "Good luck with him," she called over her shoulder. "He's not being reasonable today."

Papa answered with a harrumph.

A short while later, Annie returned to the palace, where the footman opened the carriage door with a message. "Her Majesty wishes to see you now."

She was ushered into Granny's private quarters where her great-grandmother was seated alone at her desk. "Come in, kitten, and tell us what you've learned."

"After a thorough investigation, we've cleared Uncle Eddy."

Her brows rose. "So soon?"

"Yes, ma'am," Annie said. "Between his size, his health, and his alibis, we believe he could not have committed any of the murders." She paused. "Either here in London or in Austin."

"And you're certain. All three of you."

"We are."

Silence fell between them as the queen ran her hand along the edge of her desk. Then she looked up again. "You have more to tell us. Or perhaps to ask?"

"Both." She told Granny about the events in the case up until this morning when she arrived at the conversations with Cameron Blake and Papa. "That brings me to the question. What do you know about the Black Midnight?"

"We know that the three of you—the four of us," she amended, "have been diligent in investigating these awful crimes. We believe more has been learned in these past few days than at any time during the months prior."

"No, Granny," Annie said gently. "The other one."

"Oh. That." She shrugged. "Men playing games and acting like boys mostly."

"So you know about them." Annie was both surprised and not so surprised.

"As you've said, there is very little we do not know about what happens around us."

"Who is the killer, Granny?"

Her brows shot up. "That we decidedly do not know. It is rather bold of you to ask that, kitten."

"Should I apologize?"

"No." Granny's voice held no harshness. "You think the Black Midnight is protecting one of their own."

"And I am concerned who that is."

Granny reached over to take Annie's hand. "I assure you it is no more your father than it is your uncle Eddy. For all of the same reasons."

Annie gasped. "You knew about Papa being a member."

"Thank you for not posing that as a question. Of course we knew. He is family. Though we understand his involvement is minimal at best."

"Still, Granny, he is a retired lecturer of English history, not a killer, a member of law enforcement, or a vigilante. How can he be involved at all in such an organization?"

"Oh, kitten, you don't know, do you?" The queen shook her head, her eyes softening. "The Black Midnight began as many organizations of its kind do, in secret and not out of any ill intent." She paused only a second before continuing. "Among the higher circles of education and society whose concerns are for the betterment of their peers and their country. We would hardly call them vigilantes. More protectors, if a word must be chosen."

Understanding dawned. "They're a bunch of professors with a few royals added in who want to help."

Her Majesty chuckled, though there was no humor in the sound. "You do have a way of putting things, Annie, but yes. That about sums it up. The police don't know who they are. Think about it, child. If they did, they would be obligated to stop them. Wouldn't you have when you were special constable?"

Annie nodded. It all made sense. "Why didn't you tell me, Granny?"

A smile was slow to rise on her great-grandmother's face. "We wanted a thorough investigation. Only one who had no knowledge of the Black Midnight could truly seek out the facts without prejudice."

Annie sorted through Her Majesty's words. Royals and university professors looking to save their peers was how she described the group. Uncle Eddy had said the members took an oath and swore to keep the members safe.

"And only you," Queen Victoria continued, "would have the audacity to ask me if I was hiding knowledge of a killer." She smiled. "We chose the right one for the job, and we are very proud of you. Perhaps we were too quick in siding with your father on certain matters involving your detective work."

"Speaking of my father," Annie said, "a reporter has alleged he is a member of Black Midnight. The same one who wrote that awful article about Isaiah and me. I thought you ought to know."

"The truth always has its day," Granny said with a shrug. "Unless it does not. Now kiss me on the cheek and tell me good-bye. There is work to be done by both of us."

❧

Ike awakened the next morning to a knock at his door. Without waiting, the footman stepped inside, followed by another fellow who threw open the curtains and flooded the room with light. A third uniformed man joined them, placing a silver tray on the table beside the window, then opening it with a flourish.

Ike wrapped the sheets around himself and stood, lured by the scent of fresh coffee and bacon. While staying at a palace had its benefits, he missed the privacy that his arrangements back in Texas allowed. There might not be anyone to heat his bathwater or bring him a meal, but he could walk around in whatever state of dress or undress he wished without having to be worried someone would walk in on him.

On a second tray beside the table was a single folded note. He opened it to read a message from Annie stating that Simon wished to see them at Scotland Yard as soon as possible. He finished up his breakfast, declined the offer of a valet to help him dress, then presented himself in the Yellow Drawing Room.

Today Annie wore a pale shade of blue, the dress the color of a robin's egg and the matching cloak a color slightly darker. The watch he'd given her all those years ago was pinned to her lapel.

"Time to go?" he asked, unable to resist a reference to the timepiece she'd kept hidden until now.

Annie grinned and took his arm, sparing a quick look at his midsection where the chain to the watch she'd given him was on display. "You'd know, wouldn't you?" was her reply.

Yesterday she'd returned full of enthusiasm over her conversations with her father and the queen. Between the two of them, enough information regarding the Black Midnight had been discovered to give them the reassurance that they were on the right track in targeting a member as the killer.

The fact the group was made up of college professors and not lawmen bothered him. He could tell it bothered Annie too, and likely for the same reason. They were both children of men who could be members. Worse, Annie's father indicated he likely was, and Pop was the man Ike had first heard of the group from.

Could Pop and his buddies be members too? Probably not, but nothing was impossible. He'd written his father last night, but the post was slow, and it would be a month or more before he would have any sort of answer.

And that assumed Pop decided to respond.

They rode in silence to Scotland Yard, and once again Simon met them at the entrance. "I received your message that there have been new discoveries. You also might be interested in something else we found."

"You first, I think," Ike said, and Annie nodded in agreement.

Simon gestured toward a side door, and soon they were winding through a warren of narrow hallways until they emerged at what appeared to be a property room. He went to a box on the shelf nearest the door and pulled it down to retrieve a slip of paper and hand it to Isaiah.

"Tests on the knives proved inconclusive. One of my boys went back to take a second look at the flat where they were found to see if he could glean anything else from the scene. He was about to leave when someone stuck this note under the door."

Ike opened it and read the words, then passed them on to Annie.

Alice Anne von Wettin, Buckingham Palace. Isaiah Joplin, Buckingham Palace. L

She looked up at Simon. "What is this?" Annie asked.

"I thought maybe you could enlighten us," Simon said. "The officer ran out to try to find the man who'd left the note but had no luck. All he could say was the hand that reached under the door was gloved and the sleeve of his coat was tweed."

"We only know one man who has claimed an association with that cook," Ike said.

"Dr. Langston?" Annie said. "Do you think he wrote this?"

"When we saw him in Whitechapel, he was wearing a tweed coat," Ike said.

"Like many men in London," Simon told him. "But the fact he led us to that flat by giving you the address is interesting. It's as if he wanted the man caught."

"If so, why put a note under the door with our names on it?"

"Curious," Simon told them. "But not completely unexplainable. We just need to ask those questions of the professor."

Ike frowned. "We're going to have to plan this confrontation. We could be speaking to the man who is not only the Whitechapel Murderer but also Austin's Midnight Assassin."

Annie sighed. "He was definitely in both places."

"And he has the size," Ike said. "The surprise meeting at

Whitechapel, the elaborate story of his friend the cook, all of it? No, I think we've got a new suspect. What do you think, Simon?"

The policeman nodded. "I think we do. You two need to be careful. You're the only ones who can identify him. We'll all go out to Greenwich together with the officers. I want to be sure I'm bringing in the right man for questioning. And let me be absolutely clear. Dr. Langston is a suspect, nothing more. I will make no allegations until there is proof."

Ike and Annie nodded in agreement as Simon led them back outside. "I'll ride in the carriage with the officers. If you two show up at the observatory, he will think you were just out for a drive and wished to say hello. Once you have confirmed it is him, we will step in and take him back to London."

They parted ways, and Ike helped Annie into the carriage. As they set off for Greenwich, he settled in beside her and considered how to broach the question of the odd note he'd gotten a few nights ago. He decided to be direct.

"Annie, about that message you sent me a few nights ago. I'm a little confused. I sent it back with the footman because I felt it wasn't intended for me, but until now I haven't thought to ask you about it."

She gave him a sheepish look. "You got the wrong note. I wrote my sister, Beatrice, and I wrote you. I gave both to the maid, and, well, she mixed them up. Yours was supposed to go to Beatrice."

"What did mine say? Something about the case, I assume. And your sister? You told her to marry someone?"

She gave him the shortened version of the contents of Beatrice's letter. Then she sighed. "So I advised her to marry the man. I think Granny's attitude has softened since I tangled with her. I doubt she would leave Papa and Mama penniless, though I have no doubt that Bea would be on her own with her husband."

"Which is how it ought to be anyway," Ike said. "So if hers was supposed to say, 'Marry him,' what was mine supposed to say?"

Color rose in her cheeks. Annie swiveled to face him. "Funny, I am not nearly as brave today as I was that night."

He reached over to grasp her hand. "What did it say?"

" 'I should have said yes,' " came out on a whisper of breath.

Chapter 27

I see."

It was going to take a minute for that news to soak in. Unfortunately, Annie misinterpreted Ike's silence.

"Look, forget I said that. It was late, I was tired. I got caught up in the moment. What was then is obviously not the same now, so let's just forget that I ever—"

Ike leaned over to stop her words with a kiss. When the kiss ended and he leaned back to look at her, she continued.

"That was nice, but you didn't have to do that. I certainly am able to handle the fact that you may have felt one way back then, but now you—"

He kissed her again.

When he figured he had finally gotten his message across, Ike sat back. "Annie, you're wrong."

"I am?" came out in a squeak.

Ike nodded. "I still feel exactly the same as I did back then. I told you I loved you then, and I love you now. Nothing has changed."

"Isaiah," she whispered. "I never told you I loved you back."

"You can fix that, Annie."

"I do." She grinned. "That wasn't hard."

He leaned close again but did not kiss her. "You do what?"

"Love you," she said. "I love you."

"Then everything else is going to be all right." He kissed her one more time. "But right now we have a job to do. Once we've done that job, we can handle what comes next."

"Which is?"

"I will speak to your father and probably the queen, if she'll talk to me. I think she'll want more than just a pair of boots to make this okay." He shrugged. "We will face that later. Together. Now let's concentrate on taking down a killer."

"I should warn you that you won't get far with either of them. They're both impossible."

He shrugged. "The impossible just takes longer."

They rode in silence until the carriage reached the observatory. Ike got out and helped Annie down, and together they strolled the grounds like the visitors they pretended to be. After they'd inquired as to the doctor's whereabouts from several of the observatory employees, it became plain that Dr. Langston did not work there. Nor was he doing research.

Ike went out to tell Simon. "He may have run as well," he added. "If the cook panicked, he probably did too."

Simon seemed to be considering the statement. He shook his head. "I'm stuck on something and need clarification. I was told this man is someone you've known a long time. How is it possible he's our killer and you didn't realize it?"

"I don't know," Ike admitted. "He and my father have been friends for a long time. He and Pop taught at several other universities at the same time."

"I wonder if there are unexplained killings in those towns too." Simon shrugged. "There's one way to find out. I'll need a list. Will you come back with me to the station and make one? I can send telegrams, and maybe we can get some quick answers."

"Sure." He looked over at Annie. "You don't mind?"

Annie shrugged. "Go on back with him. I think I will pay my sister a visit."

"Are you sure you're welcome there?" he asked. "I understand you've been urging her to do things they don't approve of."

"I'll have you know her beau trains horses and likes dogs."

Ike chuckled. "Well, that does make all the difference in the world, doesn't it?"

They parted with a smile, and Annie instructed the driver to take her to the townhouse. Not long after, the carriage was parked in front of the home Bea shared with Mama and Papa when they were in the city.

She stepped inside and was immediately greeted by her father. "What did you tell her?" he demanded.

"Tell who?"

"Your sister. She's gone, and your mother is inconsolable."

Annie straightened her backbone and looked up at her father. "I told her to marry the man she loves, the same thing I told you I had said. You ought to have listened to me, Papa. And for your information, I plan to do the same thing."

"You'll be left penniless," he called after her as she turned and walked away.

"I have a job I can go back to," she said. "I'll manage."

"What about your mother and me? What will we do if Granny decides to withhold her support?"

Annie shook her head. "Get a job, Papa. They're wonderful for buying not only what you need to live on but also a nice measure of freedom. Maybe one of your friends in the Black Midnight could help."

She returned to the palace and sent a message that she wished to update Granny. The response was for her to wait in the Blue Room. Annie complied but after a while tired of waiting.

"I will be in my room," she told the footman. "Please let Her Majesty know that I will be sending a note with an update shortly."

Then she went up to her room, closed the door, and kicked off her shoes. Padding over to her desk, she picked up a piece of stationery and wrote the queen about the afternoon's adventure.

Moving that letter aside, she drafted another one to Granny:

Please forgive Beatrice. She is marrying for love just as you did, Granny. And while you're at it, please forgive me as well, for I encouraged her to do it. I will marry for love soon too. I will not ask forgiveness for that, because I believe it is what I am meant to do. We ask nothing of you but your blessing. Should you wish to forgive Mama and Papa for raising daughters who follow their own minds, that would also be very much appreciated. In lieu of this, perhaps a job at the palace for Papa is in order.

Kitten

Annie called for the maid and had her draw the curtains. If Granny thought she was resting, perhaps she wouldn't send for her quite so quickly. It was a poor attempt at stalling the inevitable, but it was all she could think to do.

With the curtains closed, the room plunged into darkness. Walking across the room by memory was easily done. Finding the lamp beside the bed proved a little more difficult.

Finally, her fingers managed the feat and a circle of light rose around the little table. She reached for a book but saw a movement from the corner of her eye.

The armoire door.

Annie froze. Was someone in the armoire?

Ridiculous.

This was Buckingham Palace. There were no intruders here. Though it might be possible that she had interrupted a maid or footman who panicked and hid.

She decided the direct method was best. "Whoever you are, come out."

The door flew open and a glint of silver caught the light. "Who are you?" Annie demanded. Her thoughts raced toward the list found in the Malay cook's flat. Had he come for her?

Surely not.

"That is the question, isn't it?"

"Dr. Langston? What are you doing here?"

"Eliminating the obstacles to my freedom," he said. "You and

Ike are the only people in London who can identify me. I cannot let you live."

"No," she said. "You're wrong. I can't let you hurt me. Or him."

"Too late for him, Annie. I got him first."

Her heart lurched. Then she looked into his eyes. "No," she said. "You're lying."

"That's the funny thing," he said. "You really can't tell if I am or not. No one can. I'm very good at what I do. Even that idiot cook had to admit that, although it was under duress." He shrugged. "I might have had a knife to his throat at the time. His fault for trusting me and coming to London when I asked him to. A pity though. He truly did make the best steak I've ever had."

The professor lunged toward her, and Annie jumped out of his way. He was standing between her and the door, so escape was impossible. Besting him was not.

He lunged again, and the knife cut the fabric of her sleeve. Her arm stung, likely just a flesh wound. She ignored it.

"Come on, Annie. Stop fighting me. Accept the inevitable."

"Come get me, you coward," Annie taunted as she backed up until she felt the fabric of the window coverings behind her. She threw open the window, blinding the doctor.

Before he could react, Annie kicked him soundly in the stomach. Dr. Langston groaned and fell backward, causing the knife to skitter across the floor. She skirted the doctor and picked up the knife on the way to the door. Once outside, she ran down the hallway and shouted for help.

Her Majesty's footmen came running, and though Dr. Langston attempted to bully his way past them, he failed. He also failed at spinning a tale of getting lost in the palace and looking for his dear friend Annie.

When the queen arrived to see what the commotion was, even the professor was struck dumb. "We are grateful you are unharmed, kitten." She turned her imperious gaze to Dr. Langston. "Were we a queen of another time and place, we might order off with his

244

head. Instead, we will banish him into the care of the Metropolitan Police."

When he was gone, Granny turned to Annie. "Were you frightened, child? You are bleeding."

"It's nothing," Annie said. "The truth is, I was more frightened of you."

Her Majesty laughed. "I assure you, kitten, if anyone has earned the right to know her own mind and choose accordingly, it is you. We will approve on one condition."

"Anything, Granny," she said.

"You will see that your young man does not forget our boots."

Isaiah turned the corner and raced toward her. "Annie, you're bleeding," he said as he gathered her into his arms.

Granny cleared her throat. Isaiah ignored her.

"Young man," Granny said. "Show the appropriate deference to us."

Isaiah stood. "Ma'am," he said. "I have stopped wearing boots on your carpets and ordered a nice pair from Texas that'll be here in a few months. I have behaved as I should, and I have not pursued your great-granddaughter even though I wanted to."

Her brows rose, but she said nothing.

"It is true," Annie said. "I told him I loved him first this time."

"She did," Isaiah said, "but as to deference, you seem to be overly concerned for your carpets. Right now I am keeping Annie from bleeding on yours. How is that for appropriate deference? Oh, and I love her. Very much. Enough to marry her and stay in England so she can be close to you if that's what you want."

One side of Granny's mouth turned up in a half smile. "You will have to ask Annie what she wants. We are in agreement with whatever that is."

"Actually I would like a proposal, Isaiah. I didn't let you offer me a proper one last time."

"These things take time," Her Majesty said. "Think carefully, and if we may be of assistance, do mention it."

Isaiah grinned. "Duly noted, even if I'm not sure how long I can wait."

Annie frowned as the hallway tilted. "I might be bleeding more than I thought. I'm feeling a little dizzy. Mind the carpets though."

Annie's next recollection was of Granny seated at her bedside. "You were given something to sleep," she said. "The physician says you will be fine in a few days."

"Thank you, Granny."

She dismissed the statement with a regal wave. "We are due elsewhere. Rest, dear."

Granny kissed her forehead and left. Annie lay back on the pillows and tried to sleep.

But she couldn't.

She dressed as best she could without calling the maid and made her way downstairs to the Yellow Drawing Room where, as she hoped, Isaiah was alone at his desk.

❧

How long he'd pretended to work on the report, Ike couldn't say. Simon would have to handle this one. He had his mind elsewhere.

With Dr. Langston in custody, the question of whether he was the Whitechapel Murderer loomed large. If he confessed, there would be an answer. But what of the cook and his knives? Who in his right mind would accept the identification of the cook by a man who attacked a member of the royal family right under the queen's nose? Dr. Langston might be telling the truth, or he might not.

Then there was the question of whether the professor was a member of the Black Midnight. The consensus between Ike and Simon was that he was, but Ike also wondered about his connection to the killings in Austin. If this arrest solved two sets of murders—possibly many more than that—and put a secret society on notice that they could not successfully hide one of their own, he would be very happy.

So would Annie.

He looked up, and there she was. She'd scared him when she was bleeding on him in the hallway, but the way she looked at him now was a memory he never wanted to forget.

Ike had promised the queen he would take his time and offer up a proposal befitting this woman, and he intended to do that. Why then did he want to haul her in front of the first preacher who would marry them and make her his wife?

"I'd ask what you're doing here, Annie, but I figure you're going to tell me anyway. Get on with it," he said with a grin.

She remained where she stood, regal as any queen and still the prettiest woman he'd ever seen on either side of the Atlantic. "No, Isaiah," she told him. "You get on with it. The proposal, I mean. Because if I am going to give up any possibility of nobility and a comfortable inheritance, which still might happen, I would like to think I might at least be entitled to a proposal from the man who caused it."

Ike rose, though he wasn't sure if his knees would keep him standing for long. She wanted a proposal. Oh, he would give her the best proposal any Texas man had ever made.

But first he would kiss her.

So he did.

Author's Note and Bent History: The Rest of the Story

As a writer of historical novels, I love incorporating actual history into my plots. As with most books, the research behind the story generally involves much more information than would ever actually appear in the story. In truth, I could easily spend all my time researching and not get any writing done at all!

Because I am a history nerd, I love sharing with my readers some of that mountain of research I collect. The following are just a few of the facts I uncovered during the writing of *The Black Midnight*. It is my hope that these tidbits of history will cause you to go searching for the rest of the story. From a period beginning on December 30, 1884, and ending on December 24, 1885, a serial killer—eventually known as the Servant Girl Annihilator or Midnight Assassin—murdered eight people in the city of Austin, Texas. The killer, who was presumed to be a man based on eyewitness accounts, always struck at night and, until the last two murders, always chose servant women and their companions as his victims. Though a number of suspects were arrested, all were released. The killer was never caught.

Between August 31 and November 9, 1888, five women were killed in the Whitechapel district of London by a man who was never identified. These are known as the Canonical Five, the five whose murders are most likely related, though similar murders continued to occur up to November 1891. Today we think of this killer as Jack the Ripper, but in the vernacular of the day, the man was identified as the Whitechapel Murderer or Leather Apron.

The term *Jack the Ripper* came from the signature on a letter sent by the purported killer to the Whitechapel Vigilance Committee, along with a preserved human kidney.

Due to the violence involved in the murders and the fact that the killer preyed on women of a certain class, some believed the Whitechapel Murderer and the Midnight Assassin were the same person. This theory has been argued for more than one hundred years—from early newspaper accounts in the 1880s to a 2014 episode of a PBS television show called *History Detectives*—but there has never been a conclusive answer.

I base my novel, which is purely fiction, on fact but draw fictional conclusions. Personally I am more likely to fall into the same category as author Skip Hollandsworth, who wrote *The Midnight Assassin*, a fabulous book about the murders. Hollandsworth speculates that the answer to the killer's identity is still out there waiting to be found.

Desperate to put an end to the serial killer's reign of terror, Austin mayor John W. Robertson sent a telegram to the Pinkerton Detective Agency's headquarters in Chicago, asking for help. Unfortunately, the telegram was delivered not to the internationally famous agency as it was intended but to the similarly named Pinkerton United States Detective Agency, founded by Matthew Pinkerton (no relation to the other Pinkerton family), which was also based out of Chicago.

The mayor did not discover the error until the agency, which touted their mail-order course as a means of employment with the firm, had been paid and the detectives had arrived in Austin in late December 1885 or January 1886. By then the citizens of the city were so relieved to see what they thought were real-life Pinkertons coming to their assistance that the mayor elected not to correct the costly mistake. Unfortunately, the men did not produce an answer to the question of who was killing Austin's women.

The mayor's secret was out when the *Austin American*

Statesman ran an article in February 1887 regarding the city aldermen's investigation of the fees that the mayor had paid to Matthew Pinkerton's detectives. An open letter from William Pinkerton, director of the famous Pinkerton Agency, appeared in their March 4, 1887, issue stating that the mayor had hired the wrong Pinkertons. There is no evidence, however, that he sent any of his agents to investigate; thus that story line is pure fiction. Also, this would have happened later than the timeline in my book suggests, so I have "bent" history a bit to accommodate the story.

While Temple Houston, his wife, Laura Houston, and Comptroller William Swain are real people, the dinner party where they appear as guests of Governor John Ireland and his wife is a purely fictional event. Also fictional is the *New York Daily Gazette* and its reporter Cameron Blake and the professors Dr. Joplin and Dr. Langston. Slanton's Department Store, its owner, and the very sweet matchmaking clerk Lucy are also products of my imagination.

The quote Annie loves in chapter 14 is from Louisa May Alcott's novel *Little Women*. The newspaper article Ike is reading was an actual headline in the December 24, 1885, edition of the *Austin American Statesman*.

Eula Phillips's husband was tried and found guilty of her murder. The Texas Court of Appeals reversed the decision in November 1886, stating there was insufficient evidence to support the verdict. The court remanded the case back to the lower court. Eventually the case was dropped. To date no one has been convicted of Eula's murder or of the murder of any of the other victims.

Details of the murder of Eula Phillips were taken from the transcript of Jimmy Phillips's appeal of his conviction, a matter called *Cause No. 2271; James O. Phillips v. The State*, a transcript of which is readily available in the archives of the legal compendium *The Southwestern Reporter*. Testimony of the witnesses called by the prosecution and the defense offers a detailed (possibly too detailed for someone with a delicate stomach) explanation of what happened the night Eula died. It makes for fascinating reading.

One noted difference in the actual history of this case and my novel is in the weather on the night of December 24, 1885. Unlike my story where a blue norther came through and the ground was slushy with ice and snow, that sort of weather actually happened a year earlier on the night of the first murder: December 30, 1884. I thought the weather fit the scenes; thus I bent history for that purpose.

Details of the New Year's Eve party thrown by the Marshall Field family appear courtesy of an article in the *Chicago Tribune*. The party, thrown in honor of the couple's seventeen-year-old son and thirteen-year-old daughter, was dubbed the event of the century with two private railroad cars full of silver, china, linen, and food being brought in by Sherry's, a premier New York catering company. The rumor was the party cost $75,000.

Descriptions of the Yellow Drawing Room on the first floor (second floor if you're using the American manner of describing the palace's floors) of the southeast corner of Buckingham Palace are taken from multiple sources, but my favorite is an 1855 painting by James Roberts that shows the brilliant jewel box colors of the room: the gold silk of the walls and drapes that contrasts with the blue carpet strewn with red roses rimmed in gold, and pieces from Edward IV's Brighton Pavilion, including a pair of Chinese porcelain pagodas on Spode bases that stand nearly as tall as the ceiling. The Yellow Drawing Room was redecorated and hung in richly figured yellow silk for the state visit of the Emperor Napoleon III and the Empress Eugénie in 1855. According to the royal family's Instagram posts, the room is currently undergoing restoration.

Robert Gascoyne-Cecil, 3rd Marquess of Salisbury, was prime minister from 1885 to 1892 and again from 1895 to 1901. Since the duties of the prime minister would not have overlapped with any sort of project the queen might have created, whether real or fictional, Lord Salisbury is represented in the fictional meeting with my detectives on an unofficial basis. Fun facts: To date he is the only British prime minister to sport a full beard, and at six feet four inches tall, he was also the tallest prime minister.

In another case of bent history, the theory that Prince Albert Victor could possibly be Jack the Ripper did not appear until the 1970s. For the purposes of this novel, however, I elected to make that rumor something that was whispered about at the highest levels for a brief time. It is true that the prince's datebook did indicate he was not in London during any of the killings. Researchers believe it is unlikely that he committed the crimes.

Many experts over the years have taken on the question of the identity of the Midnight Assassin and Jack the Ripper. Some think the two are the same man—be it the Malay cook or someone else—and some think they are two different men. Whatever the case, as of this writing, these murders remain unsolved.

It is my hope that someday the names of these killers will be known and justice will finally be had for the victims of their crimes. I believe the evidence is out there waiting to be found.

Kathleen Y'Barbo is a multiple Carol Award and RITA nominee and bestselling author of more than one hundred books with over two million copies of her books in print in the US and abroad. A tenth-generation Texan and certified paralegal, she is a member of the Texas Bar Association Paralegal Division, Texas A&M Association of Former Students and the Texas A&M Women Former Students (Aggie Women), Texas Historical Society, Novelists Inc., and American Christian Fiction Writers. She would also be a member of the Daughters of the American Republic, Daughters of the Republic of Texas, and a few others if she would just remember to fill out the paperwork that Great Aunt Mary Beth has sent her more than once.

When she's not spinning modern day tales about her wacky Southern relatives, Kathleen inserts an ancestor or two into her historical and mystery novels as well. Recent book releases include bestselling *The Pirate Bride* set in 1700s New Orleans and Galveston, its sequel *The Alamo Bride* set in 1836 Texas, which feature a few well-placed folks from history and a family tale of adventure on the high seas and on the coast of Texas. She also writes (mostly) relative-free cozy mystery novels for Guideposts Books.

Kathleen and her hero in combat boots husband have their own surprise love story that unfolded on social media a few years back. They make their home just north of Houston, Texas and are the parents, grandparents, and in-laws of a blended family of Texans, Okies, and a trio of Londoners.

To find out more about Kathleen or connect with her through social media, check out her website at www.kathleenybarbo.com.

True Colors. True Crime.

The Red Ribbon (October 2020)
by Pepper Basham

In Carroll County, a corn shucking is the social event of the season, until a mischievous kiss leads to one of the biggest tragedies in Virginia history. Ava Burcham isn't your typical Blue Ridge Mountain girl. She has a bad habit of courtin' trouble, and her curiosity has opened a rift in the middle of a feud between politicians and would-be outlaws, the Allen family. Ava's tenacious desire to find a story worth reporting may land her and her best friend, Jeremiah Sutphin, into more trouble than either of them planned. The end result? The Hillsville Courthouse Massacre of 1912.

Paperback / 978-1-64352-649-2 / $12.99

The Gold Digger (December 2020)
by Liz Tolsma

In 1907, shy but loyal Ingrid Storset travels from Norway to support her grieving sister, Belle Gunness, who owns a farm in LaPorte, Indiana. Well-to-do widow Belle, who has lost two husbands and several children, provides Ingrid with enough money to start a small business. But Ingrid is confused by the string of men Belle claims to be interviewing for her next husband. When Nils Lindherud comes to town looking for his missing brother, who said he was going to marry Belle, Ingrid has a sinking feeling her sister is up to no good.

Paperback / 978-1-64352-712-3 / $12.99